Mrs. Hudson and the Irish Invincibles
(Mrs. Hudson of Baker Street Book 2)

Barry S Brown

Disclaimer

While grounded in the turbulent history of the effort to obtain Irish Home Rule, and including individuals and organizations that are a part of that history, the events described in the pages that follow are drawn entirely from the author's fevered brow.

Paperback ISBN 978-1-78705-358-8
ePub ISBN 978-1-78705-359-5
PDF ISBN 978-1-78705-360-1

Published in the UK by MX Publishing
335 Princess Park Manor, Royal Drive,
London, N11 3GX
www.sherlockholmesbooks.com

Cover design by Brian Belanger

Dedication

Ira Brown, Toaru Ishiyama, and Charles Radford Lawrence II

I stand on the shoulders of giants. The unsteadiness is mine alone.

Acknowledgement

I am indebted to Arlyne and Marvin Snyder for their careful review of this work and their many helpful suggestions and corrections.

Preface

Even less well known than Mrs. Hudson's achievements as director of the first of its kind consulting detective agency is her life before allying with Holmes and Watson. Now, all that is changed. Materials recently acquired from the Embassy of Bulgaria shed welcome light on that earlier history. Journals belonging to Mrs. Hudson's first employer, Lady Cynthia Stanhope, were discovered by Embassy officials during renovations made to the Stanhope's Belgravia mansion shortly after its acquisition by the Bulgarian government. In the Cold War spirit dominating diplomatic relations at the time, the journals were viewed as the prattle of an English reactionary from a bygone imperialist era and consigned to a distant part of the mansion's attic. When the building passed from Bulgarian hands to become again a private residence, Embassy officials made Lady Stanhope's journals available to the British Museum and we have finally become privy to the contents of those diaries. Unfortunately, many pages are missing, and others are substantially water damaged. Moreover, Lady Stanhope appears to have written sparingly about her servants. Nonetheless, whatever their deficiencies the journals are able to illuminate an area left far too long in shadows.

In an entry dated May 28, 1848, after first recounting her satisfaction with a shopping expedition to Paris, Lady Stanhope reports: "Mrs. Cavitt [her housekeeper] has recommended a girl to replace the housemaid who disappeared from service two weeks ago. Mrs. Cavitt tells me the staff is most sorely taxed and urges me to adopt the girl for service immediately. I feel I must trust Mrs. Cavitt's judgment in these things, but admit to some reservations about this girl. I am informed she comes from most trying circumstances. Her mother is a seamstress and her father's whereabouts are simply unknown. Not an unusual circumstance to be sure, but not a good omen. She is 14 and so is an appropriate age for service, and she reports having completed four years of schooling which speaks well for her diligence. I am told she is hard-working and honest, but is cursed with the fearful accent common to those from the city's eastern area. I will defer to Mrs. Cavitt's judgment, and hope she proves suitable to her position."

There is a second entry fully two years later in which Lady Stanhope again yields to her housekeeper's judgment and reports: "I must admit the housemaid I brought into service with some reluctance is not entirely lacking in intelligence and makes a generally favorable impression. I will take Mrs. Cavitt's recommendation and promote her to parlor maid. She still speaks without awareness that the letters g and h are included in the English alphabet; however, I will simply hope she has little occasion to engage in conversation with any of my guests."

The last entry in Lady Stanhope's journal of significance to us is dated September 18, 1851 and reads: "My parlor maid has given notice that she will be leaving service to marry one, Tobius (sic) Hudson, who is, of all things, the constable patrolling this area. I understand they will be taking a flat in Lambeth. Why the girl should give up her present position for a flat in Lambeth is quite beyond me. The girl's leaving will greatly inconvenience me, and Mrs. Cavitt, and I have no intention of favoring her with a good notice for the position she will doubtless require in future."

We already know somewhat more of the rest of Mrs. Hudson's life. We know from Constable Hudson's gravestone that she and the policeman were married until his death nearly 30 years later. We believe there were no children from that union. There are records as well of "a lease to property suitable for the provision of lodgings located at 221B Baker" entered in the name of Tobias Hudson. There is, however, no information to resolve the last great mystery surrounding Mrs. Hudson. That of determining the woman's given name.

Registry Office records of the housekeeper's birth and marriage were destroyed by fire and it is unclear which of the several Mrs. Hudsons for whom death records appear is our Mrs. Hudson. And then there is the further mystery of Mrs. Hudson's burial place, denying us even the opportunity of learning her name from its gravestone. There are, admittedly, those who confuse Mrs. Hudson with the servant, given the name Martha, inserted by Holmes into the Van Bork household as reported by Dr. Watson in *His Last Bow*. However, the connection seems to hang on the slender thread that Martha (if that was truly the woman's name) was an older woman, and in service. In fact, in the case in point, Mrs. Hudson remained in London, confidently waiting the return of her two protégés and their report of the success of her plan to root out the Kaiser's secret agent. At age 80, though still quick-witted, she left the rigors of field work to others.

Thus, we have no choice but to adopt Dr. Watson's custom of identifying the great lady solely by her last name, even as we reject all other limitations he and others improperly impose on the true sage of Baker Street.

—Barry S Brown

Chapter 1.
Moira Keegan Calls

Mrs. Hudson let the breakfast dishes soak a while longer, poured herself another cup of tea, and nodded her satisfaction to the empty room. Two weeks had passed since the successful, and handsomely rewarded, resolution of the murders at Parkerton Manor, and already Mr. Holmes had received two attractive offers for his services. The first had come in a visit from a representative of the Earl of Norwich conveying the Earl's wish to consult with him on a confidential matter of great delicacy.

There was, in fact, little that was confidential about the matter. It had been described in all its indelicate detail in several of London's penny papers for the better part of the week preceding the emissary's visit. The Earl's youngest son had not only formed an alliance with an actress of virtue reported as somewhere between easy and absent, he had had the bad judgment to express his devotion in letters filled with flowery prose and concrete promise. The Earl was willing to pay a very considerable sum to have Mr. Holmes use his "remarkable skills" to recover both the letters and what he could of the family's reputation.

The second offer arrived not three days later in a telegram from the Prince of Montenegro indicating His Majesty's willingness to come to London, or have Holmes travel to his country at the Prince's expense, to investigate the disappearance of his head groom together with his daughter and two very promising young stallions. The Prince specified his interest in the return of both the stallions and his daughter.

Neither were cases Mrs. Hudson believed appropriate to the work of the foremost consulting detective agency in London, but each would bring in a fair packet and both would maintain them in comfort for at least six months. All in all, the detective agency she had begun with more resolve than resources was succeeding quite well.

Indeed, it was her judgment that Mr. Holmes and Dr. Watson had come a long way, under her tutelage of course, to become quite respectable investigators, and she had come close to telling them so on several occasions. Without question, the two of them were doing far better than she had any reason to expect when they first arrived at 221B nearly ten years earlier in response to her advertisement of "rooms to let, good location, applicant should possess an inquiring mind and a curiosity about human behavior." The consulting detective agency she was ready to found would not only fill the empty days since Tobias had been taken from her, it would stand as a proper tribute to her companion and mentor for 29 years.

Every night, after the supper dishes had been cleared, the two of them would spread the day's newspaper wide across the kitchen table, open to the pages reporting crimes in and around London. A case would be chosen for its ability to challenge their imagination and skills. They began each investigation by cataloging everything known about the victim, about the circumstances of the crime, and about the likely suspects. They challenged each other to develop lists of persons to be interviewed and questions to be posed, to determine the aspects of the crime scene needing to be clarified and strategies for achieving that clarification, and to outline procedures to be followed and steps to be taken for narrowing the field of suspects. Along the way, her mentor would share the knowledge gained from a career with the London Metropolitan Police. They talked of gunshots, and stabbings, and drownings, and falls; and every night he added to her understanding of investigation as it might be conducted by the man she described as her "uncommon common constable."

In the daytime she trained herself in observation. At the greengrocer's, at the post office, on the horse car, and along the street she studied people—what their faces, hands, dress, walk, mannerisms, and speech could tell her about their character and what they were about. As often as she could, she supplemented the evening's analysis and the day's observations with trips to the Reading Room of the British Museum where her taste in literature raised eyebrows among those who scoured the stacks to find Browne's, "Reports of Trials for Murder by Poisoning," and Vigar-Harris's, "London at Midnight," then scrutinized the next day's newspaper in search of a horrific crime perpetrated by a short older woman wearing a black formless dress, and having coils of gray hair wound above a doughy face.

With Tobias's death, the lodgings at 221B, whose lease they had purchased years before, gave her the means to put to use the learning and skills she'd acquired, and to create a legacy befitting her uncommon common constable husband. She knew full well a woman could never be accepted as the head of a consulting detective agency, much less an older woman who'd never lost her Cockney accent. She would need a figurehead, a man of course, mature but vigorous, with the look and style of gentry, and the capacity to inspire immediate confidence in his judgment. Mr. Holmes had appeared very much the best man for the job. His age was right, his figure and movements were athletic and he claimed skills in boxing, fencing and with the pistol. His speech reflected the years he reported having spent at Cambridge, the high forehead and forceful assertion of his ideas might be mistaken for wisdom, and his unfailing admiration for his own thoughts seemed certain to inspire the confidence of others. He also brought a background in chemistry, and an interest in continuing his scientific investigation which—if kept within limits—might further the agency's reputation. The mottled character of his hands did give Mrs. Hudson some concern about his competence in handling chemicals, but she chose to let it pass. Of great importance to Mrs. Hudson, Mr. Holmes was accompanied by the solid, unpretentious Dr. Watson to whom she took instantly.

In the end, a bargain was struck, and Mrs. Hudson acquired two boarders and a consulting detective agency. Mr. Holmes was to be the agency's public face. He and Dr. Watson would conduct the core investigation under Mrs. Hudson's close supervision. Dr. Watson would have special responsibility for maintaining a journal of the people and events in each of those investigations. Mrs. Hudson, relying on that journal, her accumulated knowledge, powers of observation, and deductive skills, would be responsible for developing solutions to the problems the agency accepted. It had taken years, and a constant attention to Mr. Holmes's exuberant self-confidence, but her efforts had been rewarded with the development of an organization whose services were now requested by earls and princes.

The bell at the front door brought Mrs. Hudson back to her routine as housekeeper at 221B Baker Street. She caught a glimpse of herself in the parlor's mirror, pressed into place her braided gray coils, but otherwise ignored the stubby figure looking back at her.

A raised eyebrow was the extent of her greeting to the two visitors she found on the doorstep. She recognized only one of them, but he was sufficiently objectionable to make her wary of them both. Wiggins, the object of her disapproval, was the mop-haired undersized leader of the Baker Street Irregulars, as the group of unruly street urchins had been christened by Holmes. It was his contention they gathered information often impossible to collect through conventional means. Mrs. Hudson, while aware of their occasional assistance, found their more telling characteristics to be insolence and scruffiness. An agreement was struck such that admittance to Holmes's sitting room would be restricted to Wiggins, and admittance to Mrs. Hudson's parlor would be denied all Irregulars.

Drawing himself up to a height that put him at eye-level with the diminutive housekeeper, Wiggins announced the cause for his interruption to her day. "We are here to see Mr. Sherlock Holmes on official business. You may 'nounce us as Mr. Thomas Wiggins and Miss Moira Keegan. You can say Miss Keegan here has got a case for Mr. Holmes and she means to pay for his services."

In spite of the speaker, Mrs. Hudson was prepared, just this once, to allow a member of the Baker Street Irregulars to enter her parlor. Her decision had nothing to do with Wiggins and everything to do with Miss Moira Keegan. She was a girl of about twelve, wearing a spotlessly clean and freshly ironed white pinafore over a lime green dress with matching green ribbons tied in small neat bows around her two dark brown braids. Mrs. Hudson concluded that Moira Keegan was no street urchin like her sudden protector, but came from a home providing concerned and reliable care. The outfit would be a school uniform and the hour of day, and beads of perspiration on her bright pink forehead and the cheeks of her heart-shaped face, indicated she had left school early, probably in association with a hastily contrived excuse, and walked some distance to find Mr. Holmes. The contrast of soiled and dusty shoes with the rest of her carefully tended outfit gave further evidence of her journey. Judging by the rosary beads evident in the pocket of her pinafore, the crisis the child was feeling called for prayer—and likely frequent prayer. And, in the unpredictable way in which prayer may be answered, she had come to be teamed with Wiggins. Nonetheless, the child believed herself to have a serious problem and could not be blamed for the guardian she had acquired. Mrs. Hudson focused her attention on Moira Keegan, and for the girl's sake, tolerated Thomas Wiggins.

"You come into my kitchen. I've a kettle on and a fresh batch of scones from the oven. And I'm sure we can find some strawberry jam to go with them. I'll not be disturbin' Mr. 'Olmes who is workin' on one of 'is little experiments. Suppose you tell me what could be troublin' you on such a fine Spring day."

Wiggins was sorely tempted by the offer of Mrs. Hudson's scones. He well remembered the two scones he had managed to slip into a jacket pocket on the occasion of an earlier visit to Mr. Holmes, but those had to be devoured quickly and without benefit of strawberry jam. Wiggins steeled himself to demonstrate a necessary, but painful restraint. Forcing temptation from his mind, he clasped the hand of his adopted charge, and spoke in a voice intended to carry to the upstairs apartments. "Thank you, Mrs. Hudson. I'm sure I thank you most kindly. But we are here to see Mr. Holmes. I have a case for him which I'm bound to say he will find most intriguin'." Every now and again Wiggins liked to flaunt the advantage of his nearly five years of schooling.

Mrs. Hudson was prepared to rescind her invitation to tea and scones and refer the matter to the local constabulary when the door to the upstairs apartments opened and a familiar, if at the moment unwelcome voice called out cheerily, "Is that Master Wiggins I hear? Come upstairs and join me, my young friend. Pray tell me what new challenge you've brought me. Oh, and Mrs. Hudson, would you be so good as to bring up a pot of tea and some of your delicious scones. Perhaps some strawberry jam if you can spare it."

Wiggins glanced triumphantly to Mrs. Hudson before sweeping Moira Keegan up the 17 steps to the second floor landing and into the sitting room Holmes shared with his fellow boarder, Dr. John Watson. Moments later, Mrs.

Hudson followed with a tray of tea, scones and jam, and an air of barely contained fury.

Holmes was in his dressing gown, his arms stretched wide across the top of the settee, while Watson sat at his writing desk, his head encircled by smoke from his second pipe of the day as he reviewed his record of the Parkerton case. He held Wiggins in roughly the same regard as did Mrs. Hudson and so paid no attention to the young man he described as "little more than a ruffian."

Wiggins had long since identified his sole source of support at 221B and now fixed his attention on Holmes. Having completed his introduction of Moira Keegan as "a young lady what is in desperate need of Mr. Holmes's services," he gave the floor to her while he turned his attention to the scones Mrs. Hudson had placed on the round table farthest from the basket chair in which he had installed himself. Noting the gulf between himself and what he regarded as a just reward, Wiggins rose and circled behind Holmes after first signaling to Moira Keegan to begin her story.

Finding herself with the undivided attention of the great man she had come miles across London to see, she found herself without the words to tell the story she had been practicing for the past two hours. Holmes responded to the girl's discomfort with his best effort at a welcoming smile, and words he hoped would provide gentle encouragement. "Pray speak up, Miss Keegan. Tell us how we may be of help to you."

Moira Keegan bent her knees the slightest bit, uncertain whether or not to curtsy before again searching for the words to make Mr. Holmes understand how desperate her situation was. Watson had turned in his chair and was now focused on the youngster, while Mrs. Hudson was dividing her attention between Moira, and the scones she rightly viewed as subject to Wiggins's imminent assault. Mrs. Hudson decided that shifting the scene of battle might best serve her interests, and picking up the tray before Wiggins completed circling the settee, she offered its contents first to Holmes and then to Watson, placing the tray finally on a second table that made it necessary for Wiggins to retrace his path across the sitting room.

Unaware of the battle of wills unfolding before her, Moira again opened her mouth to speak, this time managing a small, high-pitched voice with a distinctive Irish brogue. "Mr. Holmes, your honor, I'm obliged to you for seeing me. I've come about me da. He's in the most terrible trouble." And with that, the enormity of the terrible trouble, and of all the terrible things she'd done to bring that trouble to Mr. Holmes overwhelmed her and tears gushed small waterfalls down her reddened cheeks. She was certain to go to the bad place Father Kilpatrick and the sisters talked about even though she was sure, and Shannon, her best friend, agreed, there was nothing else she could have done. She had lied to the sisters at St. Augustine's, telling them she wasn't feeling well so they would send her home from school, and then she had not gone home, but had walked from Kilburn over streets she'd never been on before, asking complete strangers if they could tell her where Baker Street was, all to find the man the older girls said was the only person in London who could help her.

Watson came quickly to her side, helping her into the basket chair Wiggins had vacated, while Mrs. Hudson brought her tea and a scone with a generous serving of strawberry jam, for the moment unconcerned that she had left the field open to Baker Street's most accomplished petty thief.

Watson spoke the support Holmes had intended. "Just take your time my dear. Mr. Holmes is in no hurry."

"Thank you, sir. It's very kind I'm sure. I am sorry to be so much trouble." Mrs. Hudson wiped her cheeks with a napkin and Moira gave her a tired, but winning smile. "I do thank you for the scone, ma'am. It looks ever so good."

Holmes tried again to encourage the youngster's story. "The scones are excellent. It's one of Mrs. Hudson's particular accomplishments. Now, tell us my dear, what is this about your father?"

Fortified by smiles and soft words, she found the courage that had earlier led her to spend the morning risking damnation. "It's just that he's in terrible trouble, and I didn't know what to do, and the other girls told me it was a right problem for Mr. Sherlock Holmes, although there's none I told I was coming here." Another lie, she'd told Shannon, and she shuddered as the gates of Hell yawned a little wider.

"Moira, when you say he's in 'terrible trouble,' what is it that you mean?" It was again Watson lending gentle support to the young visitor.

"There are people, horrible people, who are planning to kill me da. That's why I need help from Mr. Holmes." She spoke to Watson, with a quick glance to Mrs. Hudson, but did not chance a look to Holmes.

Dissatisfied with the progress his charge was making, Wiggins contributed his own form of encouragement. "Go on Moira. Don't go wasting Mr. Holmes's time. Give him the whole story, start to finish, just like you done with me when we was coming here."

Moira swallowed hard and began again, this time determined to see it through start to finish as Wiggins urged. She now spoke mainly to her shoes, glancing occasionally to Watson and Mrs. Hudson, but still avoiding the man she hoped would become her savior. "It's all about what happened yesterday when I come home from school. I always stop off to play at me friend Shannon's house before I go home to lay our table for dinner. Only this time Shannon's not in school because she's sick for the day, so I go straight home. I come

16

in quiet because me grandda will sometimes nap in the afternoon and I'm supposed to be careful not to wake him. I go straight to my bedroom to put my books away, and maybe work the paper doll cutouts me mam has got for me, when I hear her and me da talking in their bedroom. I know me grandda is got to be out, probably down to Caffey's pub, because my folks are talking in their regular voices. They don't never talk in their real voices about anything important if grandda is home. My brother, Liam Junior, who everybody calls Little Liam, is in our room, but he's playing with his puzzles like always and he won't talk to anybody, and likely can't hear anything when he's got his puzzles to work. Besides he's only five and don't understand half of what's going on anyway.

"Well, I know it's bad to listen to what other people are saying. I mean it's bad to listen when they don't know you're listening, and I tried hard not to hear. Except they don't know about me being home, and they're talking loud enough for me to hear even with their door being closed and me trying not to listen. And me da tells me mam how from now on she's got to be really brave, and he says to her, 'we both know there's no getting out of this alive.' In just those words, Mr. Holmes." She tried to look to Holmes as she spoke the last, but got no further than the blur of his dressing gown. "And then he says something about how he won't be putting her and the cubs— which is me and Little Liam of course—in danger. But next comes the worst part. As near as I can remember, me da says he's going away from here and this time there'll be no coming back, and later when she hears he's passed over, as she's bound to hear, she'll need to stay specially strong for me and Little Liam. Then it gets all quiet except for me mam's sniffling, and me da talking to her real soft like he does sometimes, saying things I can't make out.

"It's then I'm thinking it's time for me to get away so

they don't know I been hearing them. I whisper to Little Liam to say nothing only he's still busy with his puzzles and not hearing me. Which is when I snuck out of the house with nobody knowing, and come back a few minutes later, slamming the door so loud I'm sure even Mrs. Hogan upstairs can hear me. As soon as I do, me da comes out and grabs me up in a big bear hug like he always does and I can see me mam has been wiping her eyes, but she right away wants to know why I'm home early and I explain about Shannon being sick; so then she's got to feel my forehead and my cheeks and make me open my eyes real wide so she can look at them, and then at me tongue too. And of course I'm fine except for being scared by what I heard. Still and all, it's her thinking I'm sick that gives me the idea of how I can get out of class when the older girls at school tell me how Mr. Sherlock Holmes is the only man in London who can save my da."

Moira swallowed hard before telling of her lying to the sisters and making the trek from Kilburn to Baker Street. She smiled to Wiggins, who interrupted his chewing long enough to nod his acknowledgement, as she recounted her meeting him and his helping her to find the great detective at last. Her story complete, she looked finally to Holmes, holding his gaze for as long as she dared. "Now you see why I need your help Mr. Holmes, sir. Me da is got the devil himself chasing him."

Holmes, together with Watson and Mrs. Hudson, stared at their young visitor with a mix of wonder and concern as each tried to sort through the girl's meager facts and strong emotion. Wiggins alone had heard all he needed to hear. He smiled triumphantly to Holmes. "Didn't I tell you her story was a corker? There's a mystery for you here I am sure, Mr. Holmes. And she's ready to pay near three bob she's saved from work with her mother to get your services. Of course it's nothing like you're used to, what with the swells that are all the time asking for your help, but it's everything in the world she's got and I'll bet you never had a customer ready to pay you everything they got."

"Never." Holmes conceded after brief consideration. There were, in fact, some who'd promised they'd give everything they owned for his services; however, they always found cause to pay an ample but smaller amount. Something about Moira Keegan suggested the promise would be kept.

"Moira," Watson began in his same soft voice, "why would anybody want to hurt your father?"

"I don't know, sir, but he'd never talk about dying, or leaving me and me mam and Little Liam unless there was someone terrible after him. And then there's the things me grandda has told me. It was about a month ago. He come home from Caffey's and he had what me mam calls 'a snootful' or he wouldn't have said anything to me. He tells me I should be prepared, that me da will never live to see me marry. He says 'death is out there waiting on him.' And before I can ask him what he's meaning, he tells me he's tired and has to have a lie down and when he wakes up, he says he never said any such a thing, but I know he did. I asked me mam what he meant, and she told me to just ignore grandda, but I could see it upset her too."

"Child, can you tell Mr. 'Olmes the kind of work your father does?" Wiggins looked with surprise at the questioner although no one else seemed to take special note of Mrs. Hudson.

"He builds houses and fixes them up, ma'am. And I'm sure he's very good at it because he's always having to go off somewheres to help people put up their houses or repair them." With that, Moira wiped away tears and nibbled tentatively at her scone.

Away from Wiggins's sight, Mrs. Hudson nodded to Watson, then gathered up the teapot, the plate now empty of scones, and the bowl containing only streaks of the strawberry jam that had filled it to the brim earlier. She suggested to Moira and Wiggins they come downstairs with her while Mr. Holmes and Dr. Watson discussed the situation, but her suggestion carried a clear element of demand. As a seeming afterthought, Mrs. Hudson told Holmes and Watson she'd be back with a fresh pot of tea. Wiggins, who had envisioned gaining entree into the world of detection, was disappointed, but mollified by an explanation that he was needed to look after Moira, and an assurance there were additional scones and strawberry jam downstairs.

On her return with the promised pot of tea, and with both youngsters now safely out of earshot, Watson turned to the housekeeper. "What do you make of it, Mrs. Hudson?"

She frowned her response. "I don't know there's anythin' to be made of without first knowin' a whole lot more of what ails Mr. Keegan. And, truth to tell, ails may be the best word to describe the situation what with 'im talkin' about goin' away so as not to be puttin' the family at risk, and sayin' 'e's sure to die. And then there's the grandfather tellin' the little one death is waitin' on 'er father. Of course, there's no way of knowin' for sure, but if the child is gettin' their words right, it sounds like the poor man may 'ave got 'imself some disease 'e thinks is bound to do 'im in and is lookin' to keep it from 'is family."

Watson had been nodding to the housekeeper as she spoke. "Those were exactly my thoughts, Mrs. Hudson. Tuberculosis is rife through many parts of the city and would certainly call for isolating the patient, with death a far too frequent outcome of that disease. Then of course there's typhus, and possibly cholera or even smallpox although we're having some real success containing those two. One has to also think about the diseases that can come from contact with the women a lonely young man might choose for companionship in the course of his travels, although of course those diseases wouldn't threaten his children."

"But surely it's also possible Mr. Keegan is being pursued. He may well be the subject of a Scotland Yard manhunt." Holmes's tone reflected astonishment at his colleagues' inability to appreciate the obvious. He stood at the mantel, lavishing his attention on a favorite briar. "All of this traveling he does repairing homes provides a perfect cover for his criminal activity, which is very likely housebreaking. He doesn't dare stay long in his own home since the house is probably under police surveillance. Unfortunately for our young friend, the grandfather revealed the extent of Mr. Keegan's difficulties, and she overheard her father essentially confirming his comment."

"It's a fair point, Mr. 'Olmes, and one to explore. The truth is Mr. Keegan's leavin' could be for most anythin', disease, runnin' from the police, or runnin' from others for who knows what reason. All we 'ave is a very upset little girl, and no good way of knowin' the reason for 'er worries. I'm afraid we need to 'ear from 'er father or 'er mother, or there's no tellin' which way to go no matter 'ow each of us feels about the little one."

Watson's face was screwed into an unhappy grimace; his pipe lay on his small desk, its flame long since extinguished. "What then do you suggest, Mrs. Hudson?"

"We can make some inquiries at the Yard to see if they know anythin' about a Mr. Liam Keegan, but we'd 'ave to be careful not to alert them to a problem we don't know exists. We can try to get one of 'er parents to come and see us, but then we'd 'ave to reveal 'ow we know things which could get our little Moira into 'er own spot of trouble. And besides, 'er father is likely somewheres well away from 'ere, and 'er mother is unlikely to 'ave a great deal she's willin' or able to share. I think for now we'd best get the little one back 'ome before 'er mother is wonderin' what in the world could've 'appened to 'er. Dr. Watson, if you feel up to it, you might see to that." Watson grunted agreement. "Mr. 'Olmes, I'm thinkin' it might be well to 'ave Inspector Lestrade over for a friendly cup of tea, and a little chat."

Holmes gave his housekeeper a thin smile. "I trust we can count on you for another batch of scones. Perhaps this time with raisins."

Mrs. Hudson promised scones, with raisins, and then all three went to fetch the two visitors in her kitchen. While Wiggins was still in her apartment, Mrs. Hudson made a rapid inventory of utensils and china, satisfying herself that everything appeared in their appropriate numbers and location.

Watson sat beside Moira at the kitchen table and explained that her father could well have been talking about an illness he had, and his going away was likely all about his getting better if he could, and not making her, or her brother or mother sick. He told Moira there were hospitals and sanatoriums where people could get well, even people with really serious illnesses, and it would be good if she could get her father to come to see him. Moira nodded all through his talk and harder when Watson shared his willingness to see her father, but she said nothing. Finally, Watson told her he would take her home in a cab, and perhaps he could talk to her mother about the situation. Moira's eyes widened with the fright Mrs. Hudson had seen in the little girl on her doorstep. She shook her head vigorously at Watson's offer, explaining she could walk back now that she knew the way, and promised to speak to her mother as soon as the time seemed right.

In the end, it fell to Wiggins to continue in his role as Moira's guardian. He was given four shillings to take Moira home and get himself back, and another shilling for himself. He left with pockets stuffed with scones, and Mrs. Hudson's firm belief that a coachman was shortly to become engaged in some very hard bargaining.

A few days later, over tea and raisin-filled scones, in the same sitting room that had been witness to Moira Keegan's desperate plea, Inspector Lestrade advised Holmes and Watson that he knew of no police search for a Liam Keegan, although he cautioned that the Special Branch of the Yard had specific responsibility for monitoring the movements of suspicious Irish immigrants, and they could be very stingy with the information they gathered. Then, after accepting two additional scones to take home to Mrs. Lestrade, he took his leave amidst expressions on both sides of the need to get together both soon and more often.

It was several days later that the members of London's foremost consulting detective agency found their world suddenly and dramatically transformed. Watson was reading out the crime reports in that day's *Standard* while Mrs. Hudson dried the breakfast dishes she had finished washing. Holmes was just sitting down to his breakfast, having spent most of the night conducting microscopic study of threads from the collection of British, Indian, and American ropes and twine he had amassed. Watson read out news of a suspicious fire in the home and business of one Matthew MacMurchison, a tailor in Knightsbridge; and a report that body snatchers had brazenly removed the corpse of one Joshua Hobbes from the undertaking firm of Septimus McCardle and Son on Holborn Street. The mood turned quickly dark as Watson read out the last entry. "The savagely hacked and mutilated body of a man identified as Liam Coogan of the Kilburn area was discovered in a room at the inn in Wapping where he had been stopping. Mr. Coogan had, during his lifetime, been engaged in the building trades. The deceased leaves a wife, Patricia, and two children, a son, Liam Junior, and a daughter, Moira. The family goes by the name of Keegan. Scotland Yard has no suspects at this time."

Chapter 2.
Inspector Lassiter of the Special Branch

Watson threw the offending newspaper across the table, then turned to stare blindly out the kitchen window. Mrs. Hudson stood grim-faced, drying over and over again the dish she held. Holmes alone entered into a torrent of activity. Pushing himself from the mound of eggs, bacon, sausage and toast he had been eager to attack moments earlier, he strode from the kitchen to the adjoining parlor, traced its small boundary and returned to the table where he grasped the back of his chair and stood glaring first at Mrs. Hudson, then to Watson's back, and finally to the breakfast plate that mocked his loss of appetite. In spite of the fury that made his face an ugly mask, Holmes's voice was one of resolve not anger.

"We need to act on this." And then, lest there be any confusion about the urgency he felt, "We need to act on this immediately."

Watson turned back, nodding a vigorous assent, "Absolutely right, Holmes, but we'll need to act with a careful plan."

Holmes grunted his acceptance of Watson's qualifier, and the two men looked to their housekeeper to await a plan.

Mrs. Hudson set down her towel and the plate it covered. She took her accustomed chair at the kitchen table and the two men took their places across from her. "First, we'll be needin' to tell the Earl of Norwich and that foreign Prince we'll not to be takin' their offers because of a prior commitment." There were grunts of agreement from both men.

"Well then, let's see where things stand. Of course, we've little to go on just yet, but we know some things and it would be well to review them." Nodding his understanding, Watson withdrew a small notebook and pencil from his waistcoat and leaned earnestly forward to capture the housekeeper's report of what it was they knew. "Wappin' is in the East End, by the docks. It's where you'd go if you were lookin' not to be found. And that suggests there was someone comin' after 'im like you supposed, Mr. 'Olmes. But it wasn't the police. The killin' rules that out. And it couldn't be robbery. There's no point to manglin' your victim like was done even where there's a robbery gone bad. Apart from which, 'e's not likely to 'ave 'ad anythin' of value on 'im. And of course it's been done by a man, women don't go choppin' up people like somebody's done 'ere.

"There's other things possible, but first things first. And first, is for us to know who this Mr. Coogan was and what 'e might 'ave done to get 'imself killed. It would be good to 'ave a talk with whoever at the Yard is the one lookin' into this. More than likely it's someone from the Special Branch like Inspector Lestrade was thinkin'. It's just a couple of years ago they stopped bein' called the Irish Branch, and I'm bettin' the biggest part of their job is still keepin' watch on the Irish in London they think could make trouble. Our Mr. Coogan might well be one they 'ad on their list. A man who uses a name different from the rest of 'is family and is all the time away from 'ome sounds like a man with secrets. Mr. 'Olmes, I'm wonderin' if you could ask Inspector Lestrade to sort that out for us, and 'elp us get to the officer at the Yard we should be talkin' to in the spirit of workin' together to solve this crime, the two of us workin' different ends of the same street as it were.

"After we know a little more about our Mr. Coogan, we'll want to get over to the inn where 'e was found and talk to anyone who might 'ave 'eard or seen somethin' that can be a 'elp to us. Whatever clues there might 'ave been at the inn will 'ave long since been trampled by the police so there's no need to run over there right off. As soon as it's respectable, we'll want to talk to Mrs. Keegan or Coogan, whatever she's now callin' 'erself. And let's not be forgettin' Moira's grandfather. 'E sounds like 'e thinks 'e knows somethin' and maybe 'e does.

"Dr. Watson, I'd appreciate your pullin' from the files our 'Questions for family members of the victim.' Mr. 'Olmes you'll be wantin' to study those sooner rather than later."

Mrs. Hudson paused, allowing Holmes and Watson opportunity for questions. Watson spoke for both men. "When can we get started?"

The following day, after an exchange of telegrams between Holmes and Lestrade, and several sessions in which Watson played an inspector from the Yard, while Holmes played Holmes, and Mrs. Hudson critiqued and gave direction to them both, the visitor for whom they had been preparing rang the bell at 221B Baker Street at the appointed hour of 11 a.m. Mrs. Hudson opened the door to an inspector from Scotland Yard dressed unlike any inspector who had visited Holmes previously, most of whom could have passed for omnibus conductors in something less than their Sunday best. The inspector she greeted wore a silk top hat, dark frock coat, striped gray trousers, and showed off a perfectly knotted red tie framed against a high collared starched white shirt. Mrs. Hudson caught a glimpse of his shoes, and was unsurprised to find them polished to a high gloss although they lacked the spats she also expected. He removed his hat, revealing waves of dark hair above a thin clean-shaven face whose most prominent features were high cheek bones and narrowed eyes that gave his face a fox-like quality. Mrs. Hudson judged him to be in his mid to late 20's, his perfect carriage and punctuality suggested military training or schooling. His rank of inspector at such a young age lent weight to a military background as explanation for his rapid advancement. His bored appraisal of first Mrs. Hudson, then the small entry hall, and finally what he could see of her parlor, indicated a policeman's professional attention to his surroundings, and this Inspector's private misgivings about the appointment he'd been directed to schedule.

"I'm Inspector Peter Lassiter. I'm here to see Mr. Holmes. If you would give him my card." The clipped precision of his speech and practiced indifference of command affirmed Mrs. Hudson's judgments about his background. He waited now to be invited into her parlor.

Mrs. Hudson obliged him, but only after making an unnecessarily lengthy study of the card's eight words:

Peter Lassiter
Inspector, Special Branch
London Metropolitan Police

"If you'll take a seat, I'll inform Mr. 'Olmes you're 'ere. May I take your 'at and stick, sir?"

Without comment he gave the housekeeper his top hat and walking stick, then seated himself in one of the three armless oval-backed chairs in her parlor after first studying its green cushion for whatever hidden capacity it might possess to blemish his trousers. Turning her back to the inspector and simultaneously raising her eyebrows to nearly unprecedented heights, Mrs. Hudson left to apprise Holmes and Watson of their visitor's arrival. Watson was already prepared with pencil and foolscap to record the information obtained, and she urged Holmes, for what he informed her was the third time, to make use of the scenario they had rehearsed. He continued packing his briar with the shag to which he was partial, and made no further acknowledgement of her presence.

Feeling as prepared as seemed possible, she directed Inspector Peter Lassiter of Scotland Yard to the sitting room, promising to come up shortly with tea and scones. In fact, she would join them in exactly 20 minutes, unless Watson called for her sooner. At that time, Watson would announce his intention to review his notes with Inspector Lassiter for the accuracy of his recording while Mrs. Hudson poured tea. If she thought of additional issues to be pursued, she would ask Watson to assist her on the stairs at which time she would advise him of points needing clarification. For now, the investigation was in the hands of her colleagues while she became again the dutiful housekeeper.

Peter Lassiter rapped one time on the sitting room door. A voice from inside sang out the door was not locked and encouraged him to enter. He smoothed the frock coat over his slender frame one last time and entered, taking in the room with a single dismissive glance before striding to a place beside the settee. From his position at the mantel, Holmes waved him into a seat. Lassiter identified himself as an inspector with the Special Branch, then cut Holmes off in mid-sentence as he was introducing himself and Watson to indicate he knew of the consulting detective, and was acquainted with his occasional contributions to the work of the Yard. Nodding toward Watson without looking at the doctor, he reported an awareness of the work of his assistant as well. There was a sudden sharp crack to his left and this time Lassiter did look at Watson, finding him seated at the small secretary's desk, holding two pieces of the pencil he'd been using. Lassiter shrugged, and returned his attention to Holmes.

"I'm here, Mr. Holmes, at the urging of my chief inspector who is, himself, responding to a request from Inspector Lestrade as a courtesy to a long-time colleague. I don't mind telling you the involvement of amateurs in the work of the Yard, and more particularly in the work of our Branch, makes me very uncomfortable." His back stiffened as he pouted his displeasure. "Still, I'm here and I'll do what's been requested. However, before beginning, I've been asked to learn the basis for your interest in this case, Mr. Holmes."

Holmes drew himself to the fullness of his greater than six foot frame before responding in the flat tone of a parent dismissing a child's foolish concerns. "I assure you I wouldn't have asked for the Yard's participation if I didn't think it important. I will tell you we're acting on behalf of a family member whose own motives are wholly innocent. It would, of course, be betraying a confidence to reveal the family member's identity. I will, however, share everything with you and the Yard that is not compromising to my client when we have concluded our investigation. I seek no personal glory through these efforts, but strive only to uncover the truth." Satisfied he had provided as suitable an explanation as the question and the speaker deserved, Holmes settled back into a comfortable slouch against the wall.

"I suppose that will have to do. I doubt it will satisfy my chief inspector, but I suggest we get on with it." Peter Lassiter watched a plume of smoke twist its way from Holmes's pipe, considered the possibility of lighting a cigarette, but saw no evidence of an ashtray nearby, and instead began the task he had been assigned. "What do you know of the Irish Invincibles?"

"The Invincibles? Weren't they the group responsible for the murder of a British official in Dublin several years ago?" It was Watson who spoke to Peter Lassiter's question, but the Scotland Yard man continued to look solely to Holmes before making Watson's response the prelude to answering his own question.

"Two murders, and eight years ago to be precise. The Invincibles were—and remain—a group of Irish radicals who decided the movement toward Home Rule was going too slowly and too peaceably so they took matters into their own hands. A group of savages attacked and viciously killed two officials of Her Majesty's Government while they were taking an innocent stroll through Dublin's Phoenix Park. The murderers had gotten their hands on a set of surgical knives— carried in the skirts of one of the group's pregnant wives if you can believe it—and slashed their victims so badly their own mothers won't have known them by the time they finished. Our police colleagues in Dublin captured all those directly involved in the killings and hung five of them. As is always the case with these cowards, as soon as we put pressure on them they turned one against the other. In this case the murderers were taken down after their own ringleader, one James Carey, put the finger on most of them.

"Carey was then allowed to go free—for all the good it did him. A fellow Invincible followed him to South Africa where he had sailed in hopes of starting a new life. Carey was shot dead before he even touched land. Most of the rest of the Invincibles won't see the outside of a prison cell any time soon, but there's some who got away before the Irish Branch was organized. We know several of them have gone to ground in the Kilburn area, where they made common cause with the Irish Brotherhood. I take it you're aware of the bombings in the tubes, at Westminster, even at the Yard."

"And Whitehall," Holmes volunteered, remembering his concern about Mycroft's safety at the time.

"Yes, Whitehall as well. That's why we had an interest in Liam Coogan. Not that he had a hand in the bombings. He was doing his five years in prison when those happened. Still, we knew it would only be a matter of time he'd be back with his friends and up to his old tricks. In the meantime we've kept tabs on his family as a way of keeping track of him. All of them are in Kilburn. His wife and daughter, together with his father-in-law, got out of Dublin as quickly as they could after Coogan was put away. She had another child, a boy, a little after they got here. His wife took her maiden name, Keegan, probably hoping she could use it to disappear among all the other Irish in the area. Coogan kept his own name, maybe to protect his wife, maybe because both the Yard and the Brotherhood already had a line on him and couldn't be thrown off his trail by a name change. He did take the precaution of staying on the move. He'd get work as a mason somewhere, come home for a while and then be gone again. We'd find him and bring him in for questioning every now and again, especially right after there'd been an action by the Brotherhood, but we could never get enough on him to take him down. That's not surprising; he's always managed to stay on the edge of things.

"We have reason to believe the Brotherhood started to have its own suspicions about Coogan as well. There had always been those who looked at his getting five years, when others were getting life or being hung, and wondered whether his light sentence wasn't some kind of reward for his cooperating with the Irish Police. I suppose our taking him into custody after one of their actions, and then maybe taking down one or two members of the Brotherhood not much later, probably looked to them like proof of his disloyalty and reason enough to make an example of him." The Inspector shrugged. "To tell you the truth there's informers enough out there we never needed Coogan and never got much of anything out of him anyway. Regardless, if one of his former mates has taken care of him, I'm not going to lose any sleep over it. Frankly, Mr. Holmes, from the standpoint of the Yard, someone has saved the rate payers the cost of either a hangman or a long stay in Newgate. I'm not condoning murder mind you—this, or any murder—but if these savages want to kill each other ... well like I say, I won't lose any sleep over it."

Lassiter's voice had grown strained as he neared the end

of his account. Now, he drew back into the settee's cushion, squared his jaw and with the quick massage of one hand over the other disposed of any further consideration of the life of Liam Coogan. For a moment the only sound was the scratching of Watson's pencil and the draw of Holmes's pipe. Then, Peter Lassiter brushed some imagined lint from the sleeve of his frock coat, and stated to no one in particular, "I wonder if this wouldn't be a good time for tea."

Although unaware of her visitor's request, Mrs. Hudson was preparing to join the others when the bell rang in her kitchen. She placed the teapot, cups and saucers, milk, lemon and sugar on a waiting tray. She chose to omit scones and marmalade. It was not that it would create too large a burden, she had carried larger trays than that to guests she deemed more deserving. Dr. Watson opened the door to admit Mrs. Hudson into the sitting room, raising his eyebrows and rolling his eyes as he did so. Mrs. Hudson made a vague smile acknowledging his message. In a room gone unnaturally silent, she carried her tray to the round table at the side of the settee that days earlier had been a staging ground in her battle with Wiggins. She poured tea for her lodgers and their guest, while Watson began his summary of the earlier discussion in line with their accustomed procedure. Watson had, however, barely begun his report when Peter Lassiter interrupted.

"Really, is all that necessary. I'm certain you've taken things down correctly, Doctor, and I see no need for a tedious review. I will only ask your indulgence on one point before describing what is known about the death of Liam Coogan. I know some of what I have said may sound callous to you. For that reason, I want to try to make you understand the full horror of the Phoenix Park murders. After that you can decide how much you want to involve yourself with the death of Liam Coogan. I recognize you're acting on the family's

33

behalf, but if you're thinking to find something that will exonerate him I suggest you get it out of your head." Having reconsidered his earlier decision, he lit the cigarette he had taken from its silver case and exhaled a trail of smoke. He looked to Mrs. Hudson, then to Holmes.

"I believe we can dispense with your housekeeper for the rest of this. I don't find murder—and especially this murder—a fit subject for a woman's ears." The Inspector, a man accustomed to ready obedience, puffed at his cigarette waiting compliance. Mrs. Hudson spoke before either of her colleagues could protest.

"I'll just be goin' now. Ring if I'm needed." The housekeeper adopted the patient smile of a dutiful servant before closing the door noisily behind her. Peter Lassiter took no note of either the smile or the door's closing.

"I've tried to describe the sheer brutality of the murders, and in deference to good taste I won't repeat its utter savagery. That savagery would be reason enough to lose any sympathy for those involved. But it goes deeper. The murders were nothing less than an attack on Her Majesty's Government, and the victim of that attack was a devoted and hard-working representative of the Crown, who left behind a loving wife still coping with the shock of losing her husband so suddenly and terribly. It is for these reasons the fiends responsible for that crime remain the enemy of everyone who loves his country, and why the death of any one of them is not something I, or any member of the Special Branch, will be mourning." He stared hard at Holmes to make certain the point was not lost on him.

"With that understood, I'll tell you the state of our investigation." Peter Lassiter did his best to adopt the matter-of-fact reporting expected of the police, but his voice never lost the hard edge it had acquired. "Coogan was killed in his room at the inn in Wapping where he was staying. Not being a very imaginative sort he'd registered himself as Liam Smith. The inn is near to the docks and probably seemed a good place to disappear to; maybe he even hoped to scrape together enough money to arrange passage out of England. Anyway, as I said, we believe the Brotherhood found him. Informers are easy enough to come by and will work for anyone who's got their price. As near as we can tell, they trapped him in his rooms and very methodically proceeded to hack him to death the same way the killings were committed in Phoenix Park. They may have even used the same surgical knives since those were never recovered.

"We believe they wanted to show the punishment informers could expect from the Brotherhood and, more especially, make clear why they'd come for Coogan. They pinned a note to him with the word 'INFORMER' all in capitals to make certain there'd be no confusion on that score. We had his wife down to identify the clothes he was wearing and the change of clothing he had in his wardrobe at the inn. We spared her looking at her husband's body. There was a change purse in one of his pockets that his daughter had made for him and inside it was the key to the flat in Kilburn. You're welcome to see all that whenever you like. We showed the picture we had of Coogan from the Irish police to the staff at the inn and whatever guests would talk to us, and they all confirmed it was Coogan that was staying at the inn."

Peter Lassiter paused to drown his cigarette in the tea that had spilled into his saucer. "There's something more for you to know, Mr. Holmes, and I want you to understand what I'm about to say has the backing of my chief inspector. We're reporting to you about Liam Coogan as a courtesy for whatever favors you've done the Yard in the past. The Branch's concern, however, is to use our people to protect London's citizens from any future terrorist attacks by the Irish rebels. In a word, we have no further interest in this case, holding that with the terrorists having done in one of their own, further investigation would be a waste of precious resources. Therefore, Mr. Holmes, you'll have no assistance from the Yard on this one." With that, Peter Lassiter lit a second cigarette directing its smoke down the length of his frock coat.

Holmes eyed Peter Lassiter coldly. "My dear young man, while I appreciate your informing me of the Yard's concerns, I am not in the habit of requesting assistance from your colleagues. Quite to the contrary, I am accustomed to providing your colleagues with the benefit of *my* assistance."

Watson mouthed a silent "well done, Holmes." Peter Lassiter took no notice of Holmes or Watson. "As long as I've made myself clear." His mission complete, the inspector rose to take his leave. "Now I really must be returning to the Yard. I trust I've clarified the events surrounding Liam Coogan's death."

"A moment if you would, Mr. Lassiter. There are still a few questions I believe." Holmes had not stirred from his place at the mantel, and now looked Peter Lassiter back to the settee.

Holmes had spent too much time in rehearsal to be deterred from giving voice to the rest of his script. "Perhaps you can tell us the name and location of the inn in which Liam Coogan was staying, also who discovered the body, and what you know of the time of death."

Having resumed his seat, Peter Lassiter concentrated his attention on smoothing the lines of his trousers before answering. After satisfying himself that every offending wrinkle had been removed, he responded to Holmes. "Liam Coogan was staying at the Lord Selkirk Inn on Waterman's Way. When the housemaid went to clean his room yesterday morning she found the mutilated body. She's a youngster of perhaps 14, and I suspect she'll be a long time recovering from the shock." For a second time the Inspector attempted to stare Holmes into a shared appreciation of the events he was recounting. For a second time he had reason to doubt his success.

"Is there anything additional you wish to know?"

"Is the place of Liam Coogan's murder being maintained as a crime site? I should like to visit the inn and Mr. Coogan's room."

"The room and all of the second floor are for the moment cordoned off. However, the owner is most anxious that we take down the barriers we've erected so he can capitalize on the publicity. I understand the cost of his second floor rooms has now risen by 6d to a shilling depending on their proximity to the murder site. I'll ask my people to hold off removing the barriers for one more day, and I'll inform them of your interest in seeing the room."

"That would be most appreciated." Holmes's voice was silken.

"One more question, Inspector."

Peter Lassiter turned to face his new inquisitor, the solid looking man with the neatly trimmed moustache who had been writing at a feverish pace during the whole of his visit. He wondered if his ordeal would ever be over, or whether the old woman in widow's weeds would be called back to pose whatever queries struck her fancy.

"Can you tell me where the body of Mr. Coogan is now?"

"At her request, we've given the body to Mrs. Keegan, as she calls herself, to permit the family to conduct its wake. I'm not a Catholic myself, but I understand they're usually done with an open casket. I assure you this wake will be conducted with a closed casket. It's scheduled for tomorrow night. I intend to be there myself. It's a long shot, but there's always a chance someone in the Brotherhood might show up."

With an exaggerated sense of purpose, Peter Lassiter pushed himself from the settee a second time. "Now I really must return to the shop. I'll need to retrieve my hat and stick." He hesitated a moment before leaving, grimacing at the prospect of sharing a last discomfiting thought. "I don't mean to sound insensitive, Mr. Holmes. But I know these people and their lack of respect for the lives of others. I ...." Whatever he was about to say was lost to a second judgment. He took Holmes's hand in a firm grip, and said only, "You have my card; if you need to reach me please make contact through the Yard." And he stomped down the stairs to gather his top hat and stick from the waiting housekeeper.

"What do you make of our Peter Lassiter?" The members of the consulting detective agency were again gathered around Mrs. Hudson's kitchen table. A fresh pot of tea was now joined by a small mound of scones and bowl of strawberry jam. Their provider had raised the question for her colleagues after listening to Watson's report.

Watson set down his notes before making his response. "In truth, I found the man to be quite curious. He obviously maintains strong feeling about the murders in Dublin all these many years later, although I grant the horrific nature of that crime. And while I'm unfamiliar with the workings of the Special Branch, I am astounded by their cavalier attitude toward murder, regardless of the victim."

Holmes spoke from his place on the settee where he could once again comfortably spread his long frame. "I plain don't like the fellow. I found him supercilious and I suspect he's not terribly competent. I wonder if what we got from him is a full and accurate account of what's known about Mr. Coogan's death." Holmes sniffed a close to his remarks, and turned his attention to the large scone set within his easy reach.

"'E's not my cup of tea either, Mr. 'Olmes, and from what Dr. Watson reports it sounds like you gave 'im a good what for on that account." She smiled her support for Holmes before turning again to Watson. "I'd agree with what you say about the murders in Dublin, Doctor Watson. 'E sounds to 'ave got very upset about that indeed. But just see what else we 'ave there. When 'e talked about murders in Phoenix Park, 'e only talked about one man's death and 'e knew about the difficulty the dead man's wife is still 'avin' today. There's somethin' personal about the Inspector's work on those murders, somethin' that leads 'im to 'ave strong feelin's still about the one man's death and to still be involved with the murdered man's family. It could all be innocent enough, but I think we'd best keep it in mind as we go to investigatin' the death of Liam Coogan.

"There's one more thing. It's maybe just a small thing, but I find it a curiosity. You said, Doctor, that when the Inspector left, 'e didn't say 'e 'ad to get back to the Yard like you or I might've done. 'E said 'e 'ad to get back to 'the shop.' It's not an expression I've 'eard before. Is that some new way of talkin' either of you know about?"

Watson looked up from the entries he had continued making as the housekeeper spoke, his eyes bright with sudden inspiration. "He did say that, Mrs. Hudson, and it struck me as something odd I'd heard before, which is why I took it down. But now that you speak of it, it comes back to me where I heard it. There was a fellow posted to India with us, a man named Snowden as I remember, an artillery man who was providing training in the use of field pieces—cannon and such. When he talked about returning to regimental headquarters he said he was getting back to the shop. We ragged him about it, and he explained it was the name he and his classmates used at his old school. He'd gone to the Royal Military Academy at Woolwich which, as he told it, had been

39

a workshop until they converted it into the school's first classroom and the name had stuck." Watson's face tightened into a grimace. "It's interesting I suppose, but it doesn't seem very important, Mrs. Hudson."

"Not yet, Doctor, it's just somethin' to file away."

Watson took the hint and resumed recording while Mrs. Hudson turned her attention to Holmes.

"Mr. 'Olmes, I'm thinkin' a visit to the Lord Selkirk Inn and to its nearest pub might be in order. It'll 'ave to be by someone who can fit into the surroundings. I believe there's likely a lot more to be learned than our Mr. Lassiter cares to learn, or maybe cares to share like you were sayin', Mr. 'Olmes. I'm thinkin' somebody who looks the part could stop by the local pub and maybe 'ear things or ask the occasional question that could get us to understand better what 'appened to Mr. Coogan. That same somebody might inquire about a room at the Lord Selkirk and see what 'e can learn from a conversation with the night clerk that's there. What would you think of all that, Mr. 'Olmes?"

Holmes brightened immediately. His normally clear baritone transformed to a gravelly bass. "Simon 'Opgood at your service, just come to visit my dear old mum and the scenes of my misspent youth in Wappin'."

"Very good, Mr. 'Olmes. Perhaps we can work on some of the finer points of your story after I finish with the mornin's dishes. I'm thinkin' we'll 'ave to do some considerable work on that accent as well."

In the end, over his mild objection, it was decided Holmes would be an old man, and a friend of the Keegan family concerned with helping them better understand how Liam Coogan died. That would avoid having to provide a name and address for Holmes's "dear old mum," or an accounting of acquaintances from his "misspent youth" in Wapping. It also did away with Holmes's efforts to adopt a

Cockney accent which Mrs. Hudson found wholly unconvincing. It was agreed Holmes would call himself Simon Hopgood.

Chapter 3.
Simon Hopgood Investigates

The occasional gas lamp that might have provided something approaching safe passage along Wapping Lane had been either destroyed by vandals or left untended by the lamplighter, who had little fear of a supervisor coming behind to inspect his work. Two and three story planked housing lined each side of the street, the buildings differing from one another chiefly in the placement of their broken windows. A solitary figure held to a course that took him into the street and far from the shadows that grew large and small in the gaps between buildings. A game leg caused him to list heavily to one side. He counterbalanced the handicap with a thick staff that also served to keep at bay the night's creatures as they sought the leavings of food discarded by the residents of Wapping Lane.

Though once tall, the man was now stooped with age. He wore a faded frock coat over a much boiled white shirt and dark trousers. His clothes showed neither holes nor significant fraying, identifying him as a man of substance in the community. And yet, his gray matted hair and unruly beard, as well as the grime collected in the lines carved deep into his face, suggested he was by no means out of place on Wapping Lane. His destination lay nearly two streets ahead where light spilled out on the street from a building he could not yet see, but from which an undecipherable figure protruded. He presumed it to be the prow of the local pub, a judgment confirmed by the steady course of those entering and the unsteady course of those exiting the building.

As he struggled toward the light, two men emerged from the shadows and made their way toward him. They walked with the sureness of youth and confidence in the well-practiced task at hand. As they neared him, the old man could see that the shorter man had brown curly hair and wore an over-sized sweater. The taller of the two wore a workman's cap pulled well down over a long angular face. Both men smiled darkly at their target. The old man's attention fixed on the thick stick the taller of the two carried. Even in the dim light it glinted brightly up and down its length, the sign of its being studded with nails. They approached warily even with their advantage in numbers and youth. The taller man used his weapon to swipe at a rat lazily completing its evening meal. The animal snarled its retreat, then waited at a safe distance to resume its dinner. The old man continued his journey, apparently oblivious to the two men who now divided and began coming toward him from front and behind, until finally the taller man stood before him, brandishing his weapon at waist level.

"If you just give us the coins you're carryin', together with that nice fat stick you've got, you can go on past and there'll be no 'arm to come to you. If not, it's you and it's the two of us, and not another soul to know or care what 'appens 'ere."

The old man squinted up at the speaker, turning as he did to capture the second man within his field of vision. He spoke in a low gravelly voice. "Talk louder, lad, I don't hear quite as good as I used to. What is it you're asking?"

The spokesman for the two men heaved an exasperated sigh and relaxed his vigil for just a moment, but a moment was all that was needed. The old man swung his heavy staff in a graceful arc that smashed against the hand holding the studded club and sent the weapon clattering its way harmlessly down the street. He then brought his staff quickly straight up, catching the suddenly unarmed man a blow under the chin that sent him sprawling amidst the street's mud and refuse. His curly haired companion looked to the old man and the staff he now held menacingly aloft, and made a quick retreat to the shadows from which he and his friend had earlier emerged. The old man watched until he was swallowed up by the dark, then turned to see his other assailant first crawl, then stand, and wiping away the blood that poured from his mouth, stagger his way into the same bank of shadows.

The old man spoke into the night, his only audience the rat whose dinner had been briefly interrupted, and who now sat eyeing him and his thick staff. "And let that be a lesson not to trifle with Simon Hopgood."

With its unpainted rough-hewn planks and strategically packed daubing it was impossible to know if the pub had been built 100 years ago, or slapped together in the last few days. The buxom female figure overhanging the door, which had been the beacon for Simon Hopgood and many before him, appeared to be a carving of the pub's namesake although, if the truth were known, it was a failed effort to create a somewhat less generously proportioned young woman. The carver's inadequacy had, however, ended an argument between father and son as to whether to name the pub the Merry Mermaid or the Bonny Nymph, and led to an easy agreement on the Fat Mermaid.

A lone hansom stood outside the pub, its driver making failed effort to appear unconcerned about the patrons and vagrants gathered on the street nearby. A wraith-like woman, her blouse dipped low off one shoulder, stood just beyond the pub entrance, near enough to its light to be seen, but not seen well. She smiled an offer to Simon Hopgood as she did to each man that passed. She dared not risk speaking lest she give way to the wracking cough that might accompany an effort at speech. Simon Hopgood shook a gentle rejection of her advance, only to be approached by an elderly beggar whose watery eyes shone more with desperation than hope. He put a copper in the old man's hand, and pushed open the door of the

Fat Mermaid.

To his left was a long bar whose outer limit was nearly obscured by the crowd of men and the smoke from their pipes and cigarettes. What furniture there was consisted of mismatched chairs and scattered tables well to the right of the bar. Most of those were unoccupied since the hour for supper was past and the time for serious drinking was well under way. In the distance a game of darts was in progress. Billiards and skittles would have limited the space available for men and drink, and so had been rejected by the pub's ownership. A separate space for women, if one existed, was not readily visible. The pub's patrons stood in clusters at the bar or just beyond it, engaged in the mix of argument and hilarity that accompanied multiple pints and half pints.

Behind the bar, two men, one well into his 50's, the other 20 years his junior, labored to keep up with their impatient customers. Although father and son, as evidenced by the same dark gimlet eyes overhung by thick eyebrows, the two men differed dramatically in customer relations. The older man attended grimly to business, exchanging little communication beyond the acknowledgement of orders received, and his own demand for fresh orders from those whose glasses had been recently emptied or who were newly entering the pub. His son ranged the bar, joining the playful banter of some groups and making short work of conflicts that threatened to disrupt others, filling glasses and appearing to regard payment as a trivial, but necessary part of their relationship. The father, spying Simon Hopgood's empty hands, called for his order, somehow making himself heard above the din. His presence justified by a half pint of ale, Simon Hopgood leaned heavily on his staff surveying the room from his position at the end of the bar nearest the street.

He found himself contending with a difficulty for which he was unprepared. At Baker Street, striking up a conversation with Watson as landlord had been easy, even under Mrs. Hudson's critical oversight. With no other customers for him to serve, he had Watson's undivided attention. The Fat Mermaid presented Simon Hopgood with a uninterested landlord, his overbusy son, and the need to find an alternative source of information. As he studied his drinking companions for a likely prospect, clusters of patrons began separating in successive waves down the room's center, permitting the passage of a sandy-haired young man with flaring moustaches wearing a brown-checked frock coat, matching trousers and a pale green waistcoat. He held fast to a notepad in one hand, but had returned his pencil to a waistcoat pocket, and was making his way to the pub's front door as quickly as the patrons in front of him allowed. As the crowd parted, it reformed behind him, each of its members trying to get his attention by hollering over all the others, thereby guaranteeing the incoherence of all. The young man reached the door without looking to his right or left, and sprinted the remaining distance to the safety of the waiting cab. The crowd that had followed him as far as the door broke into small groups, some clearly delighted with the break in the evening's routine, others just as clearly angered by the events of the last few minutes.

The man standing beside Simon Hopgood had watched the proceedings with sniggering that broke finally into episodic gales of laughter. Unable to hold his glass steady, he rested it on the bar and waited for the unpredictable bouts of hysterics to run their course. Simon Hopgood decided the man's obvious good humor, together with his relative sobriety, marked him as an appropriate first contact. He creased his face into a broad smile and made effort to mimic his neighbor's high spirits.

"What in the world was that all about?"

Simon Hopgood's new found companion was a short

burly man, somewhere in his late 40's, with an extravagant mane of unruly yellow hair matched by a full beard and moustaches that seemed equally unfamiliar with comb or brush. A wide grin covered the side of his face nearest Hopgood, and he might have been described as jolly were it not for the broad streak of a scar extending from his hairline past a pupil-free glass eye to the lower part of his cheek on the side of his face that only became visible to Hopgood when he turned to confront him. "It's that fool of a reporter from the *Times* wanting to know about the killing of the bloke what's been staying at the Selkirk. If you can imagine it, he was willing to pay half a crown for whatever information anyone in the pub could give. Just you look at this crowd. For half a crown most of 'em would put their own mother in the dock. So of course, every one of 'em's got a cock-and-bull story about the dead man, and when he's not willing to pay for their lies, he gets himself run out of here by the whole pack of 'em. Did you ever see such a damn fool!"

His recounting of the events led to a renewed explosion of laughter although Hopgood was now aware that the hilarity only extended to one half of his companion's face. Hopgood was also aware that his carefully prepared questions about the death of the bloke at the Selkirk would get him labeled as fool number two, and risk his suffering the fate of fool number one. For the moment however, there was no interrupting the blond man's musings.

"Of course, if it's true, like I been hearing, that the dead man was one of them Irish blokes what's been going around blowing up everything in sight, there's some here would change their minds about knowing him, even for a half crown. Not with it meaning they'd spend half a day answering questions from the constable, or from one of them chaps from the Yard, and just maybe a night in the chokey while the police figure out what's to be done with 'em.

"Of course, there's not a man here that would care one way or the other about him blowing up half of London, as long as they're in the other half when it happens. But that's the problem with these political types. You can never be sure about 'em. They could be after the bloke down the end of the bar and blow up the whole damn pub to get him. Now, if somebody's after that same bloke's money, it's just the bloke with the money that's got to watch out. As long as you ain't him, you could be standing next to him and still be good as jam."

The man stopped to take a long sip of the half pint he picked up with one well-callused hand. "Of course, I'm not saying there ain't some spots what could stand a good airing if you take my meaning. Like the Old Bailey for one. I'd shake the hand of the man what done that, though I'd have to stand in line to do it." The blond man looked to Simon Hopgood for his response. Hopgood guessed correctly the proper response, grinning as broadly as he could manage. His companion turned to him with half a face creased into a smile. "My name's Forster. Elijah Forster."

"I'm Hopgood. Simon Hopgood."

"Pleased to know you, Simon. Have I seen you in here before? You're not familiar to me and I'm like to stop by most every night."

"You've a good eye." Hopgood looked startled for the moment, believing he had managed to say precisely the wrong thing. "What I mean is ..." But he was interrupted by renewed gales of laughter from Elijah Forster.

"I know what you mean and there's no harm done. In fact, I'll just turn a blind eye to it." And he dissolved in laughter again, this time joined cautiously by his companion. "You'd be surprised how quick you grow used to it, and it becomes just another part of who you are without its being any particular help or hindrance. Except for the shipping out of course." For a moment, Forster became silent, and Hopgood feared the man had led himself into a fit of despair in spite of his protestations of unconcern. But his mood brightened as quickly as it had briefly darkened. "You can believe there's not much call for a one-eyed seaman as long as there's plenty with two to be got. That's all right though. I about had my fill of the sea by the time of my ... accident. And I surely had my fill of the woman troubling me to death every time I was in port worrying about when I'd be going out again. So here I am on dry land and happy to be here. The woman's content, or as close to it as she can get. Meantimes, I work the barges along the river to stay close enough to the sea to keep the memories going." With that, he raised his glass to Simon Hopgood, "Your health, sir," and downed what remained of his drink. "And now, I still haven't heard what brings you to the Mermaid." He raised the question to Hopgood and his empty glass to the landlord.

Simon Hopgood waited for the small transaction to be completed, and for the landlord to go in search of patrons dallying over an empty glass. With somewhat exaggerated purpose, he looked to the right and left of his companion, then peered behind him before turning to his drink resting on the bar, speaking to it as much as to the man beside him. "I'd take it kindly if you'd keep what I'm telling you to yourself. You see, I'm sort of a friend to the family of Liam Coogan, which is the right name of the poor chap who got himself murdered. They asked me to learn what I could about his last days by way of being able to tell the little ones something different than what they'll be hearing from the police and on the street. I can't say I knew this Coogan myself, but I feel close to some of his people, in particular to his little girl, Moira. You might say she sort of adopted me. Anyway, you know how it is. I made a promise to the little one, and now I have to do right by her. Anything I can tell her and her mother will be a comfort.

Of course I'll be making sure it comes out sounding like a comfort."

The two men stood for a while side by side, huddled silently over their drinks. Having shared his mission as planned with a respondent for whom he hadn't planned, he was prepared to leave the Fat Mermaid in the hope of having better luck at the Lord Selkirk. He was not optimistic. The people at the Lord Selkirk Inn were bound to be as wary of strangers, even old crippled strangers, as the patrons of the Fat Mermaid. He finished his half pint of ale and was about to take his leave, when his companion spoke in a measured voice so different from his earlier easy humor that Hopgood found it necessary to look around to be certain he was the speaker.

"There's nobody here to tell you a thing. Those that know won't say and the rest ain't worth hearing. It just happens I know a bloke at the Lord Selkirk who can be of help if he's approached just right. He was a shipmate of mine on a voyage to the South Seas that neither one of us is likely to forget any time soon. He was a good man with the ropes, but a better one with a jug, if you take my meaning. That still might have been alright, except every time he'd get the blind staggers he was ready for a fight with anyone and everyone he could find. It didn't matter about their number or their size, or their rank come to that." Elijah Forster shook his head regretfully. "There's just so much of that you can have on a ship. Anyway, it got so no captain wanted any part of him and he's been working different places on the land, but as close to the sea as he can get. He's been fired from every job there's to be had in Liverpool and Southampton, and he's drinking his way through whatever work he can find down here. Right now, he's night clerk at the Selkirk Inn. I can take you to see him if you like. It's over on Waterman's Way no more than three streets from here. So long as you're with me, he'll tell you things he won't tell his own mother."

The Lord Selkirk Inn had been built more than 60 years earlier to coincide with the opening of St. Katharine's Dock in Wapping. Its owners saw themselves providing lodging to the builders and masters of the clipper ships that dominated ocean commerce and daily occupied piers along the several docks already available on the banks of the Thames. Shipwrights, blockmakers, sailmakers, and mastmakers would share the Inn's 18 rooms with the captains and senior officers of the ships they built, and the provisions agents who stocked the goods required for the lengthy voyages. Passengers seeking adventure, or the fresh start an ocean away from England promised, might find accommodations as well.

As clipper ship transport and passenger travel grew, the Inn gave promise of providing its owners a handsome income for decades. And for a time, the Inn met the owners' high expectations. Then steam came increasingly to replace wind in powering ships across the ocean, and the docks along the Thames were seen as too small to support the building or the mooring of the new breed of ocean-going liners. With few exceptions, shipping companies moved from London to Southampton and Liverpool. No longer the major highway to the ocean, the Thames became an artery on which goods were ferried to the long row of brick warehouses that still lined Pennington Street. The builders of ships, those who captained them, and the men who provided them with goods moved on as well, and the Lord Selkirk Inn came to serve an increasingly dubious population of lodgers for the succession of owners who sought to make a living from their patronage. The Inn that Simon Hopgood and Elijah Forster now approached had come finally to provide shelter to anyone with two shillings payable in advance, and an easy tolerance for coarse housing and coarse companions.

The Lord Selkirk was two-storied, the first floor brown

fieldstones of differing sizes joined together by mortar that had once been white and now was varying shades of gray. Whether by design or owing to the depletion of their finances, the builders had used clapboard for the Inn's second floor. The Inn was recessed from the roadway to spare its guests excessive noise from the street. Coaches carrying guests in a bygone era would follow a semicircular path to the Inn's three-stepped porch where a waiting footman would take their bags to the center hall reception. Grass had long since obliterated the semi-circular path from all but memory, and the Inn's clientele now walked directly from the roadway carrying whatever goods they felt it safe to expose to the larcenous intent of their fellow guests. Shutters hung at odd angles from windows or had gone missing entirely. On either side of the Inn, and extending halfway to the street, there were alder, oak, beech, and a thick growth of bushes that had once been neatly trimmed and were now wild from neglect. As he came closer, Hopgood could see the Inn was wedged against the brow of a hill such that the second floor facing the street was some five or six feet higher off the ground than the second floor facing the back.

Elijah Forster reported much of the Inn's history to his companion, speaking in hushed and respectful tones of what he described as "the old girl's heyday," and in more matter-of-fact fashion about the forces of "time and tide." He informed Hopgood he expected the Inn to be much quieter than usual as the prospect of a police investigation would have led many of the Inn's regulars to seek short-term housing elsewhere.

A group of five men who either had no such concerns, or were unwilling to be daunted by them, sat together on the porch's two topmost steps, taking advantage of the fine Spring evening, and filling the air with soft conversation and smoke from handmade cigarettes. They showed little interest in the two strangers, other than to look guardedly at the staff being carried by Simon Hopgood. A slope-shouldered gangly man, likely in his early 50's, but seeming older, separated himself from the group and, smoothing back wisps of dark hair, rose to welcome the possibility of new business. A fresh plaster showed over a swelling on his right temple. He squinted recognition of the blond man and dropped his mechanical greeting in favor of a genuine welcome.

"Elijah Forster, my old shipmate come to visit me. I'm glad to see the little woman is letting you out of her sight, or has she finally come to her senses and thrown you out altogether?" With that, the host of the Lord Selkirk Inn gave way to a high-pitched series of yips and cries that Hopgood gathered to be the sound of laughter. The four seated men took no notice of their companion's unusual expression of pleasure and continued their conversation in low tones inaudible to Hopgood. The host of the Lord Selkirk Inn, pointing to Forster, sought their attention. "I want you to meet the best mate I ever shipped out with on calm or stormy seas. This here's my own good friend, Elijah Forster." There were nods and murmured greetings, and a return to the discussion the men had no intention of allowing to be interrupted. The Inn's clerk, as Hopgood judged him to be, continued without regard to his recent companions. "Perhaps you and your friend would care to join me for a tiny nip. In honor of your visit, Elijah," the clerk explained.

"I would be delighted and let me introduce my friend." Elijah Forster turned far enough from one friend to the other to allow each to receive the benefit of his half-faced smile. "Simon Hopgood, I want you to meet Michael Peacock, the man I sailed with to Fiji and Tahiti on a voyage I'll never forget, and I'm guessing there are a good many in those islands that won't be forgetting us either. At least not any time soon."

"No, but there's many as would like to." And Michael Peacock went through a second series of high-pitched animal sounds in response to his own joke. As his yips and cries subsided, he turned to Hopgood favoring him with an open-mouthed grin that revealed occasional yellowed teeth sometimes in combination, often alone. "Any mate of Elijah's is my mate. Mr. Hopgood, and glad to make your acquaintance." He grasped Holmes's hand with his own, and Holmes was surprised to see his own large hand disappear in the clerk's somewhat painful grip, confirming the menace of an out-of-control Michael Peacock described to him earlier. "A pleasure to meet you," Simon Hopgood offered.

Michael Peacock waved his old and new friend into the Inn as he took his leave of the others. "I'll get back to you boys later. I'm just going to have a short one with my old shipmate and his pal." The four men gave no notice of loss.

Michael Peacock went to his accustomed position behind the counter opposite the open door, at which he registered guests, assigned rooms, and from whose depths he now withdrew an unlabeled bottle he described as first quality rye whiskey. He extracted three glasses from the same depths and, beaming to his guests and to his bottle, filled each glass half full. The counter having become a bar and the clerk its landlord, Michael Peacock provided the first toast of the evening, "To the Queen," and promptly drank the good woman's health. His companions followed, one with enthusiasm and one with an effort to look someplace other than his well smudged glass.

Elijah Forster, sensing where the evening was headed, and knowing full well the dangers associated with its reaching that destination, undertook to forestall or at least delay its progress. "Michael, in truth, I've a special favor to ask. I met Simon over at the Mermaid and come to find out he's very close to the family of the man what got himself killed here last

54

night. Not the man himself, mind you, but the wife and kiddies. And it's for the sake of them he's wanting to find out what he can about the poor fellow's death. You know, Michael, to sort of set the record straight, or as straight as may be, before the police have at the bloke, and the kids hear nothing about their father except every scrape he was ever in. Ain't that about right, Simon?"

Hopgood's eyes widened with respect for the unexpected show of diplomacy by his companion.

"It's exactly right, Elijah. You see, Mr. Peacock, even now the little ones are hearing the kinds of things that are bound to get said when a man dies violent like Mr. Coogan done, and we're hoping to get away from the bits and pieces they're hearing and kind of give them a bigger picture of who their dad was and how he passed. That's why I've been asked to sort of look into things, and see what I can come up with that can answer their questions and help get to a better understanding."

Michael Peacock stared mournfully at his empty glass and then at his two companions. His disappointment was not because he was being used by a friend, he was accustomed to that; he had expected companionship on his alcoholic flight, and now faced the prospect of putting off that journey, or, and more likely, having to take it alone. The empty glass remained the focus of his attention as he directed his question to Hopgood. "And what exactly is your relation to the deceased, if I may be asking?"

"I'm quite close to some in the Keegan family. In fact, you might think of me as a godfather to little Moira. The sweet little thing came to see me less than a week ago and in terrible straits. Anything I can learn that might help the family get past this awful blow will be that much appreciated."

The clerk's deep-set eyes fixed on Simon Hopgood. "Exactly how much would it be appreciated?"

A smile began then quickly disappeared from Hopgood's face. "If I could see the room, ask some questions and get satisfactory answers, it could be worth a half sovereign."

Elijah Forster let out a soft whistle while his former shipmate squinted a quick study of Hopgood's face before nodding his agreement. "I'll see the money before we go," but he was already bringing up a ring of keys from the bottomless cabinet beneath the counter.

With Michael Peacock a half sovereign richer, Elijah Forster greatly confused, and Simon Hopgood well satisfied with his progress thus far, they proceeded up the stairs to the room in which Liam Coogan's body had been found. Peacock negotiated the one flight quickly, then waited while Hopgood fought his way up, throwing his weight against the far wall and pushing off each step using his staff. Forster walked a single step ahead, looking back now and again with his good eye to check Hopgood's progress. At the second floor landing Hopgood made private use of his Holmes persona, cataloguing his observations in preparation for the inevitable interrogation by Mrs. Hudson.

The walls upstairs and down suggested the Inn had at one time gotten a good price on yellow paint. The frequency with which white patches interrupted the yellow indicated the paint supply had long since been depleted. Five sleeping rooms faced the front. The bath and four additional sleeping rooms faced the back including one at the far end with a large "X" whitewashed across its door. Peacock confirmed it as being Coogan's room. Beyond the door with the X was another sleeping room and the backstairs.

Peacock explained that he hadn't checked Coogan in, but he'd been told Coogan asked for a room on the first floor and, when told none was available, asked for one that would face away from the traffic and be as near to the backstairs as could be worked out—just in case. Peacock indicated that such requests weren't unusual at the Lord Selkirk which was why money was demanded in advance. They stopped while Peacock searched his key ring for number 17. He explained there shouldn't be any problem, the whole of the second floor was off limits and he hadn't seen a constable for at least a day. Still, he looked up and down the hall before opening the door, then urged them all into the room and closed the door quickly behind them, indicating "there was no point to taking foolish chances."

As Peacock lit the room's gas lantern and the room became a mix of light and shadows, Holmes thought back to his session with Watson and the questions Simon Hopgood was expected to pose. "Is this exactly the way things looked when you discovered Mr. Coogan?"

"It wasn't strictly speaking me what discovered him. It was Alice, the youngster what comes in mornings, and she reported it to Felcher—he's the day clerk—if you could call her screaming and hollering all over the Inn, reporting. Not that I can blame her much given what all she found. But your answer's yes, except for what was left of Coogan to get carried off, there's been nothing that's been moved or taken away."

Hopgood looked over the room, wishing for the moment Watson was along to take the detailed notes that so impressed Mrs. Hudson, then decided the room was so plain and sparsely furnished he couldn't imagine there would be any difficulty in describing it when the time came. There was a narrow rope bed to his right as he entered the room. Its covers were pulled back and the pillow lay askew at the head of the bed. His new-found interest in ropes and twine led him to study the tightly drawn rope below the straw mattress. He wished he could have cut off a small part of it for later study although, in truth, he saw nothing remarkable about the rope. A battered wardrobe stood on the wall opposite the door next to an open window. Inside the wardrobe there was a pair of shoes and neatly folded trousers. A ladder-back chair, its well-worn state making it a match for the other furniture, stood in the far left corner beside a round table covered with a gold-fringed green cloth that bore the scars of multiple cigarette burns, and the stains of the many meals and drinks that had been consumed with greater haste than care. Beside the chair and table, and opposite the bed, the fireplace stood cold and empty. The walls were bare, yellow like the rest of the Inn and with the same patches of white scattered throughout. What caught all three men's attention was the floor, or more precisely the blood-stained carpet that lay between the bed and the fireplace, and which each man stepped around with exaggerated care while exploring the room.

Peacock pointed to the object that fascinated and repelled the three men, "That's where they done him up."

Hopgood nodded and continued with the questioning practiced earlier at Baker Street. "Was there anything out of the ordinary you noticed on the night of the murder? Anything that got your attention?"

"Not right off. It started out just like every other night. I come on to relieve Felcher at six, which is also the time when the place is probably its busiest. There are blokes going in and out all night starting then, and there's no stopping until about one or even a little after. At six they're mostly going out to get their supper at the Mermaid or some might walk over to the White Pelican. The food's better, but it's kind of a long way to go and it's best to get with a group if you're going, if you know what I mean." Simon Hopgood indicated he knew what the clerk meant.

"The most of them start drifting back any time from nine to around one in the morning, which is when the pubs close. I lock the doors at two and there's nobody can get in without me letting 'em in. Of course, they want you to think the locking up is to keep out thieves and riffraff looking for a free night's sleep, but it's mostly to keep them as is already in from sneaking out without paying if they've stayed past their time. Anyways, after about two that night it gets quiet as a tomb just like usual. I make my rounds to check up on things every now and again like I'm supposed to. I make sure the back door is locked, which it was every time I checked. Except for my rounds I stay where I'm s'posed to back of the counter downstairs. At least I stay there until this bloke I never see comes up behind me with his cosh and gives me this," Michael Peacock pointed to his plaster, "and put me out for the night."

"Is that what you told the men from the Yard?" Elijah Forster raised the question gently, but without making effort to hide his suspicion that his old shipmate was not telling all he knew.

Michael Peacock found himself on the glass eye side of Elijah Forster. He stared at the pupilless eye and the eye at him. "Well now, there might be some things I told 'em that was a little off the mark, but nothing as would make any real difference. And here's this Coogan, just as dead as he would be if every word I spoke was the gospel truth." He tried to move to a position on Elijah Forster's other side, but he would have had to cross the blood-stained carpet to do so and therefore remained where he was.

Forster held the gaze from his good eye away from the night clerk. "Now then, Michael, you took the man's money and a right smart piece of coin at that. I think you owe him the whole of the story."

Michael Peacock looked away from his former shipmate to Simon Hopgood whose eyebrows were raised in anticipation of his response. "Well, I was just now getting to that. The way I seen it there was no point to risking my job just to add another line or two to some constable's report. But I'll tell *you* the whole of what happened since, like Elijah says, you've paid for it." He stepped gingerly around the carpet, put the ladder-backed chair between himself and his two guests, took a deep breath, and began.

"First off, everything I told you to here is true except for the part about me staying in back of the counter the whole time. There's nobody could do that a whole night. So every now and again I take a little break. Starting at three I'll go outside for a smoke, but I'll only do it once an hour and I don't start until the place is asleep. When the hall clock strikes the time, it's my signal to go for a smoke. The trouble is I'm not supposed to open the door after two unless it's an emergency so if I tell the police that I leave the door open to sit outside and smoke, I'm out of a job. Instead, I tell 'em it must of been somebody, or some couple of somebodies, who snuck into the Inn somewheres before two while the door is still unlocked, prob'ly when I'm making my rounds, and that whoever it was must of hid until it was safe to come out, then hit me from behind which is why I don't know who it was. I was just looking to keep my job, and didn't see the harm in it—and I still don't." Michael Peacock looked to his audience for the approval he thought his action deserved, but the faces, including both sides of Elijah Forster's, were expressionless.

Simon Hopgood let the moment pass before making his request. "Please tell us now what really happened."

"I said I would and I mean to. It's really not all that different from what I told the man from the Yard except for everything happening outside. Like I told you I go for a smoke when I hear the clock striking three. I unlock the front door just like I always do, only this time I see there's a fire down by the street that I figure is from some tramp who's trying to stay warm. At night it can still turn kind of chilly this time of year, and the fact is I was planning on just a quick smoke myself on account of how nippy it had got. But I'm not three steps into going after the tramp when I get clubbed from in back by one of them blokes from the Brotherhood. I know it's one of that bunch because the last thing I hear before I go down is that 'Erin go brore' thing they're always hollering.

"Next thing I know I'm waking up on the grass with a terrible headache and this bump on the side of my head. The front door is still wide open, but lucky for me—if you can call any of this lucky—I can see the stars are out so I know it's still got to be night, and I got time to get my story straight before the whole Inn is waking up. Of course, I don't know nothing about Coogan getting chopped up, I figure it's a robbery and they maybe got to the safe where we put what we take in that day. And I know if they hear about me being out cold for more than two hours, which I later see by the clock is how long it was, they will right away figure I was on a drunk and banged my head in a fall. I can handle my drinking well enough when I have to, but I got to admit there's been some trouble from time to time, and there's them as would treat me rough if they thought I'd been drinking again." He looked away from Forster, avoiding contact with both his real and his glass eye.

"So I get back in, lock the front door again, see that the back door is still locked, and find out that the safe looks just fine. Even my key ring is sitting on top of the counter where they must of left it. Which is when I figure maybe the robbers got cold feet after knocking me out, and everything is going to be okay.

"To play it safe, when Felcher comes on duty, I tell him about me getting hit from behind because I got to explain the lump that's growing on the side of my head. Of course, I can see Felcher don't believe my story and I'm thinking neither will anyone else when the girl finds Coogan and all hell breaks loose. Felcher makes me go up with him and we see Coogan is been cut to ribbons with his blood running so thick on the carpet you could have wrung it out. Elijah can tell you I've seen some things—both of us have—but never anything like that. Even now it gives me the willies to think about it. Anyway, Felcher sends around for the constable, and the constable turns around and sends for the men from the Yard. For all the good the whole lot of them did. They asked a bunch of questions about who might have visited Coogan the night before, and didn't anyone hear nothing, and where was I the whole time. I showed them the bump on my head to let them know where I was."

Michael Peacock paused, his attention again drawn to the carpet, then back to the two men. "And that's really all there is to tell. I'm afraid it's not much of a help giving you things you can boast about to Coogan's family. I can tell you this that could be a help. He didn't mix with the riffraff here and he seemed to me a respectable chap. He even come down late the first night he was here, and had a smoke with me outside on account of he said he couldn't sleep for missing his family like he did. I can tell you that's a whole lot different from what we usually get in here." Peacock paused, looked to the door, and asked in a hopeful voice, "How about we all go and have that drink we talked about?"

"Just a couple more questions, Mr. Peacock." Hopgood spoke with real sympathy for the man's needs although he couldn't remember mentioning anything about having a drink with him. "What kinds of things did the men from the Yard want to know and what did you tell them?"

"I'll tell you there was just the one bloke from the Yard with questions, and he was this young pup all dandied up like he's going to a dance instead of investigating a murder. Dainty was what he was. Except for what he done around the body. I know if you work at the Yard, you prob'ly see bodies every day, but like I been saying, this weren't no ordinary body. And still he looked at this Coogan, all bloody and cut every which way, and I could swear he smiled. Just for a second, but there it was. Then he shows me this picture he says was took when they arrested Coogan over in Ireland, and asks me if he's the same one as was registered at the Inn and I tell him it's Coogan all right.

"After, we come downstairs where he wants to know how long Coogan is been here and did he have any friends or get any visitors, and maybe some other stuff like that I can't remember. Anyway, I tell him it was Coogan's second night and he was paid up for three. I don't say nothing about giving back the money for the third night because that ain't my place. I said how he came and went the whole time just as nice as pie. He wasn't friendly with anybody, but he was regular if you know what I mean. He said a pleasant word and went on his way. And I couldn't tell him what way that was, any more than I could tell him whether he had visitors, on account I don't go following any of the customers around. In the first place, I don't figure it to be any of my business, and in the second place, I don't figure those to be healthy things to do.

"But this young pup ain't through." Blotches of red appeared across Peacock's drawn bony face and his huge hands had begun to close into fists. "He goes and gets himself all worked up about my keys, and who my folks were, and what are my 'sympathies' as he calls them."

With Michael Peacock's rage and incoherence increasing together and with alarming speed, Elijah Forster again decided to take a hand. "Michael, you're not making a great deal of sense. First off, what is this business about the keys?"

Peacock looked grimly to Forster, took a deep breath and, as his hands gradually unclenched and his complexion returned to its familiar sallow condition, he nodded his appreciation. "You was always a steadying force, Elijah. I'll give it a try. This bloke from the Yard wanted to know how Liam Coogan's 'mortal enemies,' which is what he called 'em, could of got into his room without breaking down the door. I explain they must of took my keys when they knocked me out because when I come to, my keys are sitting on the counter which is not where I left 'em. Only he gives me this big, 'uh huh,' meaning he don't believe me. So next he wants to know does my family come from Ireland, when every blessed one of them is from Manchester except my Uncle Ian who's a Welshman, and there's nobody knows how he got in the family or much cares come to that.

"And then he's got this question about my sympathies. I tell him I got sympathies for everybody and most especially for my own self, but he says that ain't what he means, and he finally gives up trying to explain, but not before asking me if I maybe didn't let Liam Coogan's murderer into his room. So I say to him, does he think I let 'em give me this lump on my head too, and he says that them hitting me in the head makes it look good. Like I'm supposed to risk getting my head bashed in so things'll look good. Tell me that ain't enough to get anybody's blood boiling, Elijah."

Elijah smiled his support. Simon Hopgood spoke for both men. "I'd say that's more than enough, Mr. Peacock. And I'd say it's time for me to be getting on and leave you be. You've been very helpful. Let me just ask again. You're absolutely certain everything in the room is exactly the way it was?"

"Exactly. That's the way the young pup told me to leave it so that's the way I left it. And to tell you the truth I'd be obliged to get things back the way they was. I'd especially like to get rid of this here carpet. Anyway, I've told you all I know. Now, how about one little drink to sort of put all this behind us?"

Simon Hopgood nodded. "I'd be delighted if you'd permit me to toast your very good health."

In truth, Michael Peacock wasn't particular whose

health was toasted, and both his as well as Elijah Forster's and Simon Hopgood's very good health were toasted before the latter was able to take his leave.

Simon Hopgood limped his way across the several streets leading to The Highway where he knew he would be able to locate a cab. The further he got from the Lord Selkirk, the less pronounced his limp became. By the time he reached the thoroughfare it had disappeared entirely. Once inside a cab, Simon Hopgood transformed himself from an elderly lame man to a vigorous, if somewhat disheveled, Sherlock Holmes. The driver, staring hard at his exiting passenger, decided the light where he had picked up his fare must have been very poor.

Chapter 4.
An Alliance With the Fourth Estate

Holmes's night did not end with the cab ride to Baker Street. Aware of the inquisition in store for him the following morning, he prepared a few notes for himself before settling down for what he deemed to be a well-earned rest. When he appeared in Mrs. Hudson's kitchen the following morning, he found his colleagues anxiously awaiting description of Simon Hopgood's exploits. He greeted his colleagues with a smile meant to proclaim that all was well, then accepted the breakfast Mrs. Hudson had kept warm. With careful deliberation Holmes selected a slice of kidney, allowing himself to savor it for the moment before cleansing his palate with a sip of tea, by which time Mrs. Hudson's patience had been exhausted.

"I'm thinking it was a good night for you, Mr. 'Olmes, and likely you're entitled to a quiet breakfast, but there's a time and a place. And now is the time to give us your story, and please be careful to leave nothin' out."

Holmes dabbed at his mouth and, aided by his own jottings, proceeded amidst forkfuls of kidneys, eggs, bacon and toast, and the scratching of Watson's pencil across his notebook, to give a full report of Simon Hopgood's nighttime activities. When all of that worthy's numerous accomplishments had been fully detailed, Holmes dabbed at his mouth a last time and sat back to await the accolades of his audience.

Watson was, indeed, lavish in his praise. "A singular piece of work, Holmes. It sounds as fine a job of playacting as you've ever pulled off."

Mrs. Hudson was more restrained in her acknowledgement. "Yes, Mr. 'Olmes, I believe you've moved things along quite well." She asked a series of questions about the room and the bloodied rug (in which Holmes believed she took an excessively morbid interest as he later informed Watson), then lapsed into the silence of her own thoughts while Holmes turned his attention to preparing his first pipe of the day.

"And what do you make of all that, Mrs. Hudson?" Watson asked.

"I'm not yet certain what to make of it. I do think some things are startin' to come together, but it's a long way from bein' clear. We may know more after Mr. 'Olmes attends the Coogan wake this evenin'."

Holmes took a long draw on his briar making certain the shag was well lit, then removed the pipe to ask his question. "Another excursion, Mrs. Hudson? And who shall I be this evening? I'm of the opinion we should retire Simon Hopgood." Before they could decide on a suitable alias for Holmes, the bell sounded the arrival of a visitor to 221B.

While Holmes and Watson returned to their apartments, Mrs. Hudson pulled shut the pocket door separating the kitchen from her parlor, and went to open the front door to their unexpected caller. He was unknown to Mrs. Hudson although he would have been recognized instantly by Simon Hopgood as the reporter who had made a swift and unceremonious exit from the Fat Mermaid the night before. Even without the benefit of Simon Hopgood's identification of the man, Mrs. Hudson recognized the visitor as a newspaper reporter. The fingers of his right hand, with which he gave her his card, had traces of ink at the tips of the thumb, and second and third fingers revealing his vocation involved writing, and the pad and two sharpened pencils in the pocket of his waistcoat indicated he was prepared to jot notes when and where the need arose. He wore the same brown-checked frock coat and matching trousers that had distinguished him from other patrons at the Fat Mermaid and which, together with flaring moustaches and a soft homburg cocked just the slightest bit in the direction of his left ear, gave him too frivolous an appearance for a clerk or businessman, but one which was fitting for a newspaperman. His card confirmed her worst suspicions. On one line, it read, "Winston Parkhurst," on the second, it read, *London Times*."

The newspapers had provided Mrs. Hudson with some of her more challenging moments over the years. Mr. Holmes professed an understanding of the need to avoid exposure in the popular press and had promised—on several occasions— to keep reporters at arm's length, and still his name managed to appear in print from time to frequent time, and always in heroic, if not mythic, terms. Immediately after its appearance there would be a cooling of relations with Scotland Yard, lasting until self-interest finally overcame intransigence, and the Yard would restore its fragile alliance with the residents of 221B Baker Street.

"If you could kindly tell Mr. Holmes I'd appreciate just a moment of his time." He adopted the practiced smile which regularly gained him entrance across thresholds guarded by housekeepers and parlor maids.

"May I tell Mr. 'Olmes what this is concernin'."

Parkhurst recognized the words had the earmarks of a question, but were not delivered in the form of a question. "It's rather personal." Mrs. Hudson made no move from the threshold and continued to stare at him blankly. The forced smile required increasing force. "You can tell Mr. Holmes, if you would, I am aware of his interest in the Coogan murder and believe I have something useful to share with him."

Mrs. Hudson was concerned with what Winston Parkhurst might expect in exchange for sharing the information he had, but knew that was beyond the bounds of her role as housekeeper, and that she had already extended those bounds well beyond her visitor's expectations. She stepped back from the doorway and admitted the reporter from the *Times*.

"If you'll just make yourself comfortable in the parlor, I'll let Mr. 'Olmes know you're 'ere." She left him to choose between the three oval-backed chairs and the couch, and went to alert Holmes and Watson about their visitor. She did not offer to take his hat or stick in the hope it would encourage a brief visit. She would urge Holmes to be wary and, failing that, she would rely, as always, on Dr. Watson.

On its face, what Winston Parkhurst sought from Holmes seemed quite modest. As Mrs. Hudson joined them to serve tea and scones, he responded to Watson's question by explaining, for a second time, that he sought only to have first access to Holmes and the rights to his story if he was successful in finding Coogan's slayer or slayers. In exchange, he could provide them with access to the Keegan family, with whom he'd established a positive relationship while doing background for the story he was preparing on the Brotherhood. He had hopes that such a story might gain him the promotion that his current position, reporting births, marriages and deaths, would not. He suggested the family had reason to be suspicious of outsiders and the use of a trusted intermediary would be essential. Watson asked how he had learned of Holmes's interest in the case. The reporter clarified that, in conducting his own background investigation, he had been engaged in discussions with people at the Yard and, most recently, with an Inspector Peter Lassiter of the Special Branch. Watson and Holmes caught each other's eye at the mention of the policeman's name.

Watson wondered if the reporter might shed light on some things they found unclear. Specifically, they would like to know his thinking about the strength and real threat of the

Brotherhood living in London, and what he believed had been Coogan's participation in their activities.

Parkhurst smiled softly at the questions. He accepted tea from the housekeeper who left him to pour tea for Holmes, then Watson, before backing her way from the room. Parkhurst allowed his body to sink deep into his easy chair as he answered Watson's questions in the effortless drone of someone well versed in his subject and accustomed to queries from people lacking his background. Although its numbers were unknown, the Brotherhood was definitely a force to be reckoned with. They had proven that through a series of bombings several years earlier and their involvement in sporadic terrorist attacks since. Their activity had been curtailed in association with the increasing sophistication of the Irish Branch—now known as the Special Branch. It was Parkhurst's belief, and the belief of the Special Branch, that the Brotherhood had access to considerable resources. It was common knowledge that the Fenians, as they called themselves in America, were a vigorous force politically in New York, in Boston, and in parts of Canada, and openly raised money for what had come to be known as "the Cause."

He thought it certain that Coogan knew a good many in the Brotherhood and had participated in some of the work of the Invincibles. He reported it to be his understanding that the Brotherhood had grown deeply suspicious of Coogan, suspicious enough to murder him. Parkhurst noted that, with their own lives and fortunes on the line, suspicion was sufficient to get a man killed.

The room fell silent for a moment except for Holmes's groan of understanding. Watson continued his note-taking, while Parkhurst finished his tea without change in his genial expression. At length, Holmes broke the silence.

"I thank you for providing that background, Parkhurst. It's most useful. Now, as to the bargain you propose. You ask that I provide you with first access to a report of the results of our investigation and in return you will provide Watson and myself access to Mrs. Keegan. Is that essentially correct?" Holmes received a vigorous nod of agreement.

He gave his own slower, more cautious nod before speaking again. "I find that a fair exchange. You must understand, however, these things take time and I'll not have you coming around here constantly or interfering with our work."

Parkhurst clapped his hands together and his polite smile became a broad grin. "Of course. That's perfectly reasonable. I assume I may inquire about your progress from time to time. I assure you I won't make a pest of myself."

Holmes nodded a gracious consent. "Your occasional visits would be quite agreeable. When can you arrange things with Mrs. Keegan?"

"I'll see her at the wake for Coogan tonight although that's obviously not the best time to work out arrangements. I should be in touch with you within the next day, or two at most. And now I've taken quite enough of your time, Mr. Holmes, Dr. Watson. The reporter stood, replaced the derby to its jaunty angle and took up his walking stick. Before taking leave he had a sudden thought. "Of course, it will be essential that we keep this entirely to ourselves until there is something to report."

Holmes's raised eyebrows and supercilious tone conveyed how unnecessary he deemed Parkhurst's admonition. "Certainly, that will be the procedure."

"Then our agreement is complete." Parkhurst crossed to solemnize their accord with a handshake before leaving. His place was taken shortly after by Mrs. Hudson, come to gather up his dishes and discover what information he had divulged.

When Watson had finished reading from his notes, Mrs.

Hudson sat with lips pursed and eyes closed for what seemed to both men an unconscionably long time. She emerged at last from her reverie with a firm nod and look of fierce resolve. "It will likely serve, Mr. 'Olmes. The bargain you struck with Mr. Park'urst should prove useful to us although you may 'ave a time with the other reporters if it comes to that. Anyway, we do need to see Mrs. Keegan and if this Park'urst fellow can smooth the way, so be it. But now we'll need to take special care about you bein' at Mr. Coogan's wake. What with Mr. Park'urst and Inspector Lassiter both bein' there, you'll need a proper disguise to avoid bein' found out. I leave that to you Mr. 'Olmes and your actin' ways. But I'm thinkin' that the mourner you'll be goin' as will 'ave to be someone anybody could feel free to talk in front of without any worry about what they're sayin'."

Holmes squinted his disbelief at Mrs. Hudson. "And how could there be such a person?"

"I 'ave in mind Mr. James Burch, who's deaf as a post, poor man."

And so, for a second night, Holmes contrived to become unrecognizable before venturing out into yet another unfamiliar neighborhood.

A particularly sharp-eyed observer might have seen a resemblance between Simon Hopgood, recently of Wapping, and the man making his way down Kilburn High Road to attend a wake on Princess Street. The matted gray hair, faded frock coat and matching trousers were all familiar, and the once tall figure was again bent under the weight of age. But this figure, though he walked stiffly, carried no staff, and his gray hair was augmented by a beard and moustaches that covered a good deal of his face. He walked along streets well illuminated by carefully spaced gas lamps with no concern about being interrupted by people or vermin appearing from the modest, but well-tended row houses he passed.

As Holmes approached 68 Princess, he briefly reviewed his latest persona. He was now an acquaintance of Liam Coogan come to pay his respects—an extremely hard of hearing acquaintance. At first he had resisted the role, feeling the handicap unnecessarily limited his development of the character. After due consideration, he decided that becoming James Burch could provide its own challenge, being unlike any role he had played before. Besides, he had to grant the part would allow him to be privy to conversations he might not hear otherwise, and to choose the questions about himself he did, and did not, wish to answer.

Approaching the open door that was his destination, James Burch took up his ear trumpet and laboriously climbed the flight of stairs where he was welcomed by a small mountain of a man who identified himself as Seamus Keegan, Patsy's brother. Holding the trumpet to one ear and jerking the thumb of his free hand to his chest he announced, "James Burch. Sorry about your loss." He shook the large man's hand, then leaned into him and thrust the trumpet toward him. "I'm afraid I didn't catch the name."

The mountain rumbled once more, louder this time. "It's Keegan. Seamus Keegan, Patsy's brother. Please come inside."

James Burch smiled vaguely, leaving unclear to Seamus Keegan what he'd heard or hadn't heard. He took James Burch by the arm and led him across the threshold of the Keegan's first floor lodgings and into the parlor. The small room would have been described as dark and cheerless, even without the casket laid across three chairs along the wall separating the parlor from the adjoining kitchen. A single gas lamp did its best to brighten the apartment, but was no match for the gathering night sky, as the room's beige walls were already darkening to shades of gray. Two round tables, set together beneath the window, and a respectful distance from the casket, contained trays filled with an assortment of small sandwiches as well as cakes and biscuits. The contents of both were regularly replenished by the several women who brought cups of tea and plates of food in continuous trips in and out of the pocket door separating the parlor and kitchen.

Some of the guests were seated on the collection of mismatched chairs Holmes guessed had been lent to Mrs. Keegan for the occasion. There were more mourners than chairs so several were left vacant lest anyone truly needing a seat be deprived of one. Most stood with a cup of tea in one hand, and refreshment in the other, engaged in animated conversation with their neighbors.

James Burch was led across the parlor by the large man of whom he took careful notice in light of the report he would be making to Mrs. Hudson. Seamus Keegan was of average height, perhaps a little more, but his broad shoulders and powerful chest easily exaggerated his size. So too, the flowing black moustaches set against his broad face, and his piercing dark eyes furthered an impression that Seamus Keegan was best regarded with caution. His only evidence of vulnerability was the small limp he revealed as he lumbered his way across the parlor with James Burch in tow.

He introduced Burch to his sister, Patricia Keegan, who sat by the head of the casket, hands folded on her lap. She was a stunning contrast to her brother, sharing only his dark hair and heavy-lidded eyes, but those eyes were set above high cheekbones and a small bow of a mouth that gave her an attractive appearance, even with the strain of the moment, and likely the whole of her life, reflected in her sad, tired expression.

"Thank you so much for coming, Mr. Burch."

He held the trumpet to his ear and showed a pained confusion.

Her voice came louder with the brogue he had heard from Moira Keegan made stronger and even more appealing. "I'm that grateful to you for coming, Mr. Burch."

James Burch nodded, the pained confusion now giving way to a show of distress. "I'm so sorry about your loss, Mrs. Keegan. He was a fine man."

"How were you knowing my Liam, Mr. Burch?"

The trumpet and pained expression returned. "Yes, I certainly did."

From behind James Burch, Seamus Keegan rolled his eyes and shook his head from side to side. Positioning the trumpet for James Burch, he called into it that he would get him settled with a nice cup of tea, and steered him gently, but firmly, in the direction of the tables of food. Staring hard at the clean shaven man with flowing dark hair and stylish dress who had chosen a seat at the end of his path, he induced Inspector Lassiter to yield the chair nearest the tables to Burch. Seamus Keegan then took his leave, calling into the trumpet that he should let the ladies know of anything he might need, before limping his way back to the door to resume his role welcoming mourners.

Viewed as a poor partner for conversation, James Burch was left alone. One of the servers wordlessly brought him tea and pointed to the lemon, sugar and cream she held to learn his preference, then to the cakes and sandwiches. He accepted a potted beef sandwich and two biscuits. The priest came up to him, touching an arm to get his attention and looking to him with eyes crinkled and lips pursed in the hope of conveying both sympathy and a need to be strong, before moving away to comfort mourners less dependent on facial cues alone. The snatches of conversation he heard seemed the things one could expect to hear at any ceremony marking a death and appeared useless to the investigation: "Patsy was bearing up awfully well ... the turnout was much larger than expected ... the turnout was much smaller than expected ... this would be a terrible blow for Little Liam and Moira ... Big Liam had been much too young a man to die ... there was no telling how Patsy would get along ... the ladies had done a fine job preparing sandwiches and cakes."

A man about the age of James Burch, and somewhat the worse for drink, shambled up to him, announcing himself to be Cornelius Keegan, father to Patsy Keegan and father-in-law to the dead man. James Burch held the trumpet to his ear, but showed no acknowledgement of what had been said. Cornelius Keegan continued unperturbed.

He spoke into the horn of the trumpet, leaning forward to do so, and seizing on the opportunity that provided to poke the shoulder of his audience as he made each point. "I'll not say Liam was a perfect son-in-law. Not by a long shot. But he done one thing there's nobody can take from him. He got himself two beautiful cubs. Jewels is what they are. Jewels in a family crown. Of course, we all know he come up crosswise of the Brotherhood and I'll not defend him there, but it's all over and done with now. And I'll tell you this ...." But before he could tell James Burch another word, he was borne aloft by two men who appeared at each side of Cornelius Keegan and transported their burden easily and swiftly out of the parlor to a destination James Burch guessed to be the man's bedroom. There was a succession of "Here now's," and "What do you think you're doing?" among some of Cornelius Keegan's less colorful protestations until a door closed, drowning out all further complaints.

With a great deal of head-shaking, and comments of "What else can you expect," and "He's at it again," the room settled back into its mix of conviviality and sympathetic understanding. James Burch noted that Patsy Keegan never stirred or changed expression at any time during the brief turmoil.

"That's really an excellent likeness of Liam. Moira is getting to be quite the artist don't you know." The words were spoken by a heavy-set woman of perhaps 35 or 40 with flaming red hair falling in curls to her shoulders. She was drawing another woman's attention to a pencil sketch set in a cardboard frame on the mantel above the fireplace. The large bright eyes in a heart-shaped face established him as Moira Keegan's father. The artist had drawn curly hair and a face without moustache or whiskers. It was an unremarkable face, but gave a sense of softness out of keeping with the nature of his death.

Her companion, an older and equally substantial woman, whose braided gray hair circled her head in a manner that put Burch in mind of his housekeeper, shook her head in vigorous agreement with her friend. "That one could almost make a living with her pictures, and the poor dear may just have to. They're bound to have the devil's own time getting on now. The old sot can't contribute any but his awful thirst and never has, not even when Seamus and Patsy was cubs. Wasn't poor Seamus up before the judge when he was no more than 12 for the housebreaking he done to get him and Patsy enough to eat? And Lord knows where they'd be if the judge, Christian that he was, didn't send Seamus over to the police stables to become a stable boy and learn an honest profession. I reckon it'll fall on Seamus again, just like it's done right along, with him taking care of the family all the while Liam was in chokey, and a lot of the time since from all what I hear. He's a good brother and a better soul, that's for sure. But what's to become of Patsy and the cubs when he goes to taking a wife for himself, as is bound to happen. There won't be money for two families."

The red-headed woman spoke in a hushed tone. "And that's if he keeps his job. You see that limp he's got. He told my Arthur he was kicked by one of the horses. Some of those rich families can be mighty finicky. How long, do you think, they'll keep a coachman who gets himself kicked by one of his own horses? You know what the gentry thinks of us Irish. They'll be saying it's on account of drink and they won't abide drink in their servants." With a punctuating sniff from one and disdainful nod from the other, the two women moved away from the food tables and beyond earshot.

James Burch sat and watched as new guests came and others left. The pattern never varied. Patricia Keegan received the visitors her brother ushered in, gave each of them a faint smile, unfolded the hands in her lap long enough to grasp the hand of her visitor, then mouthed her gratitude for that person's coming. Each guest expressed condolences and moved off to kneel before the closed casket, head bowed, eyes shut in brief prayer, before choosing a suitable knot of fellow mourners, and accepting tea from one of the women who came forward to offer a cup. Neither Moira nor Little Liam was in evidence, but he had understood from Mrs. Hudson that the children would be away being cared for by a neighbor.

When Winston Parkhurst arrived, he was welcomed with what seemed unusual warmth by both Seamus and Patsy Keegan. He bent low over the widow, shared a few words after closing his hand over hers, and moved to the tables holding refreshments. Encountering Peter Lassiter as he deliberated over the cakes and biscuits, he nodded a solemn acknowledgement of the Inspector and selected a piece of gingerbread. Knowing no one else at the wake, the two men fell into polite conversation in a corner away from the others, but close enough to James Burch for the deaf man to hear their every word without need of the trumpet that lay on his lap. Their discussion put him in mind of the careful parry and thrust he remembered from his days of fencing at Cambridge.

After swallowing a bite of cake and remarking on its flavor, the reporter raised a question in as casual a manner as he could manage. "I wondered about the Yard's view as to how the investigation is going?"

The Yard man extracted a cigarette from his case, tapped it on the back of his hand, and after lighting it directed a stream of smoke down the small space between the two men. "As I've said before, the Yard views this crime as the action of the Brotherhood to exact retribution on one of its own. The effect of those actions on family is certainly regrettable," Lassiter cocked his head in the direction of Patsy Keegan without looking at her, "but our central concern remains the continuing surveillance of the Brotherhood, and preventing the attacks in public places we experienced just a few years ago."

"And you're here in line with that surveillance?"

"I am. Although I don't mind telling you I don't expect to learn much. Anyone who knows anything, or thinks he does, will doubtless be on his guard all evening. And it's not likely anyone from the Brotherhood will be making an appearance." The Inspector looked to move the conversation to a more agreeable subject. "Have you made contact with Holmes as I suggested?"

Beyond James Burch's sight the reporter smiled derisively. "I have, and I can't say I found him terribly impressive. Indeed, I felt myself in the presence of a most pedestrian mind and couldn't help wonder about the mystique that surrounds the man. When all this is behind us, perhaps I'll write a story for the *Times* exploding the myth of Sherlock Holmes."

"I have to say that was my reaction as well, but there are people at the Yard who encourage me not to underestimate the man, that he can come up with the most ingenious solutions to problems. Frankly, I'm not sure some of the older hands at the Yard are up to modern police work. I'm sure they made a contribution in their time, but that was yesterday and this is a new day."

The two men smiled their agreement and Lassiter raised an additional question to the reporter. "I take it you're still conducting research for your story about the Brotherhood?"

Parkhurst's voice carried a note of resignation. "Still. Of course as far as the people at the *Times* are concerned, I remain their man for Announcements. It could be worse, but there's not a lot of creativity to be put into two to three line announcements of births, marriages and deaths."

"Although one could argue that captures the major events in the lives of most men. And surely there are death notices that merit a good deal more than two to three lines."

"Yes, but those are few and far between. For every Gladstone and Parnell, there are a thousand butchers, bakers and Scotland Yard inspectors."

"With perhaps an occasional newspaper reporter thrown in." Both men laughed good-naturedly before edging away to other parts of the room.

His reputation now established, James Burch found himself the object of sympathetic glances and studied avoidance. He had decided he had about exhausted the limits of his character and was planning his exit when the priest unexpectedly reappeared before him. Now wearing a smile more determined than sympathetic, he had been directed by one of the servers to intercede with the "poor deaf soul." Speaking with a volume he normally reserved for miscreants splashing holy water, he asked Burch if he could be of some help.

"Yes, thank you, Father. Everyone's been a great help, but I believe I should be leaving now and get on home before the children start in to worry. Would you give my compliments to Mrs. Keegan?"

The priest nodded deeply as though James Burch's vision as well as his hearing was impaired, and mouthed an exaggerated, "Certainly."

As he left, he found that Seamus Keegan was also taking his leave, explaining to those around him he had to get back to the Shipworths in Bloomsbury. The family had kindly lent him the use of one of their carriages and he'd have to get back in time to unharness, scrub down, and feed his horse, as well as give instruction to the new groom who had been hired. Seeing James Burch leaving, Seamus bellowed his good wishes and appreciation for the visit.

Once returned to Baker Street, and divested of all remnants of James Burch, Holmes politely refused the cold meats proffered by Mrs. Hudson and even her tea and scones, explaining that he was really quite full. He described in detail the events of the evening, recapturing as best he could, the conversations he'd heard, and the room and people while Watson again took notes. Mrs. Hudson was particularly interested in learning about the family members, drawing out all he could remember of Seamus and Patsy Keegan. She wanted to know as well whether he'd reported everything there was to tell about the conversation between Peter Lassiter and Winston Parkhurst.

Holmes understood the need for a full and careful accounting of anything that might contain some hidden clue. Nonetheless, while he indicated his name had come up in the men's conversation, he saw no need to report all the idle chitchat associated with its mention. Besides, he reasoned anything said about any one of them reflected on all of them and he was unwilling to create needless distress for his colleagues. Given that reasoning, he told Mrs. Hudson he had reported fully the conversation he'd heard.

Mrs. Hudson pushed herself back from the kitchen table and lapsed into an uncharacteristically lengthy silence. The focus of both men's rapt attention, she shared finally an observation that surprised them both. "It's good work, Mr. 'Olmes, and it's gettin' us closer to solvin' our problem. But it's takin' us down some unexpected roads I can tell you." She shook her head from side and seemed for a moment unaware of anyone else in the room, then she looked brightly to each of the men. "I'll just say there are boxes inside of boxes and we've still got a way to go."

Watson took a long draw on his briar before speaking for Holmes and himself. "Do you mean you're beginning to get an idea about Mr. Coogan's murderer, Mrs. Hudson?"

"I'll not say just yet what it is I'm thinkin', Dr. Watson. It's too early for that. If I'm right we'll be travelin' some twists and turns before we get to where we're goin', but for now we're well on our way." Rising from her chair, she drew the discussion to a close. "Now, you must forgive me gentlemen; I'm afraid these old bones need their rest." With that, Holmes and Watson withdrew to their upstairs sitting room where they shared a last pipe of the day, and a perplexity each man took finally to his own bed.

Chapter 5.
Religion and Politics

The next morning an earnest-looking youngster arrived with a note from Winston Parkhurst informing Holmes it would be convenient for him to visit Patricia Keegan at two o'clock that afternoon. The note went on to say it was Mrs. Keegan's understanding that the *Times* had commissioned Holmes to investigate Coogan's death in association with its story on the Brotherhood, and if Holmes found those arrangements satisfactory, he should so inform the messenger. Mrs. Hudson so informed the messenger on behalf of her still sleeping lodger. For a second morning she was prepared to let Holmes sleep late. This morning, however, her plans and Holmes's rest were to be interrupted.

Watching from her parlor window, Mrs. Hudson counted four hansoms and three four-wheelers arriving outside 221B Baker Street, and depositing at least 15 men in the course of a five-minute period, every one of them wearing top hats, dark frock coats, and matching trousers. In clothing and demeanor they looked to be mourners for a dignitary whose passing demanded more respect than feeling. As each carriage emptied, its occupants shook hands with those who had already arrived, then joined or sometimes formed a small group on the sidewalk. Exactly at nine, a leader emerged from the largest of the groups and, with a summary wave of his cane, led a loosely formed command to Mrs. Hudson's door. Silver crosses bounced across the stomachs and chests of several of the callers making clear the clerical concerns of the delegation. Mrs. Hudson judged they were too numerous to have come for a charitable contribution and too self-possessed to be seeking advice from Mr. Holmes. The bell signaled their mission was about to become clear.

Opening the front door, Mrs. Hudson found her small

center hall overflowing with the men she had been observing from her window, their numbers spilling down the steps and into the street. The group's leader occupied nearly the whole of her vestibule, a huge cross dangling across a substantial middle, drawing attention to both his spiritual and secular passions. He had a full gray beard and moustaches, and an air of authority appropriate to his role as the group's spokesman.

"My card, madam. We are here to see Mr. Holmes. First, however, if it please, may I know your name?" His syrupy tone did not hide the fact that the Reverend Llewellyn Farnsworth, as his card identified him, was accustomed to unquestioning compliance with his requests.

"I'm Mrs. 'Udson, the 'ousekeeper, Reverend."

"Then Hudson is your married name. What about *your* family. Where are they from?"

"I'm not takin' your meanin', Reverend."

"Your people. Where were they born?"

"I take your meanin' now, Reverend. We were all of us born at 'ome with the midwife in." Mrs. Hudson was aware that without making any effort to do so she had begun to adopt elements of Moira Keegan's speech. "If you're wishin' to see Mr. 'Olmes, I can learn from 'im whether 'e's receivin' visitors today. May I tell 'im your concern, and just 'ow many of you are wishin' to see 'im?"

The Reverend smiled with beneficent condescension. "We can sort all that out with your Mr. Holmes. Please inform him we are here."

"I'm afraid I'll be losin' my position unless I can tell 'im somethin' more than that sir." Mrs. Hudson did not budge from where she stood.

There began a grumbling in the ranks of the Reverend's command. It was unclear whether the dissatisfaction was with Mrs. Hudson or with the Reverend, but it was clear that the group was feeling itself inappropriately detained. The

Reverend decided his best strategy lay in conciliation. Indeed, the woman's stupidity and intransigence suggested it was his only viable strategy. "Tell Mr. Holmes a delegation representing the London Branch of the National Society for Christian Union is on his doorstep, and that it is essential we speak with him. We wish to meet with him as a body, but we are willing to have as many of our members participate as is feasible." The Reverend gave his response as loudly as a concern for the morning hour permitted. Those nearest the Reverend made statements of stout support for his position; those at the edge of the crowded vestibule repeated their leader's statement to their colleagues on the street.

Mrs. Hudson had also concluded that conciliation was a wise strategy. She was becoming concerned that, clergymen or not, the group was on the edge of becoming unruly, and that newspaper accounts of men of God becoming fractious, or worse, outside 221B Baker Street would not advance the reputation of the consulting detective agency. She asked the Reverend to remain, assuring him she would be back shortly.

She found Holmes looking every bit the unmade bed he had just vacated. Strands of dark hair followed independent paths across his forehead and temples, and his hollowed cheeks awaited the civilizing effect of a straight razor. He wore the lilac dressing gown he would remain in until mid-day, longer if he could exercise his plan to return to his microscope and the strands of English, Indian and American rope and twine carefully teased apart and lying on his laboratory table. Watson was at his desk, the notes from Holmes's account of James Burch's visit to the Keegan flat spread before him. Each man had his own reason for avoiding contact with the Reverend and his coterie. Watson knew of the Reverend's organization and was unsympathetic to its objectives; Holmes had been eagerly anticipating a first pipe and breakfast. Looking from the sitting room window, Mrs.

Hudson reported that a crowd of curious onlookers was already gathering across Baker Street. She advised the two men that the crowd was likely to grow and perhaps attract the attention of a passing constable, and then the press. A brief meeting with the Reverend and a very few of his followers might defuse what had the makings of an ugly situation. Interspersed between comments about the Reverend Farnsworth's audacity, insensitivity, and mindlessness, a compromise was reached whereby Holmes and Watson would meet with the Reverend, and no more than four of his colleagues, for a maximum of 20 minutes. In return for their cooperation, Mrs. Hudson would prepare a sumptuous breakfast to be leisurely consumed immediately thereafter.

It took 15 minutes for the Reverend Farnsworth to reach agreement with his flock as to which four men should join him. The Reverend, and the chosen four, handed hats, canes and umbrellas to Mrs. Hudson, and made their way soberly up the stairs; the remainder exited onto the street where all but five of them found cabs and returned to whatever parts of London had earlier disgorged them. The five attempted, without the least success, to appear inconspicuous while awaiting the report of their colleagues who had gained audience with Holmes.

Holmes assumed his accustomed position alongside the fireplace from which he could survey the room and tower above his seated visitors; Watson took his post at the secretary's desk and withdrew several sheets of foolscap from a cubicle. The Reverend Farnsworth knocked once, then burst upon the scene without waiting for response from within. He was closely trailed by his four companions arrayed in groups of two behind the Reverend. As the four men took positions flanking their leader they looked with surprise and a measure of disapproval from the unkempt Holmes to the unkempt room. They took brief note of Watson before settling their gaze finally on the substantial presence of Reverend Farnsworth.

"Mr. Holmes, it is a pleasure indeed to meet you. I am the Reverend Llewellyn Farnsworth, and these are my colleagues, Sir Arthur Tripp, Mr. Ebenezer Desmond, the Honorable Stafford Michaelson, and Sir Carter Bullingsworth."

Holmes's half-hearted effort at a smile of greeting got only as far as Mr. Ebenezer Desmond before he settled on nodding to his remaining guests, and waving a semicircle to the room's furniture when the Reverend had finished. "Please gentlemen, do sit down." The chairs and couch to which Holmes made reference were largely taken up with books, papers and, in the instance of the basket chair, with James Burch's hat, coat and trousers. Holmes took no note of the clutter. "Let me introduce my friend and colleague, Dr. John Watson. Dr. Watson will be taking notes while we talk. Please don't be put off by that, it's simply our way of maintaining a history of the conversations conducted here."

Watson nodded as his name was called and continued removing a stack of books from the easy chair nearest his desk. The Honorable Stafford Michaelson, who had been coveting that chair without the least idea how to handle the confusion laying on it, thanked Watson and took a seat. The other visitors arranged themselves as best they could. The most slender of them, Ebenezer Desmond, wedged himself between papers and the arm of an easy chair. His two more generously proportioned colleagues found pockets in the room where they leaned against walls or furniture while holding their host and each other in view. The Reverend Farnsworth, having observed the seating of Stafford Michaelson, lifted the stack of books lying at one end of the settee and carefully heaped them onto the books at the other end, waited to determine if his creation would resist the

87

demand of gravity, then seated himself and turned his attention again to Holmes.

"As your housekeeper may have informed you, we are members of the London Branch of the National Society for Christian Union. You may have heard of us?" The Reverend's raised eyebrows and eager smile were met by Holmes's wooden expression. "No, well, no matter, no matter at all." The soft groan from Sir Carter Bullingsworth, who had staked out a position beside Watson's desk, belied a consensus of indifference. "In a word, Mr. Holmes, Dr. Watson, we are concerned with maintaining our country's rich Christian heritage and independence from those who might have us bend the knee to any foreign authority. Please understand, we seek tolerance for all those claiming Jesus Christ as their Lord and Savior, but wish to be certain that none take advantage of our tolerance to advance the idea that we should heed the dictates of a foreign prince claiming to speak for our Lord and Savior."

As he neared the close of his declaration, the Reverend's voice seemed poorly contained even by his massive body. Taking advantage of a pause during which four voices filled the silence with decorous amens, he managed a return to more normal timbre. He smiled his warmest to Holmes and continued, "I trust my meaning is clear and we can count you a soldier to our cause." And, becoming suddenly aware of his other host, "And you as well, Doctor. We have a goodly number of medical men pledged to our banner."

Holmes adopted a stare of intense concentration. The Reverend interpreted it to mean he had indeed found a soldier and beamed his recognition to Holmes. Watson recognized Holmes's stare as meaning that he hadn't the foggiest notion of what the Reverend was speaking.

"Reverend Farnsworth," Watson began, drawing the group's attention from Holmes, who had turned his own attention to studying the cuffs of his dressing gown, "The science of criminal investigation so fully occupies Mr. Holmes's time that he has little opportunity to devote himself to other concerns. For my own part, I know something of your organization and its issues, and I'm having difficulty understanding why you've come to see us."

"I certainly understand the demands on Mr. Holmes's time, and I appreciate his single-minded attention to ridding our city of its unhealthy influences." The Reverend smiled his appreciation of Holmes's efforts before again becoming as grim as his mission demanded. "It is because we share that interest we are here today to pledge our support and cooperation. We have allies all over London, even in Scotland Yard, but we are also aware that not everyone in that organization shares our devotion to bringing to justice the Waterman's Way Assassins as we describe those villains." The Reverend looked to his hosts, then to his colleagues who alone seemed to share their leader's zeal.

"We are here to encourage Mr. Holmes's resolve, and to pledge our willingness to work with him to counter opposition to his investigation wherever it may be found. Speaking frankly, we believe the men responsible for the murder of Mr. Coogan are enlisted in the cause of papal domination and that those men, if brought to justice—may I say in deference to Mr. Holmes, *when* they are brought to justice—will provide a unique opportunity to make evident once and for all the insidious nature of the conspiracy within our midst. Through their capture, we can bring to light the names of all those who work with them and, most especially, of those from whom they take direction. With their purpose revealed and their leaders exposed, we can demand our elected representatives take all necessary action to guarantee the safety and integrity of our country and of the Empire, and to remove—root and branch—this poisonous tree planted on our shores. In a word, we seek to make common cause with Mr. Holmes to further our shared interest in making England safe from its enemies, both foreign and domestic." The Reverend extracted a massive handkerchief from the pocket of his waistcoat and proceeded to dab at the beads of sweat that had formed on his forehead and cheeks, taking care not to disturb his moustaches while so doing. He replaced the handkerchief, and grandly brushed aside the hosannas that echoed around the room.

"Reverend ... Farnsworth is it? Reverend, I appreciate the spirit that leads you and your colleagues to pay me this visit," Holmes smiled the room in semicircle without allowing his gaze to linger on any of Farnsworth's companions, "and I'm pleased to learn of your support which I'll keep very much in mind. If there's nothing else to discuss, I should like to prepare for the rather busy day Dr. Watson and I have in store." Holmes waved a few strands of hair from his forehead and took a step from the fireplace. Everyone else remained in place.

"Well, if I might, I wished to raise a few other points, Mr. Holmes," Reverend Farnsworth looked to Sir Arthur Tripp and Sir Carter Bullingsworth, both of whom were trying to communicate with narrowed eyes and firm jaw the confidence they placed in him. "May I inquire first as to the progress you've made thus far."

"I would say we're satisfied with the way things are progressing. Of course, it's early yet in our investigation and there remains much to do. Is there something else you wish to raise?"

"Yes, there is, Mr. Holmes. As I've been at pains to emphasize throughout our discussion, I feel it keenly that we share a bond in pursuing this investigation. I should like to make known to my organization's membership that such a bond is in place, and report to them we are jointly engaged in the endeavor to rid our blessed island of God's own enemies.

It would be greatly reassuring to my people, Mr. Holmes, allowing us to feel our prayers have been answered and our cause is being strenuously pursued. As it is written, 'A faithful friend is a strong defense and he that hath found such an one hath found a treasure.' Ecclesiastes, 6, verse 14." Reverend Farnsworth paused again, looking for the moment to the sitting room's ceiling or perhaps beyond before continuing. "For our part, we will pray for your success, and provide you whatever earthly assistance we can to make certain you are able to pursue your investigation free of outside pressures." The Reverend fixed Holmes with the piercing stare that routinely brought naysayers to their knees and his followers to their feet. "May I tell my people that Sherlock Holmes is joined with us in this ennobling adventure?"

Holmes was prepared to pledge himself to any adventure that would ensure early access to the rashers of bacon and mound of eggs that waited only the Reverend's departure. Watson however found his own appetite had disappeared and answered the Reverend's question while Holmes was gathering his thoughts.

"Gentlemen, if I might interrupt, it is most flattering for you, all of you, to make this journey to Baker Street. I know Mr. Holmes is as taken as I am with your gracious offer, but I hope you can understand and appreciate that if we appear allied with any one group we compromise our ability to work with every other that may prove essential to the investigation. In short, sir, we cannot authorize you to speak for us nor do we wish to be seen as in any way representing your organization."

"You take the words out of my mouth, Watson." Holmes nodded an acknowledgement to his friend before turning to Reverend Farnsworth. "Dr. Watson speaks to our long-standing policy, Reverend. While I too appreciate your expression of support, I share Dr. Watson's concern that we risk losing the cooperation of others if we appear closely allied with the interests of any one group. I need to emphasize as well, that we already have a client and must be respectful of that person's wishes in all of this."

As each man spoke, low growls rumbled their way from deep within the Reverend's cavernous frame. When Holmes had finished the Reverend cleared his throat with a good deal more force than the simple exercise seemed to require. "I am deeply disappointed, Mr. Holmes, deeply disappointed. We came here to make clear our willingness to ally with you in a cause I hoped we both shared—the need to deny to Rome power over the lives of Englishmen. Now, I find you are content to remain aloof from the most important struggle of our generation, and will take no part in resisting the effort to place a foreign prince over our own queen." Reverend Farnsworth pushed himself from the settee, the sudden displacement of his weight causing several of the delicately balanced books at its other end to cascade to the floor. He paid no attention to the addition he made to the room's clutter, signaling with a glance his instruction to the other members of the London Branch of the National Society for Christian Union and, in a body, they strode to the door of the sitting room. The Reverend turned at the door, again looking hard at Holmes, "Take heed, Mr. Holmes, for it is also written, 'He that is not with me is against me.' Luke, 11, verse 23." With that, the Reverend Llewellyn Farnsworth allowed the Honorable Stafford Michaelson to open the door for him, and without another word led his small entourage down the stairs where Mrs. Hudson waited with hats, canes, umbrellas, and an open door to the street.

Returning to her kitchen, Mrs. Hudson watched the ten men reconnoiter on the street. The Reverend dominated their short conversation, his tightly set jaw thrust out as he spoke.

In groups of two and three, looking sullen and disappointed, the members of the Society entered waiting cabs. Across the roadway, two men in work clothes watched the gathering and departure of Holmes's guests before walking in different directions down Baker Street. Mrs. Hudson watched them go out of sight before turning to ask Holmes and Watson, who had now joined her, whether the meeting had been useful. Watson answered for both men, "Mrs. Hudson, I fear that Reverend Farnsworth has found Holmes and myself to have a great deal in common with the Philistines of old. For my part, I do believe we share one thing with the Philistines. Both of us have been set upon by someone bearing the jawbone of an ass. I believe that can be found somewhere in Judges. I regret I'm unable to cite chapter and verse. And now as I remember, we're owed a sumptuous breakfast which, I can tell you, we have well and truly earned."

With each bite of the bacon, sausage and eggs Holmes had been anticipating for the past half hour, supplemented by kippers he hadn't dared to imagine, the Reverend Farnsworth slipped ever farther from his and Watson's thoughts and conversation. Watson read from the crimes listing in the *Standard* as part of their morning ritual. There were reports of break-ins to several shops along Oxford Street, all of them believed to be the work of a single thief or thieves, there had been a fire of suspicious origin in a Chelsea warehouse, a reward of 10 pounds was being offered by unspecified persons for information leading to the location of a Caleb Sanderson who had left his home in Hackney to visit his mother in Cheapside and not been seen since, and an altercation had taken place at the Boar and Bear Publick House on Chancery Lane requiring the intervention of the London Police. With the day's recitation concluded, Mrs. Hudson attempted to focus their attention on the afternoon's task.

"We need to go over the issues you'll be raisin' with Mrs. Keegan. I think you'll be in for a difficult interview."

Holmes spoke without taking his eyes from the last piece of toast he was in the process of spearing. "Difficult because of the recency of Mr. Coogan's death?"

"There's that to be sure, but I'm thinkin' about somethin' else. Maybe this Mr. Park'urst 'as got an in with 'er and maybe 'e 'asn't. We know she's got reason to be on 'er guard against just about everybody. The police, thanks to our Inspector Lassiter, are lettin' 'er know they're not the least bit interested in findin' 'er 'usband's murderer. She's got cause to believe the same people as might 'ave been 'er 'usband's friends in Ireland are the ones who were waitin' to do 'im in when 'e got to London. Even 'er own father is makin' noises like 'e's got sympathies for those folk. Now 'ere we come, a couple of complete strangers ready to muck around in 'er grief. We know Mr. Park'urst 'as told 'er the *Times* is payin' for us to find 'er 'usband's killers, but we don't know what else 'e's told 'er, or what she believes. And on top of all that, there's our little Moira. We've no idea what she's told 'er mother about us, if she's told 'er anythin' at all. I don't mind tellin' you I don't like us steppin' into such a deep 'ole without a better idea of what's at its bottom. Anyways, I'm thinkin' we need a sit down before you go off to see Mrs. Keegan. You both 'ave your pipes and I'll do the cleanup down 'ere. In two 'ours then we'll have some tea, and I need for you to try my raspberry scones although I'm afraid they may have got just a little burnt."

It took nearly three hours for the detectives to reassemble; Holmes required the additional time to finish recording the microscopic differences he had discovered between the hemps used in the manufacture of English and Indian rope. He was, in fact, in no hurry to rehearse interviewing Mrs. Keegan, doubting as he did that it would prove a difficult undertaking. He joined the preparations at last in the interest of group harmony, and his willingness to test Mrs. Hudson's raspberry scones.

For the second time in as many days, Holmes traveled to the Keegans' home on Princess Street, this time wearing a top hat, stylish frock coat, white shirt and tie, and with his hearing restored. He was accompanied by Watson who carried the familiar notebook and pencil in his waistcoat. They were admitted to the flat at 68 Princess Street by Patricia Keegan, her pale, drawn face contrasting with the black dress of mourning, creating a nearly spiritual quality about the woman. Holmes had only seen her seated in his earlier visit and now was struck by how small and fragile she appeared.

She looked uncertainly from one man to the other as she inquired of them both, "You are Mr. Sherlock Holmes?"

"I am Mr. Holmes, and this is my friend and colleague, Dr. Watson. May we come in?"

Each man expressed his condolences as they were ushered into the parlor, which Holmes noted was thankfully rid of its coffin and makeshift catafalque. Indeed, all trace of the prior evening was gone. Where people had congregated in earnest small voices only a day before, there was now empty space and the stillness of loss. Chairs had been returned to the neighbors, and the round tables from which those same neighbors had taken sustenance were now bare and set at either end of the couch to which Mrs. Keegan waved her visitors. She sat in a wingback chair angled just far enough away to allow the men a view of the small fire that warmed without brightening the room.

Holmes began the practiced explanation for their visit. "As you know, Mrs. Keegan, we've talked with Mr. Parkhurst and are concerned with bringing to justice the people who committed the terrible crime that has occurred." Holmes was prepared to elaborate on their association with Parkhurst and the *Times*, making brief reference to the paper's interest in the Brotherhood when, to his surprise, Mrs. Keegan waved away further need for explanation.

She gave a small, tired smile, then spoke softly, but without taking her eyes from her visitors and with a resolve for which neither man was prepared. "My daughter has told me of her visit to you. As I'm sure you're aware, it's more than a little odd for a child to be leaving school in the middle of the day, and so the sisters came by to ask how Moira was getting on. They were that surprised to find I didn't know a thing about her illness or her leaving school. She's a good girl, Mr. Holmes, and that night we had us a little sit-down where she told me all what had happened. So you see I already know of her coming to your apartments, and about you thinking my Liam had some disease that would be the cause of his going away and not returning." She paused, working a handkerchief in her lap, then spoke with unexpected force. "Now you know it was no disease that took him from us."

"So what's all this? What's going on here?" The voice preceded the appearance of the man Holmes recognized as having been the short-lived confidant of James Burch the preceding evening. He stepped cautiously into the parlor as if uncertain whether it was he or the people already there who were out of place. Cornelius Keegan's heavy-lidded eyes, high cheekbones and coloring were those of his daughter, but his face substituted dark suspicion for her gentle resolve. He came only a short way into the room, squinted at the two men, then turned back to his daughter. "So who are these, then?"

"I thought you'd already gone to Caffey's." It was less a question than an accusation.

"No such a thing." He stole a second glance to Holmes and Watson before looking again to his daughter. "She's always about getting rid of me. You'd think I had the plague

96

the way I'm treated around here. So will you tell me or no who are the guests in me own house."

She looked sharply to him at the last, but chose not to question her father's claim to home ownership. "This here is Mister Sherlock Holmes and his friend Dr. Watson come to look into Liam's killing." She gave a quick jerk of her head in the direction of the speaker. "And this is my da, Cornelius Keegan. Now, I'd be obliged if you'd take yourself to Caffey's and leave me to be with my company."

"Well now, don't I always leave you to be with your company? But give me just a minute girl. We don't often see the likes of Mr. Sherlock Holmes inside our poor little home." He looked to the two men out of the corner of his eye. "I shouldn't have thought Liam's death would kick up near such a fuss as to attract the likes of Mr. Sherlock Holmes." He waited but his comment drew no response. "I suppose this is the work of that reporter who's got hisself all sweet on you."

Patricia Keegan spoke in a voice that might have frozen hell. "I'll not be getting down in the gutter with you, old man, but I'll ask you to keep your black thoughts to yourself. For now, these men and I have some business together. I'll thank you to be on your way and not to be back until you're of a mind that leaves you fit to be with decent people."

Cornelius Keegan agreed to what had been inevitable from the outset. "I'll be going, I have friends at Caffey's and it's there I can be with people who respect their elders."

His daughter's tone became suddenly confidential. "Are you by way of needing anything before you go?"

His body stiffened before he spoke again. "I have all what I need." And then, as a seeming afterthought, "I'll be back for dinner. I take it your company will be gone by then." And he walked with exaggerated purpose to the door.

Holmes and Watson had watched the family drama unfold without change in expression, although both shared a mix of small wonder and large distaste. Watson felt it necessary to speak to the exchange they had witnessed. "A tragedy like this is terribly hard on the family. I'm sure things will get back to normal between the two of you with time."

Patricia Keegan looked at him doubtfully before allowing herself the small smile they'd seen earlier. "You mustn't mind my da. He's all wind and no rain. It's been that way since me mam died, and it's got worse since we left Dublin. He blames Liam for our leaving. In another minute you'd have heard about Liam getting himself cross-wise of them as are a part of the Brotherhood, and all of us having to leave on that account. He'll be off to Caffey's now where he and the others can share lies about how wonderful things were in the Old Country. And like as not he'll stay too long, and be falling all over himself getting home so that he's only fit for the bed when he gets here." She gave her head a small shake dismissing any further talk about Cornelius Keegan. "Still, my da is not the reason you've come to see me, and we should get on with it while I've got the neighbor watching Little Liam and Moira is still at school."

Watson continued with the script that had been developed. "Mr. Holmes and I deeply regret what has happened and whatever role we may have played in not preventing things from following the course they have. I hope you understand we felt we could not contact you earlier because we had given our word we would not. Of course, we can't change history, but we are very much concerned with making certain, as Mr. Holmes has stated, that whoever did this terrible thing is brought to justice."

With what he hoped was a warm smile and his most gentle voice, Holmes tried to further the spirit Watson had been at pains to create. "Mrs. Keegan—ma'am—it would seem Liam was the target of an organization known to many as the Brotherhood. Did he ever speak of it to you?"

98

"Yes, we talked of it." She began again to strangle the handkerchief she held on her lap. "There are no secrets—were no secrets—between us. We knew they were after him. The poor fools thought he'd informed on them, though why they should think such a thing neither of us could ever hope to know. It's God's own truth he'd never play the tattler, no matter the try to get him to. My Liam was as honorable a man as anyone could hope to find. No matter how he felt, he won't turn on them as had been his friends. But they got it in their heads and there was no getting it out. Not them and not the police who are every bit as hard a lot. Well, they all got their way, didn't they?"

"Then you think it's the Brotherhood that's responsible for Liam's death?" Holmes asked.

"It's them or the police. Oh I know you think nothing like that could happen with the likes of Scotland Yard. And maybe it don't if you're living in Mayfair. But it's a different story down here. Like with that detective that come from the Yard, the one what butter wouldn't melt in his mouth. Inspector Lassiter they called him. If I never see his like again it won't be too soon."

Watson cleared his throat, hoping to turn attention to those he saw as the more likely assassins. "Mrs. Keegan, I know this is a delicate subject and I apologize for raising it, but we'd like for you to tell us about Mr. Coogan's relationship to the Brotherhood both here and in Ireland. Could you share with us how things got started in Dublin."

There was a long period of silence. Her voice had taken on unexpected strength as she considered the injustices visited on her husband, and now again became soft and strained. "It was all to do with Mr. Carey and Liam's job, and was nothing either of us could see coming. When we was married, Liam was working for Mr. Jim Carey. It was Liam's first job, but there was more to it than that—a lot more. You see with his

99

own da long gone, Mr. Carey come to be his second father. And Mr. Carey was just the same, treating Liam practically like his own. Liam started out a hod carrier and in no time Mr. Carey learned him to be a mason, and he become a fine one too. Mr. Carey even had men working under Liam, not many of course, and not all the time, but it's how much Mr. Carey trusted him and how hard my Liam worked. So when Mr. Carey asked him to help out on some other things he was doing, Liam went along. It weren't right and I'm not asking for anyone to say it was, but it's what happened and we neither of us knew the half of what it was all about—at least not right at first we didn't. Like they asked him to haul some equipment to where they was meeting, which they put in the wagon without him knowing what it was. Later, he found out it was things they couldn't bring themselves because they was being watched. Then they started asking him to stand lookout where they was working and to let them know if anybody come near. Of course by then he knew what was happening. What with the explosions you couldn't help but know, but it was all empty buildings and the both of us could think at least no one was getting hurt. But all that changed with Phoenix Park. After the Park the police and the Brotherhood never stopped hounding my Liam."

She paused; Holmes and Watson permitted her space to pull herself together, but she needed only to catch her breath. Pain was too much a part of her life to merit special time for recovery. She drew new breath and continued. "The police was sure he'd been with the murderers, or anyways they said they was sure, and they kept after him, wanting to know what he done and what he knew. The ones what called themselves Invincibles knew he hadn't been in the Park and they wanted to know why not. Well, it was because Mr. Carey told him to stay away, not wanting him to get in any deeper than he already was. But that carried no weight with the Invincibles, especially after Mr. Carey and Michael Kavanaugh started naming folk who had been in the Park. Nothing Mr. Carey said or done counted for a hoot in Hades after he done that, and Liam using him for his alibi to the Invincibles just made it look all the more like he was a tattler hisself. And when the police come, and the judge give him the softest sentence of the lot, they was sure of it.

"It was after Liam got put away that life got to be impossible for me. Not just because he weren't with me no more, though that was the hardest, but it's then my own neighbors, ones who I'd been knowing for years, would have nothing to do with me for fear of making themselves targets for the police or the Brotherhood or maybe both. It got to where the people I did char for wouldn't have me no more, and there were even some shopkeepers wouldn't take my trade. And there I am with a six year old and another on the way. It was then Seamus—he's me brother—sent me the money to leave Dublin and come to this god-forsaken island. Anyways, London hasn't been near far enough away. I no more get a place to live than the police start coming around like we're needing to get acquainted, and the Brotherhood, which was the same as the Invincibles to me, come to let me know they wasn't through with Liam. That's why when he got out of prison and come to be with us, he could never stay long, just a night or maybe two here and there. He'd find work somewheres and bring us what money he could, but it's Seamus who's been seeing us through, and denying his own self right along. Liam and me would all the time talk about getting away, but we could never figure how to get ourselves to America or Australia." She drew a deep breath and her voice seemed to come from miles off. "And now there'll be no more dreaming."

Holmes again gave the woman a moment to collect herself, then slipped from his practiced script to follow the lead Watson had found improbable. "Was there anyone else who might have been a threat to Mr. Coogan? You mentioned the police. I believe you spoke of an Inspector Lassiter."

She began slowly. "I know you're a friend to the police so you probably won't believe me. But they said some terrible things. Like how London was a good place to live before the Irish started coming, and how everything will be better when the whole of the Brotherhood is below ground where they belong. Mr. Lassiter wasn't saying any of those things hisself, but he could hear them as good as me and he didn't do nothing to stop it. Sometimes, Liam was here when they come, and they'd tell him they don't have enough on him to make an arrest, but they will. Most times, Liam was someplace else when they come, and they'd tell me how they've almost got everything they need to run him in. And even a cub could tell they was lying and all they wanted was to scare us so bad we'd do whatever they said."

Holmes and Watson said nothing. What they were hearing about the Yard wasn't new, but always before it had come from men whose life experience might have justified increased police surveillance or whose capacity for honest dialogue made their reports questionable. Patricia Keegan posed no comparable challenge to either public safety or credibility.

"Anyway, it's all done now and there'll be no more visits from Mr. Lassiter or any of his constable friends, or anyone from the Brotherhood come to that." Patricia Keegan's brow furrowed with a sudden thought. "Have you other questions? I don't want to leave the children too long."

Holmes nodded his understanding. "Just a couple more, Mrs. Keegan. Can you tell us please when was the last time you saw your husband alive?"

"It was the time Moira described to you. He come here to leave me some money from a job he'd been on, and to let me know he'd be gone for a while. He never told me where and I knew better than to ask."

"And did anyone come by looking for him?"

"Not then, nobody I can remember."

"What about Mr. Parkhurst? How did he happen to become interested in you and Mr. Coogan, and was he here to visit any time after you last talked with your husband?"

At the mention of the reporter's name for just an instant her eyes widened and her red bow of a mouth opened in a small gasp. "Mr. Parkhurst is a good friend. He first come to see me, and then Liam, when he was doing his story, and I can tell you we was both of us suspicious of someone else wanting to tie my Liam up to the Park and every explosion there's ever been in London, even with him being in prison through most of them. But he weren't at all like that. He listened to our story like he was really trying to hear us. And then it turned out he could even pay us some for what we had to tell him, which come in handy what with work being scarce and there being five mouths to feed, yes and drink to get for one of them. Anyway, he's been a friend, and one of the few we've had in London. But I ain't seen him in a while. Quite a while I'd say. Maybe ten days, maybe two weeks—not counting Liam's wake and him coming by to work out my seeing the two of you." Holmes looked from Mrs. Keegan to the slowly dying fire. He struggled to find inspiration, but could remember no additional questions from Mrs. Hudson and had none of his own. He turned finally to Watson.

"Doctor, is there anything further you'd like to ask?"

Watson paused in the entry he was making in his notebook. "There's one actually. I hope I'm not prying, Mrs. Keegan. I can't help but wonder what you'll be doing now that your husband has passed. I fear these will be difficult times for you and the children."

She nodded her appreciation of Watson's concern. "I'm

sure I don't know yet. We have a little money put by for now and I'm doing char in some people's houses, and Seamus, God bless his good soul, has always been a help, but there'll be a need to look somewheres else before too long. I'm sure I'll be having a long sit-down with Father Kilpatrick before a great many days have passed."

Watson pursed his lips, nodded and said nothing.

The three of them fell silent in the darkening room, the sound of the crackling fire and the smell of the burning oak the only distractions from the bleak thoughts they all shared. Finally, Holmes stood, buttoning, then smoothing his frock coat. "Thank you, Mrs. Keegan. You've been very helpful. Watson, I think we've taken quite enough of this good woman's time." Holmes spied his and Watson's hats on one of the round tables and, after retrieving them, each man grasped their hostess' hand in both of his own and wished himself to be remembered to Moira before backing his way from the small, close room onto the deserted street.

From her parlor window, Mrs. Keegan watched a four-wheeler come to a stop just as her two guests approached the curb in search of a cab. She was certain she'd heard two whistles which would mean they were calling for a hansom, not the single whistle that would have brought the four-wheeler. Her concern turned to terror when she recognized one of the two men who left the carriage to stand beside them. She knew him to be a soldier in the Brotherhood, a man who would do whatever was wanted with no question before and no remorse after. She saw him point the way inside the four-wheeler with one hand while his other remained in the pocket of his traveling coat, forming a distinct bulge in the direction of Sherlock Holmes.

Chapter 6.
The Brotherhood

Patricia Keegan needed help and had no idea where to turn. She couldn't contact the police. She didn't trust them and likely they didn't trust her either. And there would be questions, endless questions. They'd want to know what was her business with Sherlock Holmes, what had she told him about Liam's death, who were the kidnappers and why were they outside her flat. And, after all that, they'd likely start back watching the house if they thought the Brotherhood might be coming around. It would be Dublin all over again with the neighbors closing their doors and looking somewheres else when they passed her on the street. Then there was the Brotherhood. What would they do if she went to the police? They'd find out, that was for sure. It was true they didn't make war on women, not usually, but what if they thought a woman was making war on them. There was always the Church. But the Church was there for comfort; Father Kilpatrick and the sisters would have no more idea how to deal with the Brotherhood than would Little Liam.

She ruled out Mr. Parkhurst as well. He'd already done more than was fair and she couldn't see dragging him still deeper into her troubles. All things considered, her best choice might be to find the Mr. Wiggins Moira had bragged on. He was a partner to Mr. Holmes and the two of them must be forever getting into and out of these kinds of scrapes. He and Mr. Holmes might have even worked out a plan for what to do when one of them gets in this particular kind of trouble. She went to the coin jar under her bed to find money for a cab, then to Mrs. Hogan upstairs to get Little Liam, and down the street to Shannon's mother to have her send Moira straight home without giving any reason for her urgency. She'd need Moira to help her find Mr. Wiggins and Little Liam would be upset if he had to stay by himself.

"When do you intend to share with us the reason we've been invited to join you, and where it is you are taking Dr. Watson and myself?" Holmes sat erect on the back seat of the four-wheeler, looking with undisguised contempt at his two captors who held their prisoners with fierce stares as though fearful they might vanish if not kept under constant observation. The one who seemed in charge showed black hair spilling from underneath his workman's cap, a flattened nose, and the small scars of numerous battles evident in spite of his full dark beard and moustaches. His broad shoulders and thick chest gave further indication he could prove a formidable adversary even without the revolver he kept focused on Holmes's middle. In contrast, his companion's thin straight nose and unscarred hairless face suggested he was unaccustomed to the violent behavior he was now abetting. His revolver followed the course set by his dark eyes, owl-like behind thick rimless glasses, as they flitted from Holmes to Watson and back. Watson recognized the inexperience of the kidnapper across from him and judged him the more dangerous adversary on that account. Nonetheless, his anger overruled whatever caution he might otherwise have exercised.

"I sincerely hope you realize what you're doing. The penalty for kidnapping is quite severe, and you can't seriously hope to get away with committing such a monstrous crime in broad daylight."

The brawler spoke for the first time and revealed a now familiar Irish brogue. "I'm suggesting you get yourself under control, Doctor, if it's really a doctor you are. We've a short ride, and then you can talk your head off about all what's been done to you. Until we're there I'll ask you both to keep your mouths shut and I'll have you put these blindfolds on. I'm hoping it won't be necessary for me to come across to tie them on or to keep you quiet." With that, the speaker produced two dark colored pieces of cloth and handed one to Holmes who viewed it with wry curiosity before daintily taking hold of the blindfold by its two edges; then dangled the other in front of Watson who pretended not to see the proffered cloth before snatching it away from the large man. Both men tied the blindfolds on themselves with exaggerated care. The thick-set captor studied the faces of each of his prisoners, simulated a punch that stopped short of each man's chin and, receiving no reaction, sat back with a satisfied smile.

Holmes broke the silence, speaking in the same casual tone he'd adopted earlier. "As you seem to already know, I am Sherlock Holmes and the gentleman with me is my friend and colleague, Dr. John Watson. Will you at least share your names so we can have a proper conversation until we get to wherever it is you're taking us?"

"Like I already told you, when we get to where we're going you can talk 'til the cows come home. For now, I'm telling you a last time to settle back and enjoy the ride." With that, the captors became silent and, except for occasional grumbling from Watson, so too did their prisoners.

As promised, the ride was a short one. By the detectives' reckoning, no more than five or six streets before the two men were helped from the carriage by unseen hands. They felt themselves on a surface softer than pavement, but smooth and flat, and guessed it to be either packed dirt or well-trod grass. They walked about 15 paces, then were helped up three narrow steps, crossed a space of another four paces, heard two knocks, a pause and three more knocks. There was a short wait before the door groaned its way open without an exchange of words from either side. They crossed the threshold, were led into what they judged to be a small entryway, got nudged forcefully to the left, and after five more steps were directed to stay where they were. The door sounded shut behind them, their guides released them, and they felt more than heard the two men move away. An unfamiliar high-pitched voice addressed them. "Mr. Holmes. Dr. Watson. You may remove your blindfolds now."

Moira recognized the Baker Street brownstone that held Holmes's lodgings and whispered the information to her mother who called out a request for the driver to stop. He held the chestnut mare in check while Mrs. Keegan exited his cab. She helped Moira step down and caught Little Liam as he jumped from the four-wheeler's top step with a scream of delight. The driver waited while Little Liam ran to the front of his coach to wave good-bye to the "red horse." He had three children of his own. Patricia Keegan gathered up Little Liam and allowed Moira to lead them both to 221B.

There was little that could surprise Mrs. Hudson. She had opened her door to royals, political figures of every rank, actors fresh from their performance on stage, military leaders returned from their regiments, and navy men so newly arrived from their ships they hadn't yet gotten their land legs. She could not recall having ever opened her door to a family. She recognized Moira and broke into a broad smile of welcome. She greeted Mrs. Keegan, and invited her to take a seat in the parlor and relax for a moment with a cup of tea. Her investigative skills weren't necessary to understand the nature of the Keegans' visit. Mr. Holmes and Dr. Watson were in serious trouble. There could be no other reason for Patricia Keegan to gather up her family and spend her precious savings on a cab immediately after meeting with her two colleagues. The harried look on the woman's small bright face only confirmed what Mrs. Hudson already knew. She was about to pour tea, and offer scones to the children by way of making her more comfortable when Mrs. Keegan made an unexpected request.

Dropping herself into a parlor chair and drawing Little Liam onto her lap, Patricia Keegan implored the housekeeper, "Can you please help us to find Mr. Wiggins, ma'am. Mr. Holmes and his friend are in some terrible trouble and we need Mr. Wiggins to rescue them."

Mrs. Hudson was bewildered for the moment by the characterization of Wiggins as Holmes's likely savior. Then she realized the source for Mrs. Keegan's assessment of Wiggins's problem-solving skills was her 12-year old daughter. Rather than challenge the youngster's judgment, it seemed wisest to yield for the moment to the alarm her guest was feeling.

"I'll do what I can to get Mr. Wiggins to come by 'ere on the double. What should I tell 'im is the problem?"

"Tell him his two partners have got themselves kidnapped. I saw it happen myself, ma'am, and I know one of them as did the kidnapping." Her voice dropped to a confidential whisper, "He's one of the Brotherhood and he's a bad lot. The Lord only knows where they've taken Mr. Holmes and his friend or what they're planning, but it's for certain they're up to no good. Something needs doing and soon. It's Mr. Wiggins I was thinking would know what to do."

"I'll see what can be done." With that, Mrs. Hudson took a dark shawl from a hook by the door, and wrapping it round her shoulders, she went in search of a boy who could find the self-proclaimed leader of the group Mr. Holmes had christened the Irregulars. She reckoned that a shilling now and a second shilling on delivery of Wiggins would attract one of the boys, and the lure of comparable reward—plus the opportunity to assist Mr. Holmes—would attract Wiggins. A likely looking youngster lingered outside the dressmaker's shop several doors down the opposite side of the Baker Street roadway. She knew him to specialize in telling female shoppers sad stories of his orphaned state while he squashed his cap, chewed his lower lip, and blinked away tears if he could manage them. At the end of the day he gave his earnings to his mother, less a small amount for sweets, and it nicely supplemented the income his father drew as a baker's assistant.

Mrs. Hudson knew the boy as Jack, but had no idea of his last name, or the last names of any of the Irregulars other than Wiggins. The boy was certain the woman he had been tracking was near to completing her fitting, and so he made a great show of pretending the housekeeper's call was for someone further down Baker Street. When at last Mrs. Hudson was too near him to be ignored, he stepped away from the shop, while keeping it well within his field of vision, and asked in an angry whisper what it was she wanted. Upon learning of the urgent need to contact Wiggins, and of the reward associated with that action, he instantly deserted his post and went in search of the leader of the Irregulars. He called to Mrs. Hudson not to trouble herself, he would have Wiggins in her parlor in double-quick time. Mrs. Hudson did not find altogether reassuring the prospect of having Wiggins return to her parlor a second time in three days.

Jack was as good as his word. By the time Mrs. Hudson had returned, convinced Mrs. Keegan to accept a second cup of tea, and completed the far easier task of tempting Moira and Little Liam with raisin filled scones and strawberry jam, a breathless Wiggins and his grinning tracker joined them. Jack accepted his payment and started back to the dressmaker. Wiggins assumed as dignified an expression as a torn shirt partly tucked back in his trousers and a small purpling mouse under one eye permitted. He smiled uncertainly to Moira, who broke into a broad dimpled grin on seeing her benefactor; then smiled with even greater uncertainty to Mrs. Keegan who still held Little Liam on her lap. Mrs. Hudson introduced Mrs. Patricia Keegan to Thomas Wiggins, prefacing his first name with the title, "Mister," in accord with the need for extreme self-sacrifice to rescue her boarders from whatever fate had befallen them. Swallowing hard, she explained the state of affairs to him while he munched contentedly on the scone he selected after careful consideration of the tray lying within unprecedented reach of the chair he selected.

"Mrs. Keegan 'as come 'ere with the news Mr. 'Olmes and Dr. Watson 'ave been snatched by the Brother'ood and are now being 'eld by them at a place we don't know. She 'as asked to see you because she understands you to be a friend and colleague to Mr. 'Olmes and is thinkin' you will 'ave a plan to rescue Mr. 'Olmes and Dr. Watson." Mrs. Hudson paused to be certain Wiggins understood the level of responsibility he was being assigned.

Mrs. Keegan nodded enthusiastically, Moira beamed, and Little Liam took a moment from pulling the raisins from his scone and stuffing as many as possible in his mouth, to look with curiosity to Wiggins. The object of their attention, who moments before had been clarifying the financial obligations of the delivery boy he had helped get hired by Simpson and Sons Meat and Poultry, furrowed his brow, nodded deeply, and issued a series of well-spaced, "umms," to demonstrate his understanding. Pursing his lips and furrowing his brow still further, he began to raise questions adapted from the several interrogations in which he had participated, although the role of questioner was new to him.

"What is it makes you think Mr. Holmes and the Doctor was snatched, if I might ask?" Mrs. Keegan described seeing Holmes and Watson directed into a carriage by two men who followed them into the coach, at least one of them showing a suspicious bulge in his coat pocket. There were more nods and umms from Wiggins.

"And what makes you think it was the Brotherhood what done it?" Mrs. Keegan explained that she recognized one of the men, a bad-tempered sort who had several times come to see her about her husband. She didn't know the other, but the Brotherhood seemed always to be finding new people.

Wiggins was silent for a moment, struggling to achieve the epiphany Mrs. Keegan believed inevitable from an associate of Sherlock Holmes. His next question, the only other question that occurred to Wiggins, was a severe disappointment to her.

"Have you been in touch with Scotland Yard about this?" In a tired voice, Mrs. Keegan explained the difficulties she would face if she went to the Yard, and added her private pessimism about the capacity of the Yard to find Holmes and Watson.

The room became silent again, but now there were no more nods or murmurs of understanding, and Wiggins's furrowed brow seemed to indicate confusion rather than thought. Mrs. Keegan concentrated her attention on the tea cooling in her cup. Moira still looked to her champion, but concern had replaced the hopeful smile. Only Little Liam continued as before, working his way through the scone from which most of the raisins had been removed. Mrs. Hudson freshened Mrs. Keegan's tea, and put forward what seemed an off-hand suggestion.

"Might I suggest we approach this problem like Mr. 'Olmes might 'ave done." The faces of Mrs. Keegan and Wiggins indicated their openness to the housekeeper's suggestion. "It's just that I've been seein' 'im work on these little puzzles for so long I sometimes think I can almost 'ear what 'e might be sayin'. Mrs. Keegan, might I ask you, ma'am, were you alone with Mr. 'Olmes and Dr. Watson the 'ole time 'e was with you? Was there anyone else who could've known about you seeing the two of them?"

"Well, there's Mr. Parkhurst. He helped make the arrangements for us to meet. But I can't believe that Mr. Parkhurst ... He's been a good friend right along." At the mention of Mr. Parkhurst, Mrs. Keegan's cheeks reddened prettily and her voice took on a small tremor.

Mrs. Hudson fluttered a hand to derail Mrs. Keegan's train of thought. "Was there anyone besides Mr. Park'urst who knew you were seeing Mr. 'Olmes?"

Mrs. Keegan's eyes narrowed, then widened suddenly. "My da. He knew. He come in on us while we was talking and then he took off to go to Caffey's."

"Caffey's?"

"It's the neighborhood pub he goes to. It's a place where a lot of the folk from the Old Country go."

"Really. Well, I count that most interestin'. Wouldn't you agree ... Mr. Wiggins?"

The object of her query looked warily to Mrs. Hudson before chancing a reply. "Interesting. Interesting is the very word for it, Mrs. Hudson." He stopped at that point, and waited to learn why he found it interesting.

"Usin' Mr. 'Olmes' methods, it seems clear there's only two people as could of told the Brother'ood of 'is and Dr. Watson's whereabouts. Mr. Park'urst knew Mr. 'Olmes would be payin' you a visit, but couldn't know exactly when, only knowin' it'd be after two. Besides 'e's got nothing to be gained from tellin' the Brother'ood about Mr. 'Olmes. It's only Mr. Keegan who knew the exact timin' of Mr. 'Olmes' visit. I'm wonderin' if 'e might 'ave shared that information with anyone? Like maybe there's some at this Caffey's that would 'ave an interest in knowin' about Mr. 'Olmes' visit to you." An open-mouthed nod from her visitor let Mrs. Hudson know one part of the puzzle had fallen into place. "Mr. Keegan would of 'ad to contact someone at Caffey's. There won't of been time for 'im to get to anywhere else. Mr. Wiggins, is that what you understand might be our Mr. 'Olmes' thinkin'?" She received a slow nod of agreement from a bewildered Wiggins. "And could your father be in touch with any of the Brother'ood at Caffey's pub, Mrs. Keegan?"

"He could, ma'am. It's quite the meeting place for them."

Mrs. Hudson relaxed back in her chair, "Well then, simply applyin' the deductin' principles Mr. 'Olmes might use, it sounds to me, Mr. Wiggins, like a trip to this 'ere Caffey's pub would be in order."

"Do you think I should contact my da and get him to tell us who he might of spoken to?"

"It's a fine idea, but just thinkin' the way Mr. 'Olmes might, and you can back me up with your thinkin' on this, Mr. Wiggins, I'd say it might be best to let that lay. Your dad might not want to admit to any part of this. If 'e says 'e done it 'e could be in trouble with the law, and if 'e says anythin' about where they've taken Mr. 'Olmes and the Doctor 'e could be in trouble with the Brother'ood. No, as Mr. 'Olmes might say, we could be wastin' time runnin' up a blind alley on that one. Is that what you think, Mr. Wiggins?"

Wiggins was now returned to familiar territory. He knew about people selling each other out for a few bob or less, then lying to cover it up. "It's just like you say, Mrs. H. And I'll bet he got hisself a little something for selling out our Mr. Holmes—begging your pardon Mrs. Keegan, Moira, but it's what Mr. Holmes would say." Neither Moira nor Mrs. Keegan appeared aware of any reason to take offense. "We need to be making the kind of plan Mr. Holmes would think up." With that said, Wiggins again screwed up his face in a careful imitation of deep thought.

Mrs. Hudson took it from there. "And I can just 'ear Mr. 'Olmes sayin' we need to know all we can about the people we might be dealin' with." Mrs. Hudson looked intently to

Patricia Keegan. "Mrs. Keegan, would it be your opinion that the men you saw with Mr.'Olmes are leaders in the Brother'ood?"

"I only know one of them, ma'am. That would be Brandon Cavanaugh, and I can tell you Brandon Cavanaugh is certainly no leader. I'm afraid Brandon was gone for a smoke when the good Lord handed out brains. He's wanted only for his muscle and his nerve, and takes his orders from Mr. Fogarty, just like all of them do."

Mrs. Hudson leaned far back in her chair. "And do you know where this Mr. Fogarty is stayin'?"

"I don't, ma'am. It's quite the secret really, and he's not in any one place for long. At least that's what everybody says. I believe Mr. Caffey knows because he can get to Mr. Fogarty when there are things needs to be told. My da says he'll send the potboy with a message if it's important enough."

"And is there anythin' further I should know about Mr. Caffey or his pub? Any peculiarity about it I should know?"

"I don't rightly know ma'am. I never been except two or three times to collect my da when the boy came around to tell me he was feeling badly and there was no one to carry him home. Mr. Hogan and myself would go to get him those times." Patricia Keegan shook her head with a sudden recognition. "There is one thing my da has mentioned. Mr. Caffey has this deadly fear of germs. He's got to have his tables and bar clear of anything that could have the least bit of dirt on them, and he's forever mopping things clean as soon as anyone's done with their eating or drinking. He's that afraid of someone coming down sick from things not being spotless. There's been landlords lost their business because of customers getting stomach problems or worse and Mr. Caffey don't take no chances. He keeps his place as clean as the riffraff he serves allows, and I've heard from others that his potboy has to look sharp if he's to keep his job."

"That's good to know, Mrs. Keegan. I thank you for all that. Well then, Mr. Wiggins, I'm suggestin' we do what Mr. 'Olmes would do and get ourselves over to see Mr. Caffey. We can think about 'ow Mr. 'Olmes would go about gettin' Mr. Fogarty's address from 'im durin' our cab ride. Mrs. Keegan, I thank you again. You've done Mr. 'Olmes a great service. Just now, I think you should be gettin' yourself and the little ones back to 'ome. Mr. Wiggins and I can take it from 'ere. I'll get a few shillings together for your trip back, and I'm askin' you to let me pay for your trip comin' as well. Mr. Wiggins, would you get a four-wheeler for Mrs. Keegan? I need to get a few things together and then we can be off to pay Mr. Caffey a visit."

Freed of their blindfolds, Holmes and Watson blinked their adjustment to the muted light of the drawing room to which they had been led. Heavy plum-colored drapes concealed two large windows on the wall to their right which might have otherwise relieved the room's dreariness. A piano filled the space between the nearer window and the wall behind them, the damask cloth covering it suggested that filling the space was the instrument's sole function. An oak sideboard stood below the second window and extended nearly to the far wall. It held bottles of clear and brown colored liquid at one end and a tea service at the other, the choice of refreshment separated by a tall vase filled with artificial dahlias, the reds, blues and yellows of the wax flowers providing the only color in the room, apart from the flag that stretched above and beyond the marble fireplace on the wall facing Holmes and Watson. The banner showed a corner of golden sun with 13 rays jutting dagger-like into a field of blue. Watson knew it as the Sunburst Flag and the banner of the Irish Republican Brotherhood.

Before leaving them, their two captors pressed Holmes

and Watson toward a green-cushioned couch set in a broad oval of unmatched chairs and small tables at the room's center. The bearded man and his clean-shaven ally had gone to join two other men at the room's far end. After a hurried conversation, the four took to eyeing Holmes and Watson with cold curiosity, all the while taking long draws on hand-rolled cigarettes and using the fireplace as their outsized ashtray. They took no more responsibility for explaining the abduction of Holmes and Watson than did their colleagues from the four-wheeler. It was left to the fifth man in the room to provide that explanation.

"I do apologize for the inconvenience we have created for you, Mr. Holmes, Dr. Watson, even if you've brought it on yourselves." The words were spoken in the anticipated Irish brogue by a man seated at a roll-top desk along the windowless wall to the detectives' left. He looked a near twin of their clean-shaven captor, having the same dark eyes, thick rimless glasses, pinched nose and small, slight build. Unlike the man in the coach, he possessed both a neatly trimmed black moustache and the self-assured air that marked him as the group's leader. He gave Holmes and Watson a perfunctory smile, and squinted across his desk in search of the cigarette he'd been smoking. With its discovery, he took a long draw, exhaling smoke slowly through his nose and mouth before resuming.

"I've had you brought here because we need to talk, and I couldn't be certain you'd join me of your own volition." He turned his attention again to the cigarette, tapping its long ash into a bowl already well studded with ground out cigarette butts amid small mounds of ash. Holmes seized the moment to renew his earlier request.

"You have the advantage of knowing our names. We are obviously not to know where we are, may we at least know to whom we are speaking?"

The owlish man replied with only minor irritation. "No, you may not. When you leave here—if you leave here—I have no intention of providing you with information to take to your friends at Scotland Yard. And please do me the courtesy of not denying you're in league with the police. We know all about Sherlock Holmes, and knew all about you even back in the Old Country."

Holmes waved away the charge while smiling his acceptance of the inadvertent compliment. "Then you must know that Sherlock Holmes is independent of the Yard, and of any governmental agency. I pursue justice alone and wear no man's collar." Watson nodded a vigorous agreement which carried as little force with the owlish man as Holmes's statement.

"Yes, yes, very nice. It just happens that when you hire yourself out to whoever will pay your price, you then ally with your friends at the Yard to turn whatever poor devil you find over to an English court so he can receive English justice. I've seen quite enough of English justice, thank you. I can do without any more of it."

With that, the speaker crushed out his cigarette and advanced toward Holmes and Watson. He settled himself in an easy chair angled across from his prisoners, where he was quickly joined on either side and behind by three of the men who had been watching the exchange between their leader and Holmes. The man who looked to be his brother emptied the considerable refuse from the bowl on his desk into the fireplace, then set the bowl and a small pouch of tobacco and rolling papers on the round table next to him before taking up a position beside Holmes and Watson.

"There's no need to drag things out, Mr. Holmes. We know who it is that's paying you and we know you're working with the police. You see the Irish Branch watches us and we watch the Irish Branch. I know they're now calling themselves the Special Branch, but it's the Irish Branch as they were created and it remains the right arm for Irish persecution. Fortunately, their Inspector Peter Lassiter is about as easy to keep an eye on as any man alive. You just look for the best silk topper and the fanciest coat and trousers, and you've found your man. So we know all about his coming to see you, and I trust you won't tell me he was there to pay you a social call." His look to Holmes made clear the pride he took in his organization's intelligence gathering.

"Lassiter could have your cooperation, but there's still the matter of your pay. Because Sherlock Holmes doesn't take on anyone's troubles without being well paid for it, and there's no one to pay for investigating the death of a poor Irishman. No one, except the Reverend Farnsworth and his ban-the-Irish Christian Union come to put money in your pocket if you'll just pin the murder of Liam Coogan on the Brotherhood. And so everybody gets what they're hoping for. Farnsworth can make the Brotherhood out to be a bunch of crazed murderers, Inspector Lassiter has his excuse to come after us, and you can have your fine dinners and fancy clothes bought with the blood money you get from friends of that sort. Except this time, Mr. Sherlock Holmes, you're dealing with someone who's just one jump ahead of you."

The owlish man stopped to tap tobacco into papers he licked closed in time to light the fresh cigarette with the one he then ground out in the bowl held for him by his double. Cigarette smoke trailed behind the words he spoke. "Not that I'll pretend to be in mourning for Liam Coogan. Of course, I'm sorry about how it leaves Patsy Keegan and her cubs, but there's plenty of her sisters and brothers who've suffered worse than she will on account of Coogan and traitors like him. And there's plenty more will suffer if the work of our organization doesn't go forward. Which brings us to you, Mr. Holmes. What are we to do with you? We can't very well leave you free to help Farnsworth spread his lies and hate. And we'd be plain fools to sit back and wait for you to turn us over to Inspector Lassiter so we can be exposed to your English justice. Do you see the dilemma you create for us, Mr. Holmes?"

It was not, however, Holmes who answered the questions posed. Watson could contain himself no longer. "You speak as though you represent some great noble purpose that can justify whatever behaviors you find appropriate to promoting your cause. The plain fact is you've rejected any way for achieving the goal of Irish Home Rule short of violence. You talk of high moral purpose, and you engage in a series of explosions without even the smallest regard for human life. There is a political process at your disposal, you have a well-placed champion for your cause in Mr. Parnell and a sympathetic ear in Mr. Gladstone, yet you choose the path of underworld thug to achieve your goals. Can you really believe a course of unprovoked violence will sway public opinion? I say to you your course is repugnant to the English mind, and so alien to our way of doing things as to lead to certain failure."

Watson expected neither apology or expression of sudden remorse, but was unprepared for his captor's burst of laughter. "Really, Doctor, you are the perfect Englishman. 'A course of unprovoked violence repugnant to the English mind.' How in the world do you think the English Empire was put together? You went about destroying one civilization after another without the smallest regard for the human life you're going on about. Why death and destruction are so much a part of your English way, you've even convinced yourselves that all these folk what are now chattel, with no more purpose than to feed your bellies and make your riches, are better off for having the honor of being Englishmen. They may be slaves to your Queen, but they should count themselves fortunate because they're English slaves. Well that's not the good fortune we're wanting, Doctor. And it's not the good fortune anyone what calls himself a man wants for himself or his country. We're only wanting our own land and our own way of doing things and if it's a fight you want—well, it's a fight we'll make, and we'll make it on our terms, not yours." As the owlish man lit yet another cigarette, the men around him appeared to stand a little straighter, grow a little taller, and their scrutiny of Holmes and Watson became even more disapproving.

"Whatever is true or false of what you say about the Empire—and I credit none of it—it provides no excuse for your behavior. You are responsible for your own actions regardless of the way in which you think others—even your enemies—have acted, and your actions involve the weapons and tactics of cowards. You cheapen your cause, and lose the support of those who might otherwise sympathize with your struggle when you choose to fight with bombs and stealthy attacks."

"Ah, once more the English gentleman speaks. We should fight fairly. We should fight like Englishmen." The owlish man punctuated each sentence with a sneer. "You will no doubt arrange for an even distribution of arms, as well as food and uniforms so that we can fight on equal terms and not have to rely on the tactics available to the victim. Only the side that has all the guns ever accuses the other side of not fighting fair. We use the weapons we can make or steal just like every revolutionary before us. And in some of those bombings and 'stealthy attacks' as you call them, there'll be lives lost, our own lives and yes, the lives of some you think of as being innocents. We take no joy in that, but our cause demands it. We know if we fail to act there will still be lives lost, and there will be a great many more lives that won't be worth the living." The owlish man paused, and with a wave of his hand dismissed further argument. "But none of that gets us any the closer to deciding what to do with the two of you. You present quite the problem, Mr. Sherlock Holmes, you and your apologist for Her Majesty's Empire. The likes of you can't just disappear off the London streets, and I'll not have you destroying the whole of what we've been building just so you can make more quid than you have need of."

With that, he ground out yet another cigarette in the nearby bowl and waved off the offer of the makings for its replacement. He leaned back in his chair and searched the ceiling for inspiration. While he waited for invention to make an appearance, there was a sharp knock on the door, then another, and a voice familiar to Holmes and Watson called out, "'Ello in there, is there anyone to 'ome?"

In the cab she shared with Wiggins, Mrs. Hudson described a plan she assured him "was straight out of Mr. 'Olmes' own thinkin'." She told him it was a strategy Mr. Holmes used in a case involving a dwarf Hungarian prince and the Burmese python he employed to murder a music hall actress in Budapest. She stopped there, explaining that to go any further would be to divulge a confidence. As she suspected, her exotic creation led Wiggins to embrace her staid plan without challenge. He was concerned only with learning the fate of the python who seemed to him as much the prince's innocent victim as the deceased actress. Mrs. Hudson reported the authorities agreed entirely with Wiggins, and the animal had been adopted by the Hungarian Zoo. Satisfied with that case's resolution, Wiggins was now prepared to join Mrs. Hudson in resolving this one.

They took the four-wheeler to a street just beyond Caffey's pub, which they noted bore the more formal name of The Winking Duck. A sign protruding above the entrance to the modest stone building showed the head of a white duck with elongated eyelashes, one of which half covered an eye, thereby providing a vaguely lascivious greeting to each entering patron. Mrs. Hudson gathered up the small bundle she had put together before leaving Baker Street and, after directing the driver to wait for them, she and Wiggins made their way back to Caffey's. They entered the door to the pub's parlor area where two women sat together at one of the five tables set aside for unaccompanied ladies and families. The two were having pasties and half pints of what Mrs. Hudson suspected to be ale—the housekeeper herself being a teetotaler—and maintaining a steady stream of good-humored banter with the landlord, who mopped a spotless bar within sight of the women without once looking in their direction. The larger room beyond was only partly visible through the open half of a Dutch door, and Mrs. Hudson could see the fully aproned host and two men standing at the section of the bar within her sight.

With a wink and a nod to the two men and however many more were behind them, the landlord was well into a bantering with the two women about the age and digestibility of his pasties when the stub of a woman all in black, accompanied by a youngster who appeared to be unfamiliar with the basics of personal hygiene, stepped between him and his female audience and plumped a bundle of God knows what on the open part of the Dutch door. His thick eyebrows shot well into his forehead and, with shaking jowls maintaining a rhythm with his speech, the landlord addressed the sudden intruder.

"Here now, I'd appreciate your keeping your package off of that door. It's food and drink that's to be placed there and nothing else. I'd be obliged to you for keeping your package on the floor where it belongs and off any of the places we use for eating and drinking." Several male patrons now came into view, anxious to see for themselves the target of the landlord's concern.

Seeming to take no notice of her audience, Mrs. Hudson set her bundle beside a table across from the one occupied by the two women, who had become as quiet as their male counterparts on the other side of the Dutch doors. Mrs. Hudson used the moment to make a quick study of the landlord. Caffey was 50ish, with heavily pomaded gray-streaked hair parted precisely at the center, well-tended handlebar moustaches, and a habit of looking frequently to the men around him for reaction to his words, all suggesting a man eager to impress others and anxious about his ability to do so. Above the bar there was a large cut-glass mirror on which Mrs. Hudson could see the single word, "FAILTE," printed in bright green letters large enough to give greeting to the Winking Duck's Irish patrons, without being so large as to give offense to any patrons lacking association with the Old Sod. Mrs. Hudson concluded that Mr. Caffey's concern with the impression he made on others was combined with a calculated effort to accommodate the wishes of his varied customers, and that both those interests might prove useful to her.

With the offending bundle removed, the landlord's commercial charm returned. "Now, is there something I can get for you?"

"Bless you, yes. Mr. Caffey, is it?" A brusque nod encouraged her to continue. "Didn't I tell you we'd find 'im, Thomas?" Wiggins did his best to look properly chastened. "The boy and me 'ave 'ad quite the time getting 'ere I can tell you. This is the last time I take work what is properly belongin' to your aunt. The very last time." Confusion briefly clouded the landlord's face until he determined the strange woman likely meant the boy's aunt rather than his. During the time he was working that out Mrs. Hudson took the bundle from the chair and absently set it on the table beside her.

"Madam, I'd appreciate it if you'd keep your ... things off the surfaces where we put the food and drink. Now may I please take your order so I might serve my other customers as well."

Mrs. Hudson chose not to point out to the landlord that no one was clamoring for drinks or food as everyone in the pub was now fully attentive to her and her exchange with Caffey, exactly as she intended.

"You're right, Mr. Caffey. Quite right. In fact, we both of us 'ave businesses to run though yours is a good deal grander than mine. And I'm late, dreadful late for my char duties, so if you'll be good enough to give me Mr. Fogarty's address I'll trouble you no more."

At the name, the pub's patrons, already holding themselves still so as to not to miss a word of the exchange, now appeared to delay breathing lest a syllable of conversation be lost. Everyone knew the members of the Brotherhood who came by for drinks and who sometimes met in Caffey's private room, but everyone knew as well their names were never to be spoken. And the name to be avoided most scrupulously was that of Mr. Fogarty. Caffey had come across to the Dutch door, and began to slowly wipe the area where the offending bundle had lain. "And might I know who was it told you I knew the address of that gentleman?"

"Why, of course. There's no secret to it. Mr. Brandon Cavanaugh's own cousin's boy come to tell me I was needed on account of the regular char being down with the ague, poor thing, and I was wanted to fill in so to speak. I don't mind tellin' you I need the work with my old man down with the deliriums. Only the boy didn't 'ave an address and told me that I was to learn where to find Mr. Fogarty from Mr. Caffey. Mr. Cavanaugh 'ad told 'im that Mr. Caffey, which is to say you, was a man to be trusted, whatever is the meanin' of that."

Michael Caffey looked warily to the old woman and

received a vacant stare in return. It was true enough he knew exactly where Mr. Fogarty was staying. He always knew where Mr. Fogarty was staying as he had the task of sending the boy around to tell Mr. Fogarty whenever he learned of anything suspicious that was happening, most particularly if any strangers were asking for him. Like this old lady and her son, or whatever he was to her. He couldn't really see the old char and boy as a danger, and it would be just like that fool Cavanaugh to give the woman his name. If the potboy had been there, he could have sent him to learn Mr. Fogarty's wishes. But the boy wasn't due until later. There was little point to paying a potboy when there were no drinks to carry and few glasses to clean. And whatever he thought of the char and her son or grandson, Mr. Fogarty was quite particular he was to send no one to him but the boy. To do otherwise involved risking the loss of the Brotherhood's business, and that wasn't a risk he could afford taking.

With a pub on nearly every corner a man had to have an edge to stay in business. The Brotherhood was his edge. It was their trade that kept the crowd coming back each evening in hopes of seeing the men who yesterday might have blown apart a building and tomorrow might kill somebody, or more exciting still, might get themselves killed. The crowd came to see the men who acted as they thought they might have done were it not for families, and jobs, and fears. They came to stand beside them, maybe even buying one of them a drink and getting a word of thanks in return. They would take that home and hold to the memory of a time they visited a world more thrilling, more dangerous than any they would ever know. Caffey might not understand the psychology of his trade, but he knew what kept his pub crowded nights when other pubs were half full, and he had no wish to risk his business for an old char.

"I'm afraid I can't help you, ma'am. I can't say I know

126

the gent you're looking for. But I'll stand you and the boy to some ginger beer if you'd like unless you're wanting some tea." The landlord looked hopefully to Mrs. Hudson. He wasn't a hard man and would feel better if he could give the old woman something to drink, maybe even one of the pasties.

"Are you certain you don't know a Mr. Fogarty? Mr. Cavanaugh was that sure you would."

Caffey was aware there was a sudden moving about by the men who had stood silent as death until now, and the two women with whom he was happily bantering moments before had caught each other's eye and were now looking at him with dark wonder. Caffey crossed, then uncrossed his arms, and finally set his hands on the door and leaned across, speaking to Mrs. Hudson as confidentially as the small space and the curiosity of his customers allowed.

"I wish I could be of service to you, ma'am, but I'm afraid I just can't help you."

It was at that point that Mrs. Hudson, and everyone else in the pub, became aware of a wretched wailing that worked itself into a whimper and finally to speech. "Oh mum, whatever are we to do. He'll beat us, you know he will. He always does if we don't have no money. I can't take another beatin'. I just can't. If we don't find Mr. Fogarty, I'll run away, mum. I have to. I don't care what happens. I won't be beaten. You know it's why sister run off and I will too." Wiggins, having briefly summarized a life of torment, now returned to wailing, not as loudly as before, but piteously nonetheless. He covered his face with a handkerchief that had once been either gray, brown or green, all those colors being evident in its different parts.

Mrs. Hudson recognized that, however competent her performance had been, she was in the company of genius and happily adopted a supporting role. "There now, Thomas, the old man might be so drunk as not to take notice when we come in. We'll just need to get a little somethin' to eat from the neighbors again, and everythin' will be alright. That's if they've anythin' to spare of course." She turned to the two women behind her. "The boy worries so. He takes the biggest part of the beatin's now with 'is sister gone."

"Mr. Caffey, surely it can't do any harm to let this poor woman and her boy go and clean up Mr. Fogarty's place." The voice came from a man Mrs. Hudson couldn't see. It held both age and strength, and carried the melodious brogue to which she was now accustomed. Instantly, several voices took up the appeal. As she anticipated, the women she now looked to with as wretched an expression as she could manage were the most strident in her defense. "For the Lord's own sake, Mr. Caffey do the right thing. You don't want something like this on your conscience." Others cited Mr. Caffey's obligation as a Christian, gave assurances they would stand by him in his action, opined there was already too much misery in the world, and declared him too good a person not to help this poor woman.

The argument holding the greatest sway for Caffey was that there could be some in the neighborhood as might not be comfortable giving their business to a man who would deprive a poor woman of her earnings, and leave her and the boy at the mercy of a poor drunken excuse of a husband. Caffey protested his only concern was with maintaining the confidentiality he felt for all who entered his pub, then yielded to the inevitable. He wrote an address on a piece of scrap paper after first establishing the char could read. Mrs. Hudson and Wiggins left with the blessings and good wishes of everyone at the Winking Duck; she in turn showered them with her heartfelt gratitude.

Once back in the four-wheeler, she allowed that Wiggins might yet have a career on the stage, and gave measured praise for his performance. For his part, Wiggins only wanted to be assured Mrs. Hudson would tell Mr. Holmes of his help. Mrs. Hudson directed the driver to go past the address they had been given, taking note of the curtains covering every window in the house. She had him stop at a point around the corner from the house where she asked him if it would be alright to leave the horse and carriage for a while, that she had a little job she wanted him to do. The driver made it known that the horse knew his business, and he'd be glad to help if there could be something in it for the two of them. Mrs. Hudson indicated the task was a simple one, requiring no effort on his part, but she agreed finally on two shillings as the driver's due. He was to stand beneath a street lamp across the road and part way down the street from the house and look earnest. When that proved a difficulty, she asked him to look troubled which worked well. She next took the helmet and a truncheon that had belonged to Constable Tobias Hudson from the bag she had brought. She told him to fit the helmet on as best as he could, and to slap the truncheon into his free hand every now and again. She reasoned he was far enough away that the coachman's dark blue jacket combined with helmet and truncheon could be mistaken for a constable's uniform. After seeing the driver settled at his post, she and Wiggins proceeded to the address given by Mr. Caffey where she rapped loudly at the door and called out, "'Ello in there, is there anyone to 'ome?"

Fogarty turned sharply from Holmes and Watson to glare at the interruption to his plans for their disposal. Each of his confederates stood poised to take direction while their leader continued to squint hard at the door from behind his thick glasses as if convinced he could penetrate the solid object if he only stared at it furiously enough. A sudden thought seized him and he turned back to Holmes and Watson, squinting even harder at them and with as little success in penetrating their impassive expressions.

He turned to the man who looked to be his brother and told him to see who it was. The conscripted scout went to the door and, discreetly pulling back its curtain, found himself face to face with an older woman all in black, carrying a bundle he suspected to contain rags, and accompanied by a boy of about 15. She shook her head at him to make clear her disapproval, and signaled for him to open the door. He dropped the curtain and backed quickly away to report his observation, but before he could do so she called out, "Mr. Fogarty, now I know you're to 'ome. I'm only 'ere to do the cleanin'. Will you be so good as to open the door so's I can earn my keep." And then more loudly, "Mr. Fogarty, are you 'earin' me?"

For his part, Fogarty remained rooted to his chair while all except his brother drew revolvers and trained them alternately on Holmes and Watson and the front door. "Who the devil is out there?" he hissed to his brother.

"As best as I can judge, it's an old char and a boy. She's carrying her bundle which doesn't appear to have anything but rags in it, and they look to be alone."

By now, Wiggins had taken up the cry, "Mr. Fogarty, please open the door," with an emphasis on the "Mr. Fogarty" that carried well down the empty street.

The leader's face tightened into a fierce scowl as he again looked to Holmes. "If this is some of your doing, I'll have your hide for it. Let the two of them in before they have half the neighborhood down on us, and no guessing about their being alone. You make certain there's no one with them."

On entering the room to which Holmes and Watson had been led blindfolded, Mrs. Hudson gave no recognition of her two boarders, and Wiggins looked the room over as if in search of an appropriate souvenir of the day's adventures. Mrs. Hudson had told Wiggins that Mr. Holmes would not want them to reveal the purpose of their visit until they were well inside. With only one man seated, and all eyes darting regularly to him, it was apparent to her that the small bookish man was the elusive Mr. Fogarty. The absence of personal items or decorations, with the single exception of the Sunburst Flag, indicated the address was temporary and the Cause was permanent.

"Mr. Fogarty, we've come for Mr. 'Olmes and Dr. Watson. We mean you no 'arm and 'ave no interest in your politics. We mean to leave 'ere all together and will be content to mark this 'ole business as closed."

Fogarty stared at the woman open-mouthed. His mood had proceeded from fury to incredulity and was now working its way back to fury. "And who in all that remains holy may you be?"

At that, Wiggins puffed himself up to as much size as he could manage, stared triumphantly at Fogarty, then at each of his henchman, and finally provided the requested clarification. "We are the partners of Mr. Sherlock Holmes, and we are here to rescue him exactly according to his plan."

Fogarty, now feeling in command of some of the facts and all of the situation, surveyed his young antagonist and smiled broadly before he spoke. "Rescue him. Young man— boy—do you not realize that I have only to say the word and your precious Mr. Holmes will no longer meddle in affairs he can't possibly understand."

"I don't think so, Mr. Fogarty." It was again the old char who spoke. Fogarty drew the line at harming women, but might have found the line fading were it not that this woman bore a disturbing resemblance to his Aunt Agatha, his father's oldest sister. Except his Aunt Agatha had the good grace to cook, clean and keep house for his two bachelor uncles without giving direction to their actions or challenging their ideas.

"Mr. 'Olmes is not such a fool as to leave us to come to see you without our takin' proper precautions. If you 'ave a look to the lamp post a bit down the street you'll see there's a constable who's waitin' to see us come walkin' down the steps we come up. And if we don't come down those steps, and come down them real soon, 'e'll be having 'alf the London police force down on you. I believe you may be familiar with Inspector Peter Lassiter of the Special Branch. You may be able to steer clear of bein' charged for your revolutionary shenanigans, but kidnappin' Mr. 'Olmes is another matter."

The small man moved the drape from another window and nodded grimly to his brother. Mr. Fogarty was a beaten man. He gave a small fluttering motion with his hand and the guns disappeared from view.

"You're a clever man, Mr. Holmes. I give you that. I don't know how you pulled it off, but I credit you for getting the job done. Still and all, this is just a battle—not even that— a skirmish—in a very long war. So take heed, Mr. Holmes. Everything I said before still goes. If you try to make the Brotherhood the goat in this, I'm guaranteeing you'll get no pleasure from the blood money you take from Farnsworth and his bunch of Christian hypocrites. You've been warned. Next time there'll be no warning." He gave a nod to the man nearest the door. "Now get yourselves out of here, and don't think about telling your Yard friends where to find us because by the time you're back to Baker Street we'll be gone."

The three members of London's premier consulting detective agency, accompanied by the leader of the Baker Street Irregulars and a newly minted constable, turned the corner allowing the policeman to reclaim his cab and "proper job," and Mrs. Hudson to reclaim her valued possessions. The four passengers climbed into the four-wheeler where they were cautioned by Mrs. Hudson about speaking. Although the glass separating them from the driver likely made eavesdropping impossible, Holmes and Watson were happy to sit silently with their thoughts. Only Wiggins appeared likely to burst if he didn't soon get the opportunity to revel in the day's events.

Once returned to the sitting room Holmes and Watson shared, Wiggins curled himself into an easy chair and congratulated Holmes on "the sheer ilegance" of his plan, reported his confidence that Mr. Holmes would never "let himself get cornered by them revolutionaries," and marveled at "how cool Mrs. H was in working out his plan." To their surprise, the woman identified as Mrs. H continued about her business of readying a pot of tea without appearing to take notice of the abbreviation of both her name and her role in the day's activities. Wiggins settled back, happily completing his attack on the raisin-filled scone Mrs. Hudson had set on his plate. Holmes cheerfully dismissed Wiggins's praise while concentrating on his tea and the noticeably smaller scone Mrs. Hudson had served him.

"It was nice work; that's for certain, Mrs. Hudson, and well done by you, Wiggins." Watson's words were merry, but his voice and long face reflected the weariness he felt. It was a weariness Mrs. Hudson felt as well.

With a single dissenting voice there was agreement that Wiggins needed to be getting home, although none of those supporting that position were certain Wiggins had a home in the usual sense of that word. Before he left, Mrs. Hudson reminded Holmes of his plans to have Wiggins return early the next morning to carry messages to the *Times* and Scotland Yard.

With Wiggins gone, Mrs. Hudson held up the three calling cards that had been left on the tray in the entryway outside her door. She handed them to Holmes who reported their contents. "It seems we've received visits from Mr.

Parkhurst of the *Times*, Inspector Lassiter of Scotland Yard, and a Captain Henry Harrison, MP, who called on behalf of Mrs. Katherine O'Shea on a matter of great urgency. He indicates he will try to reach us again tomorrow after two unless he receives word that the time is inconvenient." Holmes grimaced his recognition of the tasks ahead before speaking. "It sounds a busy day for us all."

Watson nodded, then turned his attention to committing to paper the details of his and Holmes's visit to Mrs. Keegan, and their abduction by Mr. Fogarty's men. Holmes returned to his study of hemp, and Mrs. Hudson went downstairs to clean her spotless kitchen.

Chapter 7.
The Press, Police, and Parliament Come to Call

Wiggins arrived at 7:30 the next morning. His punctuality was rewarded with a rasher of bacon, two slices of toast and a cup of tea, after which he was sent on his way to inform Mr. Parkhurst he could be seen at 10:15, if convenient, and Inspector Lassiter he could be seen at 11:30, if convenient. Wiggins returned a little after nine to report that both men found the times convenient. He was disappointed to learn he was too late to receive the second breakfast he'd been contemplating, although the half crown he received from Holmes and the scone from Mrs. Hudson did much to console him.

Mr. Parkhurst arrived 15 minutes late, explaining that as he was about to leave the office, he was informed of the death of Alexander Hamilton-Gordon, the second son of Sir George Hamilton-Gordon, the former Prime Minister, and himself an Honorary Equerry to the Queen, as well as having been a general in Her Majesty's Army. An obituary had to be prepared for the next edition which meant Parkhurst could only stay a short time. Having made his intentions known, he set himself on the edge of an easy chair in the sitting room at 221B and, after some consideration of the mound of raisin-filled scones Mrs. Hudson had set out, yielded finally to a scone and tea.

"I mainly wanted to follow up on your visit with Mrs. Keegan, and learn how you see things developing. I know it's a little early yet, but I sort of wondered if you had any leads at this time. Nothing for publication of course, just for background to a story." With that, Mr. Parkhurst extracted paper and pencil from the recesses of his waistcoat, licked the pencil's tip and adopted a scowl of concentration.

Holmes and Watson were unaware of the General's

death, but other than that were prepared for Mr. Parkhurst. Their task was to reveal as little as they could and learn as much as they were able. In concert with Mrs. Hudson, they had developed a set of responses to likely questions to accomplish the former, and a series of their own questions to accomplish the latter.

"As you say, Mr. Parkhurst, it is quite early yet and we could not hope to have developed any solid leads at this time, although I would say we have some promising lines of inquiry." Holmes had adopted the tone of teacher lecturing an earnest if not terribly gifted student. "We have, of course, met with Mrs. Keegan as you arranged. As you may not know, I also attended Mr. Coogan's wake." Holmes paused to gauge the effect of his revelation on the reporter. He allowed himself a small smile on seeing it hit its mark.

"I was at the wake, Mr. Holmes. I didn't see you there."

"Of course not. I didn't intend you would. But you may remember an older gentleman—very hard of hearing."

"That was you, Mr. Holmes?"

"Indeed. In addition, Dr. Watson and I had opportunity to visit with a Mr. Fogarty, of whom I believe you're aware, and shared a coach with two of his colleagues."

Parkhurst was wide-eyed and open-mouthed for just a moment before recovering the solemnity appropriate to his profession. "I say, Mr. Holmes, you are a wonder. If I felt cause to be concerned about your investigative skills, you've certainly done away with that. But tell me if you can—not as I say for the readers of the *Times*, at least not just yet—what are these promising lines of inquiry of which you spoke?"

"This may surprise you, and I only share it with you now because of your assistance to date, and our understanding that you will honor a confidence." Holmes paused to check the cuffs of each sleeve of his dressing gown. Finding them both in order, he continued. "It is my opinion Mrs. Keegan is a person of interest to us. I suspect she is not all she seems."

Parkhurst's eyebrows sought new heights in his expanse of forehead and he swallowed hard. When he spoke the words gushed ahead of the measured pace he was hoping to achieve. "Whatever do you mean, Mr. Holmes? What is it that you're saying?"

Holmes appeared in danger of having to stifle a yawn. "It's surely nothing new. A young, attractive woman with a husband away from home for long periods. Any such woman might form a friendship that could progress to a more romantic relationship. Oh, I'm not saying she didn't care for her husband—once, but I'm struck by the absence of the grieving widow. Surely you've taken notice of her extraordinary calm in dealing with Mr. Coogan's death. One has to consider whether Mrs. Keegan and her new ... friend might not have become convinced of the need to remove the single impediment to their happiness. Once that was decided it would be easy enough to carry out their crime in such a way as to throw suspicion on the Irish radicals by simulating the Phoenix Park murders. I'm sure they might have preferred a gentler solution to their problem, but with divorce being out of question in the Catholic faith ...." Holmes allowed his voice to trail off rather than elaborate the indelicate detail, then resumed in a more deliberate manner. "We're currently looking into the legacy from some of his activities that Mrs. Keegan may receive from Coogan's death."

"Legacy! There's nothing! Absolutely nothing! The man had nothing to give. How can you possibly pursue such a line of reasoning about Patsy ... Mrs. Keegan." Words did not so much leave the reporter's mouth as they exploded from it. He looked in vain to Holmes for some relaxation of his views, then to Watson whose eyes never left the paper that he seemed at pains to fill as rapidly as he could. "Mr. Holmes, Dr. Watson, I can't believe you find this line of inquiry useful.

137

As I've told you earlier, I had lengthy conversations with both Mrs. Keegan and Mr. Coogan and have found them a devoted couple without a hint of scandal. I simply can't believe there's another man. I'm sure I would have heard of one if he existed. And as for some inheritance from Mr. Coogan, it's frankly laughable. The man provided what he could, but the couple was virtually impoverished and had the devil's own time making ends meet what with two children and a worthless father. You've seen the flat and its meager furnishings. You really must rethink your position and develop some other, more credible theory."

The groundwork laid, Holmes now challenged the reporter directly. "Perhaps this would be the time to tell us your *real* interest in Mr. Coogan's death, Mr. Parkhurst. If we are to follow another line of inquiry, it would be essential we get the truth about everyone's involvement with Mr. Coogan and Mrs. Keegan."

The only sound came from Watson's pen scratching its way across the sheet of foolscap; when he had finished, there was no sound at all. Parkhurst glared from Holmes to Watson as if deciding whether to demand swords or pistols, while Holmes looked first to Parkhurst, then to the bookcase behind him, then to his fingernails, all with equal interest. Watson kept his attention on the paper in front of him, now carefully reviewing the jottings he'd been making.

The silence was broken first by the sound of Parkhurst's feet striding in place beneath his easy chair, and then by the soft clearing of his throat, "Mr. Holmes, I have described my interest in the activities of the Brotherhood and my intent to develop an article for the *Times*. I have ambitions, Mr. Holmes, and they are not satisfied writing obituaries and birth announcements. I need a scoop as we say in journalism, and a story that attracts the attention of my editor can be my scoop. I have his encouragement to pursue a story as long as I get my assigned work done. That is really all I have to say on the subject of my interest in this matter. I'll not deny my sympathy for the plight of Mrs. Keegan, but I assure you there is nothing more. And now I will bid you good day. I'm afraid I'll need to spend some time reviewing the life of General Hamilton-Gordon to do justice to his obituary. I will look forward to our next meeting with the hope, and frankly the expectation, you'll have seen the errors in your reasoning and will be embarked on a more promising course."

With that, Winston Parkhurst rose stiffly from his chair and advanced to exchange the obligatory handshakes signaling the absence of the hard feelings he still harbored. Watson thanked him for coming, Holmes said nothing, and Parkhurst nodded grimly to them both.

As Parkhurst climbed into a waiting hansom, Watson went downstairs to share the substance of their conversation with Mrs. Hudson while Holmes took his violin from its case beside the bookcase and, after plucking each string of the instrument to ensure it was properly tuned, cradled it under his chin and filled the apartment with Mendelssohn. He believed his addition of a legacy to the prepared script had been nothing short of inspired. All in all, he was content he had played his role with Parkhurst to perfection.

Peter Lassiter was prompt as expected. He nodded to the housekeeper, placing his top hat and cane in her care without further acknowledgement of her presence. He rejected Mrs. Hudson's offer to announce him, indicating he knew the way and could announce himself which he did with a single knock on the sitting room door followed by his entry seconds before Holmes's call for him to do so. Once again he commandeered the room's settee. He explained this latest visit to Baker Street was being made to satisfy his chief inspector, who had asked to be kept informed about the progress Holmes was making with his investigation, simply in the interest of ensuring there would be no unpleasant surprises the police would have to deal with.

The scene to be played with Lassiter was far more complex than the one played with Parkhurst, so much so that Mrs. Hudson wasn't content to leave it entirely in Holmes's hands. On his desk, beside the customary foolscap, Watson had placed an open copy of *Peerage, Baronetage and Knightage* and his notes from its study that morning. It was decided that questions from that volume would be put by Watson while Holmes pursued a more general line of inquiry.

Employing that division of labor, Holmes responded to Lassiter's question about the state of the investigation.

"I'd say progress is being made. Dr. Watson and I have questioned several key people although it's still early in the game. And may I ask whether the Yard has made any progress?"

The young man looked at Holmes as though he had reason to question his sanity. "I've told you there's not the time or personnel to go chasing after murderers who kill other murderers. Frankly, we've no desire to interfere with their killing as long as they concentrate only on each other. We've got our hands full dealing with those who are engaged in blowing up buildings and bridges—or are trying to—and who pose a danger to innocent citizens. As I have already said, you are on your own on this, although it remains necessary we stay informed of your work since the Yard will need to step in if things get out of hand."

"Yes, well, we will continue to take things in hand while the Yard discharges responsibilities other than investigating murder," Holmes replied. "We have made a series of inquiries which you may report to the chief inspector. We have been questioning Mrs. Keegan, to learn if there are things she's not been sharing." Holmes paused, and Watson took up his pen and looked to Lassiter. The Inspector's face showed only his impatience. "We believe there is the possibility that a romantic interest on her part could have led to Coogan's murder by Mrs. Keegan and the man with whom she became involved."

"Yes, yes. I suppose that's a reasonable line to pursue although I would think the hand of the Brotherhood in all of this is clear enough. Of course, I know you'll pursue whatever leads you see as useful. Anything else I should tell my chief?"

"Well, there is one thing." The comment came from the man Lassiter regarded as Holmes's scribe, and he frowned as though the obligation to turn in Watson's direction was a pointless taxing of his energies.

"Yes, and what is that?"

"A curiosity. Probably nothing more. But there is an area we've not yet pursued and we thought we might get your opinion about it. We felt it might be useful to explore the families of the two victims to understand whether the murder of Liam Coogan could be seen as retribution for the killing of their relative. You mentioned that the short term of imprisonment given Coogan was seen as suspicious by members of the Brotherhood who believed it to be a reward for informing on others in the movement. Might it not also be that someone in one of the victims' families saw five years imprisonment as insufficient punishment for the brutal murder of his relative? Might that person view it as his responsibility to right the wrong that had been done?" Watson looked to Lassiter and found a cold smile had replaced his earlier indifference.

"One of the two victims, Mr. Burke, was a long-time civil servant, whose sin—in the eyes of his killers—was to be an Irishman working for the British Government. Mr. Burke, in fact, appears to have been the real target for the Invincibles' attack. However, there is no evidence that anyone in Mr.

Burke's family ever left Ireland.

"The second victim, Lord Cavendish, presents a more complex picture as described in the volume on peerage." Watson indicated the thick volume on his desk. "Lord and Lady Cavendish are themselves childless. There is an older brother to Lord Cavendish, Spencer Cavendish, the Lord of Devonshire, who is himself a distinguished member of the government and clearly above reproach. Moreover, he's a life-long bachelor, so there is no younger Cavendish to carry out retribution, if retribution was to be sought. There is, however, a sister, Lady Louisa Egerton, and she and Lord Egerton have two sons who would have been nineteen and twenty at the time of the Phoenix Park murders in 1882 and are now well into their twenties. Both would be of an age to stand for family honor if an avenging of their uncle's murder was so interpreted. One of the brothers, the older as it happens, is with the Third Bengal Fusiliers stationed in India, and could have no hand in the actions taken against Coogan. The second brother, a Frederick Egerton, now Commander Egerton, appears to be still in England and, indeed, is here in London. I come now to the curiosity, Inspector."

Pointing to the open volume on his desk, Watson continued. "According to *Peerage, Baronetage, and Knightage*, Commander Egerton is a graduate of The Royal Military Academy at Woolwich. It happens that I'm an old army man myself, having been a military surgeon, and one of the men with whom I served used an odd expression that we came to understand was peculiar to the Academy at Woolwich. He talked of getting back to 'the shop' when he returned to the barracks. It's the same expression you used for returning to the Yard. A quick check of our peerage encyclopedia reveals that a Peter Lassiter did indeed attend the Academy the same years as Commander Egerton. We wondered if you might have known the young man and can enlighten us about his character."

Peter Lassiter had proven himself a rapt audience for Watson's account. The cold smile seemed to have become sardonic as he inclined his head the slightest bit toward Watson then Holmes before clapping three times, allowing a dramatic interval between each round of applause. "Bravo, Dr. Watson. Bravo to you both. You get full marks for your effort, but I'm afraid I must grade you down for your conclusion, if it's a conclusion you've come to about Freddie. You're absolutely right we were classmates at the Shop. Indeed, we were good friends at the Academy and we are to this day although we see each other infrequently now. Freddie used his degree to continue in the army and ultimately became a brigadier commander. I had gotten the education and training I'd wanted and chose a career at Scotland Yard, and work with its newly formed Irish Branch."

Peter Lassiter withdrew a cigarette from his silver case without offering one to either man. After lighting it and dropping his spent match onto a nearby plate, he resumed his rejoinder to the charge implied in Watson's query. "Now you appear to have deduced that eight years later, in a fit of uncontrollable rage, Commander Egerton tracked down this Coogan and chose to dispatch him by the same heinous means used to kill his uncle. You imply, but are far too circumspect to state, that I am now covering up the crime in deference to my former classmate. Well, Freddie does indeed live near enough to have committed the crime, having a most pleasant home in Mayfair, and he would certainly appear to have the capacity to plan and carry out such a crime, having been trained in the art and practice of combat. There's only one problem." And Peter Lassiter now leaned into his explanation, his eyes glowing at the prospect of besting the lion of criminal investigation in his own lair. "Commander Egerton has been confined to a chair ever since some poor fool he was training in the use of explosives panicked during a routine exercise, causing Freddie to throw himself at the explosive, saving the lives of his fellow officers, but losing a sizable portion of one of his legs. With respect, gentlemen, it sometimes pays to do some shoe leather investigation to check out your armchair speculation." He sat back against his cushion, tapped the ash from his cigarette onto the plate he had converted to an ashtray, and contemplated the story he would tell and retell many times after getting away from Baker Street.

Watson's jaw dropped, then quickly squared again, although the moment was not lost on Lassiter. "I am, of course, saddened to learn of the Commander's difficulties. May I ask, were you, yourself, acquainted with members of the Cavendish family additional to Mr. Egerton?"

"Of course. I've already said Freddie and I were good friends. His home was near enough the school that I visited it many times. Freddie was popular and his home was a frequent destination for many of us who lived a distance from the Academy."

"And would you say the family was close?"

"I don't know that they were especially close or distant. Everybody seemed to get along well whenever I was there. They appeared an ordinary family to me. People got together at holidays and occasionally in between." Lassiter ground his cigarette onto the plate that had become his ashtray. "Really, this grows most tiresome. I can assure you, Freddie— Commander Egerton—is incapable of exacting vengeance for his uncle no matter how he felt, and I know of no one in the family who would—and I have met all but the youngest members of the family at one time or another. Do you have any other questions? I really must get back to ... the office."

"Only one, sir, can you tell us where you were on the night of Mr. Coogan's death?" It was Holmes who had reentered the conversation and was once more departing from

144

the established script, this time in consequence of his dissatisfaction with the pace of questioning and with Peter Lassiter.

"You have got cheek, Mr. Holmes, the both of you have." He glowered at them in a way that left Holmes and Watson thankful the Yard's inspectors did not routinely carry firearms. "I'll answer to questions of that sort from my betters and not from the likes of you." Lassiter sprang from the settee and began for the door. "I'll see myself out, and I'll thank you not to send one of your street toughs around to summon me any time in the future. Indeed, I doubt we'll ever see each other again, Mr. Holmes, Dr. Watson." Without waiting a reply or looking back, the policeman started down the steps. He stopped at the foot of the stairs to collect his hat and cane from Mrs. Hudson without speaking a word or favoring the housekeeper with a look. Seeing no cab immediately available on Baker Street, he continued in the direction of Marylebone and quickly disappeared from view.

As Inspector Lassiter was speeding his way from Baker Street, Holmes and Watson left their sitting room to follow the scent of fresh baked scones to its source in Mrs. Hudson's kitchen. Holmes had stopped to fill a pipe and soon the acrid smell of tobacco battled the savory aroma of baking in the small room. The three of them sat at the kitchen table that had once been the desk at which Mrs. Hudson learned the intricacies of criminal investigation from her "uncommon common constable." Now she was the teacher, the two men were her partners and students, and the table was again a desk for the investigation of a crime reported in the London dailies. But this investigation was no academic exercise, and its findings might well prove the basis for future newspaper reports.

At Mrs. Hudson's urging, Watson read from his notes

the events of the meeting with the Inspector. Holmes added some points he felt to be missing from Watson's account and highlighted several others he felt were not sufficiently stressed by him. Mrs. Hudson asked Watson to elaborate on some points about Lassiter's contacts with the Cavendish and Egerton families, winced at his report of Holmes's accusation of Lassiter and, after bringing a pot of tea to the table, pursed her lips as she prepared to engage with her colleagues in making sense of the morning's events. Watson set his notebook and a pencil beside his cup.

"So we've 'ad two guests as you could say are persons of interest in our little problem. What are we to make of them?"

Holmes made a waspish grin before commenting. "Whatever we're to make of them, we might do it quickly, we're not likely to see either one again."

"Oh, I doubt we've seen the last of either one, Mr. 'Olmes, but be that as it may I'd say we learned a bit from each of them today."

"Will you share your thinking, Mrs. Hudson? I assume you have in mind the feeling Mr. Parkhurst showed for Mrs. Keegan, and the information Inspector Lassiter provided regarding Commander Egerton's physical condition, assuming the Inspector was being truthful with us."

"You're right about our Mr. Park'urst. It's certain 'e's got feelin's for Mrs. Keegan. It's the kind of feelin's 'e's got that makes me wonder. We know 'e's been callin' on 'er pretty regular, more times than 'e'd 'ave to for just a newspaper story, and we know it's got 'er own father thinkin' there's somethin' goin' on between them. But just look at what Mr. Park'urst says, and what Mr. Park'urst don't say. 'E visits with the 'usband as well as the wife, and talks about the two of them as a 'devoted couple'—I believe that was what you said Doctor—and about Mr. Coogan as providin' for 'is

146

family the best 'e could. Now, won't it be strange to meet with the man you're supposed to be wantin' to replace at the same time you're meetin' with 'is wife, and to build 'im up and talk about 'im and 'is wife as devoted. 'E don't say Mr. Coogan is dangerous, or is been runnin' out on 'is wife, which is things 'e could say with no one to argue. And when Mr. 'Olmes talked about Mrs. Keegan maybe 'avin' a romantic interest in somebody besides 'er own 'usband, 'e defended 'er without once seemin' to think it could be 'im what's suspected of bein' the other man. It wasn't until Mr. 'Olmes practically accused 'im that Mr. Park'urst even thought to defend 'imself. And then, too, there's 'im commentin' on 'er family situation what with the financial 'ardship of two children and a father that's good for nothin'. Put it all together and 'is feelings sound like they got a lot more to do with protectin' than with passion."

Watson nodded and added his own observation. "It's of a piece with the discussion we had with Mrs. Keegan before we were waylaid by Fogarty's thugs. She described Mr. Parkhurst as 'a good friend' to both her and Mr. Coogan. I wonder if maybe the payment she's receiving from Mr. Parkhurst isn't a little more generous than the *Times* has apportioned. But what are we to make of it all?"

"Maybe somethin', maybe nothin'. For now, I'm thinkin' we can rule out a romantic attachment between them two, or the two of them cookin' up a crime of passion, but there's somethin' between them, I'd bet on that."

Mumbling about a need to stretch his legs, Holmes had moved to the kitchen window where he stood for a moment, ostensibly studying the traffic on Baker Street, before turning to confront his colleagues. "I must say I don't see what else we need to look for. We have a gentleman offering an appropriately gallant defense of a lady. For my own part, I sympathized with Mr. Parkhurst's position. I wasn't happy making those insinuations."

"Which you nonetheless did very well, Mr. 'Olmes. And there may be nothin' more to it like you say. We'll see. It won't be too long before it all starts to come clear."

Watson grimaced his awareness that, like Mr. Parkhurst, Mrs. Hudson was not sharing everything she knew. He was aware, as well, it was pointless for him to raise that concern. "Well then, what about Inspector Lassiter? Should Holmes and I make a trip to Mayfair to follow up with Commander Egerton and learn the truth of Lassiter's story about him?"

"No, I don't think that will be necessary, Doctor. Our Mr. Lassiter sounds much too satisfied with 'imself to 'ave made up such a story. Besides, just think 'ow it would look for 'im if we was to catch 'im out in a lie. 'E knows Mr. 'Olmes 'as friends at the Yard who would learn about it. 'E's too clever by 'alf to let that 'appen. I'm sure we can take Inspector Lassiter at 'is word about Commander Egerton. Still, it's interestin' 'e's kept in regular touch with 'is old college friend. I suppose there's them as do, but 'e must be near to 10 years out of that academy they went to, and the two of them would look to 'ave gone their separate ways as it were.

"But there's somethin' more that's been troublin' me about Mr. Lassiter since the first time 'e come to see Mr. 'Olmes. It's to do with what you called a 'cavalier attitude' to Mr. Coogan's death, Dr. Watson. Each time 'e comes 'e wants us to think the Yard has no interest in this case, but then 'e lets on as 'ow 'is chief inspector wants to keep tabs on what Mr. 'Olmes is doin'. The two things don't go together. And if the Yard, or its Special Branch, is interested in takin' down some in the Brotherhood, Coogan's murder would look to be just the ticket. So why would the Branch turn a blind eye to the whole business?"

Holmes, having settled himself again at the table, nodded agreement. "That's exactly what I've been saying all along. There's something about the man that's just not right."

"And so you 'ave, Mr. 'Olmes, and now we need to know why 'e's sayin' there's no interest in Mr. Coogan's death when everythin' points to there bein' just such an interest. And I won't go askin' about our Inspector Lassiter 'avin' a part in the murder in quite the way you were goin' about it, Mr. 'Olmes. You can bet 'e's got an explanation, and a good one, for where 'e was that night."

Watson was torn between wanting to know more of Mrs. Hudson's thinking and his awareness of the time of their next appointment. A concern about the lateness of the hour won out. "I'm afraid we may have to postpone any further discussion Mrs. Hudson if we are to prepare for our next visitor."

"You're right, Doctor. We 'ad better move on to a discussion about Mrs. Katharine O'Shea before this Captain 'Enry 'Arrison, MP gets 'ere."

"And might we also get some lunch, Mrs. Hudson?" Holmes asked. "All this playacting builds an appetite."

After setting out a plate of cold meats and a pot of tea, Mrs. Hudson asked Watson what he knew about Mrs. Katharine O'Shea that went beyond simple gossip.

"I'll share what I can, Mrs. Hudson, but there is little to tell that isn't newspaper speculation, which is to say, gossip. Frankly, it's all that passes for information about Mrs. O'Shea," Watson paused to spear a spatchcock drumstick that had somehow escaped attention at dinner the night before. "In any event, it would appear Mrs. O'Shea is very soon to be sued for divorce by her husband, Captain William O'Shea, and that he will name as co-respondent in the suit the Right Honorable Charles Parnell, the head of the Irish Parliamentary Party, and the foremost champion of Home Rule in government." Watson paused to study the faces of his audience. "I take it we're all understanding what is meant by

149

the term co-respondent?"

"It means Mr. Parnell is the woman's lover," Mrs. Hudson sniffed.

"Really, Watson, this is 1890 after all." Holmes's easy smile made clear his amusement with Watson's cautious handling of Parnell's incautious behavior.

"Fine, I only wanted to be certain. It does threaten to be a rather nasty time for both Mrs. O'Shea and for Parnell. Everything suggests that Parnell and Mrs. O'Shea have a long-standing relationship and it's not clear why Captain O'Shea is seizing this moment to bring his charges. It can, of course, be very damaging to the lady's reputation, and perhaps to Parnell's as well, although he remains so extraordinarily popular with his followers he may well survive it all. These are, after all, the people who have taken to calling him 'the uncrowned king of Ireland.' And of course this comes right on the heels of his having won a huge settlement from the *Times*, 5000 pounds according to the *Standard*. You're probably aware of that story." Holmes met Watson's glance with a blank stare, leading Watson to provide a brief summary of the information unknown to one member of his audience. "A short time ago there was a great uproar about Parnell's supposed complicity in the Phoenix Park murders. The *Times* claimed to have letters from Parnell proving his involvement. Well, all of the letters turned out to have been forged by one of the *Times*' own people, a man named Piggott, who fled to Spain and committed suicide after being exposed."

"Yes, I had seen something of that although I didn't immerse myself in the details." Holmes waved away Watson's report. "It is a most extraordinary tale, although precisely what one might expect from people who rely on tittle tattle and consequently publish rubbish as news. It's why I prefer to concentrate on crime reports and the agony columns, and ignore the rest."

In the silence following Holmes's comment, Watson expressed a concern he had been harboring since learning of the visit from Mrs. O'Shea's emissary. "I do hope this Harrison fellow isn't thinking to retain our services in association with the divorce proceedings. I, for one, find any such prospect decidedly unappealing. I know Mr. Parnell is a very prominent figure, but I propose we use our involvement in the Coogan investigation as the basis for rejecting any such request."

"I agree absolutely, Watson. He can be the crowned king of Ireland for all I care. I have no interest in becoming involved in his messy divorce."

Mrs. Hudson spoke to their concerns. "I 'ear you both, and I've no taste for taking sides in a fight over the good silver. But Mr. 'Arrison will be 'ere shortly, and we can get it from the 'orse's mouth, as it were, just what it is they've got in mind. You might straighten up your sitting room a bit, at least enough to let the poor man 'ave a comfortable place to stretch 'is legs. I'll come up with tea and scones after you've 'ad a chance to get settled with Mr. 'Arrison. I'll be back later with a fresh pot and to clear dishes when it's time to review your notes, Doctor. For now, you'd best get back upstairs while I get a kettle on." The ghost of a nod from Watson assured her that sufficient cleanup would take place to permit their guest a place to sit comfortably.

Captain Henry Harrison was not at all what Mrs. Hudson expected. He was a young man, about the same age as Parkhurst and Lassiter, but at first glance he looked considerably older by virtue of rapidly thinning hair, and a full dark beard and moustaches. He had an open face that seemed impossible of guile, and left no doubt of the earnestness he felt about his mission. He fixed Mrs. Hudson with deep-set gray eyes and announced himself. "Captain Henry Harrison, MP, to see Mr. Holmes," and handed her a card confirming his identity.

"Thank you, sir. If you'd like to go right up and knock, I know they're expectin' you. I'll be there in an instant with tea and scones."

He handed her his umbrella and top hat. "Thank you, Mrs. ...." The grim expression transformed to a surprisingly good-natured smile which he kept in place while waiting for the housekeeper to finish his sentence.

"Mrs. 'Udson, sir."

"Thank you, Mrs. Hudson." The warmth of his speech, and the smile that seemed to fold around her left Mrs. Hudson with the feeling she had done something more significant than simply taking a hat and umbrella, and promising refreshments, but she had no idea what it could be.

When she brought the tray to the sitting room, Mrs. Hudson found Captain Harrison seated in an easy chair and Holmes and Watson in their accustomed places, Holmes at the mantel gravely regarding his guest and Watson at his secretary's desk, pen and paper at the ready. Introductions had been concluded and Harrison was laying the groundwork for the problem he wished to share.

"It is, as I say, an undertaking of the greatest delicacy, and both Mr. Parnell and Mrs. O'Shea would be extremely grateful for your participation. It is also a matter that demands total confidentiality. You are known, Mr. Holmes, as a man who can keep a secret. As, of course, are you, Doctor. This is a secret the both of you will be asked to carry to your graves. I want that to be very clear before we start. Everyone involved in this matter must regard its confidentiality as his solemn obligation." With that, he cast a wary eye toward Mrs. Hudson who, having poured his tea, had turned away from him while she served Watson.

"Oh, you mean old Hudson. Don't worry about her. She's deaf as a post." Holmes raised his voice slightly to make certain the newly handicapped housekeeper won't miss a word.

"But that's extraordinary. I was just speaking to her downstairs and would swear she understood me completely."

"Oh yes, and I'm sure she did—as long as she was facing you. She's become quite adept at reading lips. So many of these poor souls are able to pick up that skill. It appears to have nothing to do with intelligence, just a knack some of them have. And of course it allows us to keep her on. She's a passable cook, doesn't do too badly with scones, and we can't very well toss her out in the street." To accentuate the extent of his charitable impulses, Holmes took a substantial bite of the scone he had been handed and smiled his appreciation to Mrs. Hudson.

"To be truthful, the scones are really some of the best I've ever had," Harrison reported. "Anyway, I must get back to the dilemma of which I spoke. I count on your discretion and will say no more about it. As you are probably aware, Mrs. O'Shea is being sued for divorce by her husband, Captain O'Shea, and Mr. Parnell is to be named as a co-respondent."

"Yes," Holmes said, "I had heard something of that."

The housekeeper, having provided scones and tea to the three men in the sitting room, replaced the teapot on its tray, and eased herself from the room so noiselessly her hearing colleagues took no notice.

In her own kitchen Mrs. Hudson set the tray on her table and frowned her displeasure at the conversation she imagined to be occurring upstairs. It would be difficult, perhaps impossible, to refuse a request made on behalf of Charles Parnell. The fee would be a very handsome one of course. It was rumored Mrs. O'Shea had come into a significant inheritance with the death of her aunt. For once, Mrs. Hudson was not concerned about the fee, or at least did not find it an overriding attraction. She shared her colleagues' concerns that the divorce would be sordid and pose little in the way of intellectual challenge. Already, the *Times*, after paying Parnell the court's judgment for their efforts to blacken his name, was trying to get a little of its own back by implying there was indeed a dark side to Parnell's character, they had simply been attending to the wrong dark side. Not yet willing to rely solely on facts, the *Times* was employing innuendo in reporting on their adversary's less than private life. The *Times*, as well as other papers, was reporting that for the past 10 years of her marriage to the Captain, "Katharine O'Shea had been frequently seen in the company of Mr. Parnell."

Mrs. Hudson agreed with Watson that Captain O'Shea seemed a little tardy in declaring his outrage, but there was no question there would be sufficient mudslinging on both sides to cover anyone standing near to either party. There was, nonetheless, one thing to consider if they did get caught up in the O'Sheas' divorce action. If what she believed about Coogan's death was correct, the assistance of a grateful Parnell and Mrs. O'Shea might later prove helpful, indeed, very helpful.

She made herself some tea and ate half a scone while waiting for her cup to cool. She found the scone adequate, but not all that it should be, then smiled as she thought about Holmes getting some of his own back for James Burch's deafness some nights earlier. She had to admit, as trying as he was at times, working with Mr. Holmes was rarely dull. She looked out the window where the hansom Captain Harrison had hired waited his return. Both horse and coachman appeared pleased with the opportunity to take a brief rest. The dapple gray stood silent, asleep with its eyes open, while the driver at his back slept more conventionally with eyes closed.

Before she could return to her cooling tea she became aware of first one man, then another across the street, in soft homburgs and frock coats, one a little the worse for wear. The two men made slow progress along Baker Street, finding things of interest in the alcoves of several merchants without ever losing sight of 221B. Mrs. Hudson could not determine if they represented the Special Branch, the Brotherhood, the Christian Union, or the *London Times*. She came away from the window resigned to the difficulty of keeping track of all the enemies they were accumulating in the investigation of Liam Coogan's death.

Mrs. Hudson knocked softly at the sitting room door. Remembering her loss of hearing, she entered without waiting for reply. She had brought a fresh pot of tea which she now offered to each of the men as she moved with great deliberation around the room. Captain Harrison alone mouthed an exaggerated "thank you." Holmes took no notice of her and Watson pretended not to. The Doctor turned his attention to their visitor. "Captain Harrison, if I might just review my notes with you to make certain I've gotten everything down accurately. You say Mrs. O'Shea's four daughters have gone missing from their home in Brighton and haven't been heard from for ... I believe you said three days."

A quick nod confirmed Watson's unfailingly accurate note-taking.

Two of the girls, Norah and Carmen, are older, Norah being seventeen and Carmen fifteen; their sisters, Clare and Katie are quite a bit younger at six and seven. The last anyone knows all the girls had gone together to downtown Brighton for an outing with one of the maids, a Rose O'Connor, who's not been heard from either. Miss O'Connor was the newest member of Mrs. O'Shea's staff, but had been known to Mrs. O'Shea for years as a member of the household staff of her late Aunt—you did say the name was Ben?"

"Mrs. Benjamin Wood. Everyone called her Aunt Ben."

"I see. Rose O'Connor is a somewhat older woman, who appears to be having some difficulties in her mental functioning associated with aging." Watson glanced warily in the direction of Mrs. Hudson, who was, as decreed earlier, deaf to his comment.

Captain Harrison was not one to mince his words, or to have his words minced. "The woman is plain balmy, and Mrs. O'Shea is as much her protector as her employer. She was a poor choice to take the children out but, as I told you, Katharine—Mrs. O'Shea—has been staying in London during this time, and the housekeeper felt that, with Norah along, an outing would pose no problem. Norah has frequently taken a similar responsibility for her sisters. And let me dispel any notion you might have of Rose being involved in any plot against the family. Apart from her not having sense enough to be a part of someone's plot—let alone having any capacity to design one—her loyalty is beyond question. Not only was she with Aunt Ben until the woman's death last year, but she fairly doted on the girls, and had done for the ten years the O'Sheas and Aunt Ben lived across the park from each other in Eltham."

"Yes, thank you, Captain Harrison." Watson took a sip of the fresh tea and continued, "As you describe it, Mrs. O'Shea and Mr. Parnell—who has taken an active interest in this problem—do not want to go to the police because of the negative publicity that would inevitably be created on the eve, as it were, of the divorce trial, particularly as Captain O'Shea is professing a great concern about the children's well-being if they remain with their mother. The oldest child, and the O'Sheas' only son, Gerard O'Shea, a young man of 20, is living with his father although he sees his mother and sisters regularly. It is suspected that Gerard assisted his father to entice the girls to his care, and Captain O'Shea is waiting for the right moment to embarrass Mrs. O'Shea and Mr. Parnell. Regardless, Mrs. O'Shea's first concern is the children's safety, and if Mr. Holmes believes she should go to the police she will do so. If, however, Mr. Holmes can resolve this dilemma without calling in the police both she and Mr. Parnell will be most grateful."

Captain Harrison pursed his lips and Mrs. Hudson was reminded of the earnest young man she had seen downstairs. "I believe you have all the essential points, Doctor. I thank you for omitting the discussion regarding the younger children's parentage which I shared only to make clear the extreme delicacy of the situation." Harrison turned his attention from Watson to Holmes. "Mrs. O'Shea and Mr. Parnell have directed me to inform you of everything that might bear on the girls' disappearance. In that regard, you should be advised that Mrs. O'Shea has come into a very handsome inheritance from her Aunt Ben's estate. Indeed, her aunt has singled her out from all other nieces and nephews to receive the mansion in Eltham and the vast bulk of her considerable fortune. The property and money are to be awarded to Mrs. O'Shea outside the marriage settlement, which as you know means Captain O'Shea will have no access to it. Not coincidentally, we believe Captain O'Shea instituted divorce proceedings soon after learning the contents of Aunt Ben's will. We have reason to believe that O'Shea, being a perfect scoundrel, will join the action taken by four of Mrs. O'Shea's brothers and sisters who are seeking to overturn the will.

"All this unpleasantness led Mrs. O'Shea to take the house in Brighton in the hope that getting away from London might insulate the children from the endless speculation of the penny press. The girls, especially the two older ones, were made increasingly upset by the publicity and attention from the newspapers. I'm afraid the escape has been only partly successful as some reporters have learned of the house in Brighton and followed the family there. You should also know that, in addition to Rose, Mrs. O'Shea took to Brighton her own three servants, and is providing for Aunt Ben's staff at Eltham Lodge—as the home is called—until the courts resolve the status of the estate. Mrs. O'Shea, herself, hasn't set foot in Eltham Lodge since her aunt's death."

Captain Harrison sat for a moment, his face a frown of concentration while he considered what else he needed to convey. Nothing occurring to him, the frown disappeared to be replaced by his more customary open, eager expression. "I'm sure that's everything of importance. May I set Mrs. O'Shea's mind at rest and tell her she can engage your services?"

Mrs. Hudson had been setting unused lemon, milk and sugar on her tray, and stood now at the small table to the Captain's back. Catching Holmes's eye, she gave a deep nod before taking up her burden and starting for the door.

As she exited, Holmes was giving smiling assurance to Captain Harrison, "Tell Mrs. O'Shea and Mr. Parnell that Sherlock Holmes will be pleased to take their problem in hand."

With Captain Harrison on his way to Fox's Hotel to inform the waiting couple of Holmes's decision, the sitting room at 221B Baker Street passed back into the sole possession of the three members of the consulting detective agency. Holmes suggested the course of action he believed essential. "It seems to me our first step will be to travel to Brighton to question the servants. Then it appears a visit with Captain O'Shea will be in order. Since we have reason to believe there's been a kidnapping, it might be well for you to carry your service revolver, Watson. I doubt you'll have need of it, but we should be prepared."

Watson nodded his grave assent.

Tilting her head hard in his direction, and wearing a sly smile, Mrs. Hudson responded to Holmes. "If I'm *'earin'* you correct, Mr. 'Olmes, you're suggestin' that Captain O'Shea is to blame for the children's disappearin' from Brighton."

"I am delighted your hearing has returned, Mrs. Hudson. You and Mr. Burch have a great deal in common, having each made a spontaneous recovery from the same infirmity." Having reclaimed possession of the settee, Holmes leaned back into its cushion and threw his arms across its mahogany frame. "Yes, Mrs. Hudson, I'd say O'Shea's abduction of the children seems the obvious explanation. O'Shea gets a leg up at the court hearings by establishing the girls' mother as unfit to provide for her children's safety and well-being. She can be described as staying with her lover in London while her children go unprotected. No doubt young Gerard will affirm his father's lies."

"It could make sense, Mr. 'Olmes, except I can't 'elp wonderin' 'ow much sympathy there'd be for a father who's kidnapped 'is own children. It would seem a poor strategy to prove to the court you're a fit father, and one to be trusted with the care of your four daughters. No, I think we 'ave to look elsewhere for an understandin' of what 'appened."

Watson broke off from his pencil jottings. "What are you suggesting, Mrs. Hudson?"

I'm suggestin' the children are safe and are well away from Captain O'Shea. I'll just clear away these dishes, then we can talk, and after, we'll want to 'ave Thomas take a message to Captain 'Arrison for 'im to deliver to Mrs. O'Shea."

Both Holmes and Watson looked blankly at the housekeeper. Watson asked for both of them, "Thomas?"

"Wiggins. Thomas Wiggins."

159

Mrs. Hudson was unaware their blank looks had turned to astonishment as she had already started downstairs for the kitchen with her tray of dishes.

Chapter 8.
In Search of Katharine O'Shea's Daughters

Early the next morning, before local merchants had opened for business and the crush of morning traffic had developed, a carriage arrived at 221B Baker Street. The passengers inside were curtained from public view, their identities known only to the residents of the lodgings at which they stopped and the leader of the Baker Street Irregulars.

Thomas Wiggins, having made possible the meeting between the nation's foremost crime-fighter and one of its most recognizable politicians, had arrived early and stationed himself at the bootmaker's shop across the roadway, waiting to catch a glimpse of two of the giants on the London scene at the precise moment they joined forces.

In spite of the empty street, Holmes and Watson only left their apartments as the team of coal-black stallions was coming to a halt. They then hurried to the coach whose door was swung open by an invisible hand. Holmes looked to the distant sky, where gray clouds were massing with what he believed unmistakable intent, and grasped his umbrella tightly. He wished he had similar protection against the disastrous journey on which he felt certain they were embarked.

He had never had less confidence in Mrs. Hudson's reasoning. He only agreed to the action after Mrs. Hudson provided him a justification of sorts she believed unnecessary and he believed essential to explain the inevitable disaster. He would explain the mission's failure as the result of faulty intelligence received from his underworld sources. That way, Holmes would lay blame on figures that could be seen as both exotic and understandably subject to error. Mrs. Hudson hastened to add her conviction that such an explanation would be wholly unnecessary and that, in fact, as soon as the problem was resolved, Holmes was to inform Mrs. O'Shea he might be calling on her in the future to assist in resolving a little problem of his own. He was not, however, to identify that problem as the Coogan affair. The likelihood of his resolving Mrs. O'Shea's problem was too remote a possibility for him to take seriously Mrs. Hudson's concern with alerting the woman to the possibility of her later providing assistance.

Watson said nothing, having heard Holmes's objections at the planning session with Mrs. Hudson the previous day, then again during a contentious dinner that night, over a less than relaxing after dinner pipe, and for as much of the morning as they were together before the carriage arrived. He kept his own counsel, but he too feared a flaw in Mrs. Hudson's analysis that would result in an embarrassing admission for Holmes, and a need for him to come to his friend's aid in some as yet undetermined manner.

Wiggins, having no doubt of Sherlock Holmes's success whatever the undertaking, watched in unabashed awe as the carriage carrying his hero and the Parliament's celebrated orator disappeared from sight.

Mrs. Hudson was well aware of her colleagues' apprehension, but felt certain of her judgment. Regardless, she hadn't time to think any more about it, she had her own chores for the day. First of which was to take advantage of the men's absence, and conduct the cleaning that was impossible when they were home. The firm could easily have supported a full-time maid for the lodgings, even the hiring of a maid and cook, but bringing in other people risked revealing the secret of the consulting detective agency's operations and had been rejected outright. Unable to tolerate the men's disorder for long, it fell therefore to Mrs. Hudson to undertake periodic cleanups whenever she could get them out of the house.

A thorough cleaning of their rooms would require the

whole day or more and, as much in need of such attention as the lodgings were, she had two other tasks to accomplish before the men returned. She would look to the sitting room, and even there the best she might hope for would be the appearance of order, which could nonetheless be sufficient to create conflict with her boarders. Setting books into the places on the shelves from which they appeared to have been drawn could stimulate an hour-long harangue from Mr. Holmes beginning with his inability to find critical materials due to her meddling, progressing to her lack of respect for his research, then to a want of appreciation for his contribution to the agency, and ending with the threat of his undertaking a career in beekeeping. She kept her tongue at these times, having once expressed concern for the bees, leading Holmes to sulk in his room for nearly a week. And, while Dr. Watson was in all things the soul of reason, the disturbance of his sacred *Lancet* magazines could lead to an expression of disappointment more hurtful than Mr. Holmes's lengthy rebuke.

Squaring her small shoulders and issuing a long sigh, she began the thankless chore with the collection of plates, cups, and drinking glasses from desks, tables, the mantel, under the settee and, at some personal risk, from the top of the bookcase. She was firmly of the belief that Holmes, alert to her mission, had deposited a tea cup where he thought it to be inaccessible to the diminutive housekeeper. She emptied ash trays and trash baskets, taking care to add to her refuse collection the numerous wadded balls of paper that gave evidence of the poor aim and lack of concern of her lodgers. The comparatively noncontroversial portion of her cleaning completed, she turned her attention to the books and papers occupying the sitting room furniture. She set those on either Holmes's or Watson's desk depending on their proximity to each. She next dusted the room, giving Holmes's laboratory table and everything on it a wide berth. She got her broom, dustpan, and the carpet sweeper she had insisted on purchasing in the firm's name, taking care in the course of its use to avoid the bear rug in which Holmes took inexplicable pleasure.

As she guided the sweeper's movements through the room, she gathered clothing as it appeared in the sweeper's path, and entered her lodgers' bedrooms only long enough to deposit articles of apparel in accord with her best judgment of the ownership of each piece. She closed the doors to their bedchambers quickly, telling herself then, as she had many times earlier, that what she—and the clients—couldn't see was of no consequence. She didn't believe a word of it. Her own apartment was now, as it had always been, a model of organization.

Having satisfied herself she had done all that could be done with the sitting room, she had a light lunch and, after wrapping her black shawl around her shoulders, she stood before the mirror a while adjusting her high crowned hat so that the three ostrich feathers fitted into the blue band at the proper height and spacing. She then took up a carpetbag with outsized green leaves set against a maroon background, and was ready for the second task of her day. She would take the horse car to Fleet Street and a meeting with Charles Frederic Moberly Bell, editor of the *Times*, after first sending Wiggins on one more critical errand.

Moberly Bell was facing financial ruin. Or more precisely, the *Times* was facing financial ruin and threatening to take Moberly Bell down with it. He was not naive to the danger. He had been asked to take over the *Times* precisely because of the dire straits in which the paper found itself. A well regarded journalist, his friends publicly congratulated him on his appointment and privately questioned his sanity. His competitors, most notably the editors of the fast rising

Daily Telegraph and *Morning Post*, publicly questioned his sanity and privately worried he might just pull off the newspaper's rejuvenation. They were right to worry. The Parnell fiasco was finally behind him, and Moberly Bell had ideas about putting the *Times'* stodgy image to rest as well. A bright modern look and spirited reporting could yet restore the *Times* to its former status as London's premier daily, provided his energies and the paper's financing held out.

Raising his eyes from his desk and the mocked up front page of tomorrow's news, he found one of the copy boys—he had yet to learn all their names—standing in the doorway, waiting to be recognized. Moberly Bell looked at the boy, peering over his half spectacles and only barely raising his head from tomorrow's news. "Yes, what is it, son?"

The boy had come as far into the room as he dared. No one yet knew the rules for working with the new editor. He pushed back long brown hair that insisted on dropping without warning across his forehead, and shared his dilemma with the editor. "It's this woman, Mr. Bell, a Mrs. Hudson. She says she's housekeeper to Mr. Sherlock Holmes, and she wants to talk to you about Mr. Holmes's obituary. She says she won't talk to anyone except you. She says if you don't see her, she'll take her story somewheres else. I told her you were busy—I told her you were very busy—and besides it was Mr. Parkhurst she should be seeing. But then I found out Mr. Parkhurst wasn't here because a boy came by earlier to tell him he was wanted at a funeral over in Knightsbridge. I talked to Mr. Franklin and he said I should tell you about it. I could put her out, Mr. Bell, but she's just this little old lady." Having delivered the message Mr. Franklin had instructed him to deliver, and adding only a plea for respect for the elderly, he cleared his forehead of another wayward shock of brown hair and waited for instruction.

Moberly Bell pushed back from the desk, rose to his full

165

five feet, three and one half inches, and smoothed the waistcoat over his plump form, ignoring the vest's rich history of lunches and dinners taken at his desk and at The Quill and Hammer, his favorite Fleet Street pub. He urged the boy to escort the woman to his office. He pushed back the russet colored hair that ringed his head having long since ceased to cover it, and patted back a full beard of the same reddish hue that recently had come to contain random streaks of gray. If there was something to the woman's story, if there was reason to be thinking about an obituary for Sherlock Holmes, he would, by God, have it over all the other papers.

The woman who entered his office was perfect. If pictures were wanted she would fit every reader's image of a housekeeper. The shapeless black dress of perpetual mourning, the coils of gray hair above a doughy face, even the outlandish hat was right, giving her the desired touch of character. With a sweeping motion he indicated the only chair available to a visitor, and beaming at the housekeeper stated the obvious, "So you're Mrs. Hudson."

"I am, and are you the editor of this newspaper?"

"Moberly Bell, at your service, ma'am. Am I to understand you are the housekeeper to Mr. Sherlock Holmes?"

"For nearly ten years."

"Then you've been with him throughout his career as a consulting detective."

"You might go so far as to say 'e got 'is start with me."

"And now it appears there's something amiss with the great detective? And you want to talk to us about his obituary?"

Mrs. Hudson drew as far back in her chair as she could, grasping the carpetbag on her lap firmly to her bosom. "Goodness no! That is, I want to talk to you about Mr. 'Olmes' obituary, but there's not a thing in the world wrong with 'im

166

so don't go puttin' that in your paper."

Moberly Bell's face clouded over; Sherlock Holmes's good health came as a blow. "But I don't understand, what then is the urgency of his obituary?"

Mrs. Hudson's voice sounded her disappointment at his inability to grasp the obvious. "It's very simple really. Mr. 'Olmes is everyday riskin' 'is life for others and the good of this great city. 'E could get done in, as it were, at any moment. You might just wake up tomorrow and there's no Mr. Sherlock 'Olmes, or 'is friend Dr. Watson come to that. You do know they're near always together on these investigations of theirs." Mrs. Hudson paused, taking note that the editor's eyes were straying to the newspaper front page and his fingers had begun drumming on the desk. She would need to add a note of urgency to her tale.

"Well now, 'ere's two of the most important people in the country what could go at any time, and the both of them completely alone in the world except for each other, and me of course. And they're wantin' to be sure that what gets said about them, when the time comes for sayin', includes all the things they'd want people to know. Like what they consider to be their biggest challenges and most important cases. But, of course, it's not the kind of thing they can very well write themselves. And it's not somethin' they can come into your office to ask to get done. That's 'ow come I 'appen to be 'ere. You can think of me as a sort of ambassador to arrange what gets written is what should get written. But of course if you're not interested I can go and talk to people over at the *Telegraph* or maybe the *Post*." With that, Mrs. Hudson closed a fist on the handle of her bag, but made no move to leave.

The smile had returned to the face of Moberly Bell. It was the smile she'd seen on Mr. Parkhurst's face when they first met, and the smile she received from the butcher and the greengrocer whenever she placed an order. "I'm sure that

167

won't be necessary. I'm delighted you've come to see us and very pleased to learn that Mr. Holmes is well. I quite appreciate the need to be prepared for any eventuality, even as we hope no such calamity befalls the great detective or his associate, and that Mr. Holmes and Dr. Watson have a great many productive years ahead of them. I would very much like to have our Announcements writer, Mr. Parkhurst, work with you and your two gentlemen to put together an appropriate story."

"Well now, that's all fine as far as it goes and I'm not sayin' anythin' against this Mr. Park'urst, who I'm sure 'as got 'is good points, but what I'm wonderin' about is 'ow soon all that can be arranged. I know your paper 'as got its 'ands full what with workin' up stories about Mrs. O'Shea's divorce and all what's goin' on with the Irish terrorists—that Brother'ood thing—and your reporters must be up to their eyeballs just tryin' to stay on top of all that. I do want my gentlemen to get the attention their lives are deservin'.'"

"I quite agree, madam, the life of Mr. Holmes, and of Dr. Watson, demand the undivided attention their lives and considerable accomplishments are due, but let me assure you we have a whole fleet of very able reporters at the *Times*. Each man knows his particular area of responsibility and I make certain he sticks to it. Mr. Parkhurst handles Announcements on our behalf, and that includes the preparation of obituaries. That's his particular area of responsibility, and I pledge to you he will do all that's needed."

Mrs. Hudson relaxed her hold on her carpetbag and smiled for the first time since entering the office of Moberly Bell. "I am relieved to 'ear that. And I know you're probably used to payin' somethin' 'andsome for inside information so to speak. I'm thinkin' there's no other way to learn about some things for the stories you do, like the goin's-on inside of the Brother'ood for an example, but my gentlemen of course want nothin' for themselves and neither do I. Just seein' things are done right by Mr. 'Olmes and Dr. Watson will be reward enough."

Moberly Bell was again drumming his fingers on the desk, but now he was staring hard at Mrs. Hudson. "That's the second time you've mentioned a story about the Brotherhood. I'm sure I have no idea what you're talking about, madam. Of course, we will print any factual material we discover about Irish terrorism, but we have no plans for such a story and I haven't authorized any expenditures to develop such a story. If that is Mr. Holmes's belief, I must urge you to correct it on behalf of the *Times* and myself. We're very interested in the Home Rule debate of course, but, as you may know, we've recently experienced some difficulties around the purchase of information for stories, and there is now a policy that I must approve all such expenditures—and I've not seen fit to approve any. It would be important to make that clear to Mr. Holmes before any unfortunate rumors get started."

"I can tell you I will be doin' just exactly that with my Mr. 'Olmes. And can you tell me what I should be tellin' Mr. 'Olmes about this Mr. Park'urst. 'E does like to know somethin' about the people who come to call."

"By all means, please tell Mr. Holmes I feel certain he'll enjoy working with Mr. Parkhurst. He's a young man, but quite a good writer and already has several years of experience doing Announcements for the *Times*. He has a background I think Mr. Holmes will find most interesting. He came to us from the Royal Military Academy, although it's my understanding he was just dabbling with the possibility of a military career at the time. I'm sure you'll find him a most down to earth, pleasant chap. And now, Mrs. Hudson I'm afraid I have a paper to be getting out. I do appreciate your coming by and you can rest assured that when the unfortunate day arrives, the *Times* will handle the story with the respect and consideration these two great men deserve. I will have Mr. Parkhurst make contact with Mr. Holmes at his earliest convenience, which I assure you will be within the week."

Moberly Bell rose and circled his desk to open the door for Mrs. Hudson. She rose from her chair with a show of considerable effort, smiled her appreciation for information the newspaper editor had no idea he had provided, and went to complete her third and last task of the day, and the one to which she had been most looking forward.

Mrs. Hudson walked from Fleet Street to the Aldwyd omnibus station on the Strand, and waited in the queue for the horse car that would make the loop from London's south to Euston and Marylebone Streets, then north to Finchley before returning south through Whitechapel to complete its circular path back to the Strand. As she had anticipated, the morning's swollen gray clouds had kept their distance from the city, and while the day remained overcast, it was unlikely to dampen anything more than the spirits of those Londoners who ventured out of doors.

When the omnibus arrived and the horses were brought to a stop, Mrs. Hudson followed a family of four to the rear of the bus, gave the conductor the 3d fare, and searched out a seat on the lower deck while the family climbed the stairs to the upper deck. A boy of about 14 led the way, trying, with little success, to appear nonchalant about a London excursion. His sister, perhaps two years younger, had no such qualms and threatened to trample him in her eagerness to mount the stairs. Their mother held tight to a nervous smile that she bestowed on the backs of her children and the faces of the passengers she passed, who took pleasure and umbrage in roughly equal numbers as they looked with curiosity to a family amidst the horse car's solitary riders.

The children's father followed behind, grinning with the

pride of a man able to take his family for a London outing on a day of his choosing. Through force of habit, Mrs. Hudson began to assess the man. That he could take a day at leisure with his family established him as someone who worked for himself and was moderately successful. If he were more successful he would be taking a four-wheeler rather than an omnibus. His powerful upper body suggested, and the dirt caked under the nails of two well-calloused hands confirmed that his work involved skilled labor. The burn mark from the flat of a poker on the palm of one hand, and ruddy complexion consistent with daily exposure to the heat of a forge, were of a piece with his attention to the fetlocks of the omnibus horses as the coach pulled up, and confirmed for her he was a blacksmith in a village not far outside London.

As the family disappeared up the stairs, Mrs. Hudson found a seat on a bench near the center of the bus, and opened her carpetbag to extract JK Harrington's *Principles of Criminal Investigation*. She had gotten as far as Chapter 3. "Examining the Scene of the Crime," and was not finding Professor Harrington as enlightening as she had hoped. To her right a university student stole a glance at the title, then at Mrs. Hudson before rolling his eyes and burying himself once more in *The Spirit of the Laws* by Montesquieu. The slender white-haired gentleman to her left, whose eyes also strayed to Mrs. Hudson's reading material, moved as far away from her as the large man on his other side permitted. Mrs. Hudson had long since become accustomed to a questioning of her choice in reading materials. She ignored her neighbors now, as she had ignored the disapproving staff who filled her requests at the British Museum Reading Room, and all the disparaging eavesdroppers between then and now.

At Marylebone Road she turned from Professor Harrington's prosaic thinking long enough to watch the blacksmith and his family exit the bus at Madame Tussaud's.

171

The Chamber of Horrors had been just down Baker Street a little way from 221B until a few years earlier, but Mrs. Hudson had never gone, the blood and gore repelling her. The student closed his Montesquieu and departed the horse car at King's College on Wellington Road, and the old gentleman left at the medical clinic on Park. When the driver called out St. Marylebone Cemetery, Mrs. Hudson settled Professor Harrington deep within her carpetbag and made her way to the omnibus exit.

She approached the familiar wrought iron gates through which she had first come with Constable Tobias Hudson more than ten years earlier. Together, they selected a plot in a distant corner of the cemetery, a considerable way from the prized center section, but near enough to a sturdy English oak to provide shade in the summer and shelter through the worst vagaries of a London winter. They never spoke of the burden they bore that day. Tobias Hudson was dying, and in a very few months they would make unhappy use of their terrible purchase.

Mrs. Hudson stopped to buy fresh violets at two bunches a penny from the blind lady at the gate from whom she had been making purchases at least once every two weeks ever since the Constable's death. She thanked the flower seller by name and was rewarded with a great crinkling around the sightless eyes and a hearty, "Bless you, Mrs. Hudson, it's a fine day," as she was told at every sale regardless of the weather. Mrs. Hudson made her way along a winding path past as many angels as the Constable told her she was likely to see this side of Heaven, and mausoleums the Constable said might have been houses for the little people they'd seen once at a carnival in Brighton. She left the path at the site of a gated obelisk, turning right to walk diagonally toward the English oak they had both admired. As always, she took great care to

172

skirt the ground that lay before each of the headstones along her way. Stopping just within the shade of their tree, she took a coverlet from her bag and spread it beside the grave whose headstone read:

Tobias Hudson
October 22, 1828—August 23, 1880
Beloved Husband
Member, London Metropolitan Constabulary
A life well lived

Mrs. Hudson had added the last to the simple epitaph they had agreed on. Tobias would have felt it to be boastful, Mrs. Hudson felt it to be accurate.

She took faded violets from the small vase below the stone, and replaced them with her fresh purchase. Then she repaired the modest damage made to the grave by a spring storm, clearing twigs and leaves, and smoothing a disturbance to the area only she could see. With the site restored, Mrs. Hudson could bring the Constable up to date on events at Baker Street.

"We've taken another case, Tobias, and it's one that's been a grand puzzle. It's startin' to come clear now, but I'm thinkin' there's some twists still to come. And there's somethin' about it will surprise you. You were always sayin' I was a fine one for figures, and for makin' pennies into shillings. Well this time I'm makin' shillings into pennies, or more likely pounds into pennies. I turned down royalty, Tobias, to take the case of a little girl with no more money than a newborn babe, and I 'ave to say it was a decision that Mr. 'Olmes and Dr. Watson never questioned. They're good men, Tobias, even if Mr. 'Olmes can be a bit of a 'andful every now and again. And truth to tell, and it's not just boastin', every once in a while we can afford to take a run at a case that don't bring in so much as would fill a thimble. Which I'm not forgettin' is, every bit of it, your doin', Tobias. It's all those nights at the kitchen table studyin' cases and workin' out solutions that's made for what success we've 'ad." Her soft voice turned to a whisper. "And I'd give it all back, Tobias, every part of it, to be still sittin' at that same table with you." Mrs. Hudson smoothed an imagined wrinkle in her dress and gentled the grass that lay nearest the Constable's headstone.

"But you'll be wantin' to know about this case. It's not only a fine puzzle, but it's got us into politics if you can believe that. We're clean in the middle of the 'Ome Rule question, which 'as got us mixin' with revolutionaries, and with Bible thumpers that are just about as blood-thirsty as the revolutionaries. And right now, Mr. 'Olmes and Dr. Watson are ridin' out to the country with no less than Mr. Charles Parnell, the same Mr. Parnell who is leadin' the Irish cause, to take care of a problem that could 'elp us later on when we get to resolvin' our little girl's difficulties. That's one of the twists I been talkin' about. But I want to tell you all about the case and share my thinkin' with you." Which Mrs. Hudson proceeded to do for the next half hour. She was not a religious person, neither had been the Constable, and if anyone had asked, she would have said that hearing herself report events in the investigation sharpened her thinking. How else to explain the sudden insights she sometimes had at Tobias's graveside.

When she had completed her account of the case to the Constable, she pressed two fingers from her lips to his headstone, gathered the blanket into her carpetbag and, with a single backward glance, retraced her steps to the omnibus station where she would catch the horse car back to Baker Street. She would be home in time to fix a hearty dinner, feeling certain Holmes and Watson would have appetites to match the day's exertions.

Once inside the carriage and with introductions

concluded, conversation quickly flagged. Only Watson kept trying. He expressed his sympathies to Mrs. O'Shea, and received a polite smile. He expressed his appreciation to Parnell for taking time from his busy schedule, and received a grunt of acknowledgement. He remarked that these situations often looked bleaker than they turned out to be, and received both a smile and a grunt. Having no additional topics of conversation available to him, Watson leaned into the cushioned back of his seat, and watched the streets of London unfold into each other under skies nearly as leaden as the mood inside the coach.

For his part, Holmes had no wish for conversation. Conversation would lead to questions about his thinking, and he had grave doubts about the thinking he would have to declare to be his own. He curled himself as far as he was able into his corner of the carriage, and stared at the coach ceiling as he waited his inevitable doom.

At length, either good manners, or an inability to endure the oppressive silence, led Mrs. O'Shea to speak for herself and her partner. "I want to tell you, Mr. Holmes, that both Mr. Parnell and I were very much comforted to learn of your willingness to take a hand in resolving our problem. And, of course, your willingness as well, Dr. Watson." Her smile to each of them was not the polite smile that had greeted Watson's earlier effort to induce conversation. It was warm and engaging, and Watson felt himself captured by it much as it must have captured Charles Parnell and Captain O'Shea before him.

It countered Watson's first impression of Mrs. O'Shea. He had expected to meet a woman so alluring she could lead a man to risk his career for her love. Mrs. O'Shea did not seem to be such a woman. Her dark hair, falling across her forehead and edging her cheeks in small tight ringlets, could not hide a face too broad for its features, nor the fur trimmed coat hide a figure that had begun to reflect her 44 years. Only the great soulful eyes gave promise of something more, and now her smile made good that promise. Beside her, Parnell clasped the hand from which she had discreetly removed a glove. His long face, made to appear longer still by a full beard, was fixed in hard lines that seemed unlikely to relax during the long ride to Eltham. Dark, piercing eyes took in Holmes and Watson without evidencing any interest in them; he never looked to the woman by his side, who nonetheless held his full attention.

Chastened perhaps by his companion's statement, Parnell addressed his own comment to the brooding figure across from him. "I appreciate that each of us has his own methods, Mr. Holmes, but can you tell me why you think a carriage ride to Eltham is in order?"

Since this was a variant of the same question Holmes had pursued when the trip was first proposed by Mrs. Hudson, and at every opportunity thereafter, he had little appetite for debating his housekeeper's reasoning with the spokesman for Irish Home Rule. "I must ask you to bear with me, Mr. Parnell. I quite understand the extent of forbearance I'm asking of you and of Mrs. O'Shea. But I assure you all will become clear after we arrive in Eltham."

Parnell's response was cut short by a firm clasp of his hand and Katharine's reply. "We are in your hands, Mr. Holmes, and have every confidence in your judgment."

While the lines in Parnell's face deepened, Holmes inclined his head in genuine regard for the woman, or perhaps, Watson thought, in uncharacteristic appeal for divine intervention.

The town of Eltham appeared intent on proving itself a quiet and dignified contrast to the undisciplined commotion of London a little more than an hour away. The streets were lined with three and four bedroom homes topped by gabled roofs, and set far enough apart to provide each owner an ability to sit on his wraparound porch and feel himself alone with his well-tended lawn and ancient trees. The route the coachman chose followed the road below North Park leading to Wonersh Lodge, the home Katharine's Aunt Ben had purchased for her, in which she had lived for 10 years with both her husband and lover, sometimes with both under the same roof. The horses slowed as they approached the familiar yellow-brick house, its lower level covered with vines that wound haphazardly around windows and sent stray shoots up to the second landing. Unlike its neighbors, the house was dark and no smoke rose from any of its several chimneys. The coachman slowed for his passengers, then gently chucked the reins across the backs of his horses urging them on to Eltham Lodge, Aunt Ben's home that lay on the road above North Park. Katharine and Parnell, together and in silence, watched Wonersh Lodge disappear from the coach window. Parnell's face reflected the fierce resolve he had maintained since leaving London while Katherine's took on a small sad smile. One of them squeezed the other's hand and was squeezed back.

The coach wound its way around the eastern edge of the park, then doubled back across the road above the park. More than a hundred meters and a thicket of trees separated the comfortable world below North Park from the luxurious world above it. Eltham Lodge fit easily into the world above the Park. The carriage turned onto a path leading to the Georgian mansion that stood astride a small mountain of closely manicured lawn. Six sets of outsized multipaned windows covered each of the two floors and were made to look still larger by milk-white frames that contrasted with the building's red brick. At the mansion's center, curved balustrades led to a center door overhung by a molded cornice and framed by twin sets of columns joined to the building's walls. Between the outer columns, a triangular crown extended from the second story to the roof, holding within it the frieze of an urn and spray of flowers. From either side of the crown, between the roof and second floor, a repeated pattern of dentil molding circled the house. Columns, crown, and molding, like the frames around the windows, formed an alabaster contrast to the fiery brick against which they were set.

In spite of its size, Eltham Lodge had been home to a single resident and her servants for the preceding ten years, although Katharine and her children had been frequent and welcome visitors to the mansion. With Aunt Ben gone, and the home's ownership in dispute, only the servants remained in residence. Katharine had maintained the servants at the Lodge in deference to her aunt's wishes and her own hopes for an early resolution to the family conflict. In truth, it would have been difficult, under any set of circumstances, to discharge the people who knew the food and treats that made hers and her children's birthdays and holidays special, and who, on their many visits, put her girls to bed with a song or story when they were well, and with worry and prayers when they were sick. They were as close to being family as anyone who wasn't a blood relation could be, and they acted a good deal more like family than most of those who were her blood relations.

As the team trudged its way up the hill to Eltham Lodge, Watson thought he saw drapes pull back from different windows and faces appear for a moment before disappearing as the curtains fell back in place and the great house returned to its earlier anonymity. The carriage too became a hub of small activity. Parnell, his back to the approaching mansion, twisted his body to capture the same view of the house as was available to Watson. Katharine made no effort to see the house. She replaced the glove on the hand that had clasped Parnell's, folded both hands on her lap and emptied herself of any obvious emotion. Holmes shrugged himself out of the corner in which he'd spent the carriage ride to look to Parnell and Katharine with studied determination. His effort to suggest a confidence he did not feel was wasted as the attention of Parnell was directed elsewhere, and Katharine's attention was directed nowhere at all.

As the horses slowed to a stop, a white-haired, clean-shaven man opened the center door, and came scurrying down the stone steps a good deal faster than his age suggested as either wise or possible. He buttoned a short black jacket over his white shirt while he rushed wide-eyed to the carriage. He looked to the coachman for explanation, but received none and turned his attention to the coach's occupants. He bowed a, "Good day, sir," to Parnell, nodded a more hesitant, "Gentlemen," to Holmes and Watson, and turned a worried smile on Katharine.

"My lady. It's wonderful to see you again, but I'm afraid we weren't aware you would be arriving. Will you and your guests be staying overnight? I'm sure Mrs. Grafton can put things right for all your party if that's what you're planning." He looked hopefully to his new mistress.

Katharine guessed what he hoped for and acted to set his mind at ease. "We won't be staying long, Carruthers, although it would be good if Mrs. Ebert could prepare some tea and sandwiches. We've had a rather long trip from London and I'm sure everyone would like to have some refreshment."

Carruthers, now fully buttoned over his narrow chest, fluttered a hand at his throat where a tie should have been, and nodded a sober acquiescence, "Very good, my lady," and scampered to the front of the procession he then led up the stairs and into Eltham Lodge.

The housekeeper and parlor maid greeted the entourage as they swept through the entry hall; only Katharine O'Shea acknowledged the servants, favoring them with a warm smile and greeting each by name. Holmes hung back, in hopes of witnessing a miracle in the form of a small or large child materializing on the broad staircase at the rear of the hall. He witnessed no miracle small or large, and joined the others in the drawing room where he slumped into a wingback chair set between the settee on which Mrs. O'Shea sat and a round table wholly taken up by a Chinese vase on which red dragons appeared to snarl the contempt for him he was certain the entire household would soon share. Watson sat in an easy chair across from the two of them with his eyes fixed on Holmes. His unhappy expression was meant to communicate sympathy. Holmes took it to be Watson's acknowledgement of how truly impossible the predicament was. Parnell stood at the fireplace and, after satisfying himself everyone was in place, removed a watch from his waistcoat pocket, frowned at what he found, and directed his remarks to the person he appeared to hold responsible for creating his difficulty.

"You have us here, Mr. Holmes, as you requested. What can you now share with us? Or do you have in mind our traveling somewhere else on this wild chase?"

The same interest was stated in a gentler tone. "I know you have your reasons for asking us here, Mr. Holmes. Can you now tell us the purpose of our trip, and what you may know about my girls?"

Holmes interlocked his fingers over his chest, then raised the joined index fingers to his lips as he nodded his understanding of their concern. He looked to Katharine O'Shea and Parnell before speaking, then spoke only to Katharine. Watson thought he had never seen Holmes looking quite so pale. "You are right. There is no longer any point to keeping secret my intentions and the purpose of our excursion. It is time to share all."

But before Holmes could share anything, there came a high-pitched voice from outside the drawing room whose door

Carruthers had left ajar. "Mommy, is that you?"

For a moment, no one dared move or even breathe, while each of them strained to hear again the voice that could assure what they only dared to hope. Assurance came in a single word spoken in a small querulous voice, "Mommy?"

Holmes and Watson bolted from their chairs and advanced to the center of the room together with Parnell, where all three stopped, seized with the realization that the celebration, but not the reunion, was theirs to share. Katharine O'Shea, meanwhile, dashed to the door of the drawing room, dodging easy chairs, an ottoman, and a round table that lay in her path. She stopped outside the door and, seeing no one, called out in a voice whose forced calm only made clear the fear she felt. "Katie. Clare. Where are you my darlings?"

And then the world came right. Two small children appeared at the foot of the stairs and mother and daughters threw themselves into each other's arms. Parnell took a few strides closer, wrapped himself in his own arms and watched the scene with a sad smile. Watson and Holmes hung back, observers of the happy and disjointed family reunion.

Katharine came back to the drawing room, holding a child's hand in each of hers, and was soon joined by the housekeeper who wheeled in a tea cart loaded with sandwiches, cakes and biscuits, beaming her pleasure at seeing the family reunited. Katharine's own smile had disappeared now that the first wave of relief had passed. "But where are Norah and Carmen?"

Before the housekeeper could answer there was a voice so soft its owner seemed to fear being heard. "We are here, momma." Two teenage girls stood in the doorway making no effort to join their mother and sisters.

Katharine glared at her daughters as sternly as her relief would allow. "Please come in here immediately."

The girls came forward to brush their mother's cheek

181

with their lips, then retreated to await the inevitable reprimand. The littlest girls sat on the settee with their mother, Watson returned to his easy chair, Parnell and Holmes exchanged places as Parnell placed himself nearer Katharine and Holmes now lounged by the fireplace. The older girls found chairs as far from the others as the furniture arrangement permitted.

Katharine waited for the housekeeper to complete pouring tea and providing small plates to everyone, asked her to please close the door to the drawing room, and then turned to the older girls demanding an explanation. Carmen, the younger of the two, was red-faced and near to crying; Norah was too much her mother's daughter to allow fear to overwhelm her. She faced her audience, pushed back a wayward curl that had dropped onto her forehead and declared her unwillingness to explain anything in front of "that man," indicating Parnell, and "half of London," jerking her head in the direction of Holmes and Watson. With that, she embraced the challenge of trying to outstare her mother.

As the two youngest O'Sheas looked to their mother with eyes wide with fright, and Carmen, Watson, and even Parnell took sudden interest in the condition of their footwear, Holmes's voice sounded measured and reassuring. "Perhaps I can be of some service here."

Mother and daughter relaxed their stares; Carmen, Watson, and Parnell looked up from their shoes and the eyes of everyone in the room now turned to Holmes. Even little Katie and Clare looked to the lean, hawk-like figure slouching next to the fireplace before returning their attention to their mother.

"I won't be too hard on Carmen."

Holmes was briefly interrupted. "I think you mean me, Mr. Holmes. I'm Norah."

"Yes, of course, but I won't want your mother to be hard

on either of you. Still, I believe this adventure to have been your idea, Norah." Holmes had developed a sudden confidence in Mrs. Hudson's analysis and was now prepared to repeat her words, only inserting h's and g's as the need arose. "If I may, Mrs. O'Shea, I believe it's important that we take account of the situation in which Norah and her sisters found themselves and look at the world the way Norah might have." Holmes waited, eyebrows in ascent, for comment. There was none.

"Norah and her sisters found themselves in a situation in which the difficulties their parents were experiencing were causing a good deal of unpleasant attention to be focused on them. Leaving the house in Brighton at any time might involve facing reporters or having strangers point them out on the street. For young ladies who despised being the center of attention, it was all very disturbing, and very unfair. And so Norah, no doubt making use of an intelligence inherited from her mother, hatched an ingenious little plan. One which would hurt no one, and would allow her and her sisters to be out of the public eye, indeed out of sight altogether. Norah got the housekeeper to agree to an outing for her and her sisters with Rose O'Connor going along with them to help take care of Clare and Katie. With all that the Brighton staff had to do, it probably provided a welcome relief for them and seemed a pleasant diversion for the girls. Am I about right so far, Norah?" The youngster gave a cautious nod.

"Once the young ladies were away from the house it wasn't too difficult to convince Rose that Mrs. O'Shea wanted them to go back to Eltham Lodge for a brief stay, probably explaining to the confused old woman how it would be easier for their mother to visit them there. And so they walked the few streets to the depot to catch the Brighton Line to Greenwich and from there a short carriage ride to the Lodge, probably using money given them by their Brighton

183

housekeeper. Staff at the Lodge were likely surprised, but would have no reason not to take Norah at her word that it was Mrs. O'Shea's wishes they be cared for, and their presence at the Lodge be held in confidence while they waited for their mother to appear. When we appeared today, we were unexpected in terms of our timing and our numbers, but Mrs. O'Shea was expected to arrive at some time in accord with Norah's instruction. Is that not right, Norah?"

The older girl shook her head slowly from side to side, but it was to express wonder not disagreement. "That's almost perfect, Mr. Holmes."

A smile creased Holmes's face. An hour ago he never dreamed he would be the focus of an admiring audience or his interpretation of events would be characterized as "almost perfect." An hour ago he was certain he would be skewered by an articulate and influential Member of Parliament and his reputation would be in tatters. His reputation secure, his curiosity was roused. "And what may be in error, little lady?"

"The money, Mr. Holmes. Carmen and I each received money from mother when we went to Brighton and before that from father in London, although neither knew what the other had done." She gave a sidelong glance to her mother, but couldn't contain the ghost of a smile from appearing. "We had quite enough for a train and cab even before the housekeeper gave us additional shillings." Norah turned to her mother, a flash of fire in her dark eyes, "I'm sorry to have hidden these things from you, mother. I really am, but it is just as Mr. Holmes has said. Our every day was a torment. We couldn't go anywhere without feeling we were being watched and talked about. I ... I know we should have gotten word to you sooner, but I knew that when I did you would send all of us back to Brighton and I wanted to avoid that for as long as I could. Anyway, you should know it was all my doing and Carmen and Rose only did what I asked them to."

Katharine's hard squint and furrowed brow had begun to disappear with Holmes's account of her daughters' trials and vanished completely with Norah's apology. The need to escape from an omnipresent press and the gawking of strangers was something she understood all too well. For now, Carmen was heaving great noisy sobs with no one to comfort her, and the two littlest girls were leaning hard against their mother, aware something bad had happened, but not knowing what it was or whether it was over. Norah, having told all and defied all, looked to no one. Her jaw was firmly set, although yielding to a small tremble every now and again. Katharine had her daughters back and it was once more time to be their mother.

"We will leave you men for a while to have your drinks and smoke if you like. We women," with a nod to Norah, "will take our refreshments in the morning room. We will join you after we've had a chance to be together and talk. Norah, would you be so good as bring a plate of biscuits we can all share." Still holding the hands of Clare and Katie, she somehow managed to sweep Carmen into her fold and left the room giving soft kisses to the 15-year-old. Norah followed them from the room after first making careful selection from the biscuits on the tea cart.

As the door closed behind them, Parnell rang for Carruthers, then turned his attention to Holmes fairly exploding with compliments and questions. "Mr. Holmes, I must first apologize. I don't deny I doubted you. It was far too obvious for me to pretend otherwise. I'd have wagered a kingdom, if I had one, that you'd bungled this badly. But now you must tell me how you knew the children would be in this house. Do you consult some sort of oracle who lifts the veil of mystery for you?" Parnell laughed himself into a small bout of coughing while Holmes sniffed his rejection of the ludicrous suggestion. Neither of them saw Watson's sly smile.

"I'm afraid the explanation is rather simple, Mr. Parnell. When I have finished sharing it with you, I fear you will find it so plain your only wonder will be why you didn't see it yourself."

The three men stood together at the fireplace where they shared the Turkish cigarettes Parnell made available from a leathered case. Holmes was about to do his best to make his discovery of the missing children sound anything but plain when he was interrupted by the butler who appeared to have tiptoed into the room and was now asking their wishes.

Parnell spoke for the three of them. "Carruthers, would you bring us some brandy and glasses. Gentlemen, I'm assuming it's not too early in the day for us to share a glass together. It seems to me we should have something special to celebrate Mr. Holmes's accomplishment."

Both men signaled their agreement that the events of the day demanded something stronger than tea, and Carruthers was discharged to fulfill their request. While they waited Carruthers's return, they made small talk about the house, without mentioning the conflict about its ownership, the lovely O'Shea girls, while avoiding the name O'Shea, and the London spring, which required no censoring of thought or speech. After Carruthers had returned, Parnell had poured, and their good health and the success of their mission had been toasted, Parnell urged Holmes to share the thinking that led to his locating the children.

Holmes crushed out the last of his cigarette, and swirled the drink in his glass before speaking. "There were always only three possibilities. The children could, of course, have been abducted for profit as terrible as that was to contemplate. The children could have been enticed to join Captain O'Shea. Or the children could have run away. It was easy to eliminate abduction. A number of days had passed, and there was no ransom note or effort to contact Mrs. O'Shea seeking money for the children's return. It appeared just as unlikely that Captain O'Shea would have lured the children to his home. There were several things arguing against such action. There was no indication that either the Captain or Gerard had been seen in Brighton, and they were the only people likely to have the capacity to entice the children away from their mother's home. Also, it would seem an obviously unwise strategy to kidnap one's own children on the eve of divorce proceedings if one wants to obtain the court's sympathy. Finally, if O'Shea were to take the children why would he take Rose O'Connor as well? Here was a confused elderly woman he barely knew. The poor woman brought him no benefit and could prove a considerable burden. Indeed, the disappearance of Mrs. O'Connor together with the children is the crucial piece that allows us to put together our little puzzle." Holmes looked to his glass, eyes wide and bright as though a treasure lay at its bottom.

"Why did you consider the servant's disappearance to be critical?"

"Consider how a bright young lady like Norah might see the situation. Mrs. O'Connor—Rose—has three important characteristics. She has known the girls for years and is completely devoted to them, her mental condition is such that she is very impressionable and easily led, and she has long been a part of the staff at Eltham Lodge. In short, Rose would believe without question whatever she was told were the family's wishes. And the Eltham Lodge staff would have no reason to doubt Rose's reporting that the girls had come at Mrs. O'Shea's request. Nor would the staff receive any competing information. Whatever press was in the area might go prowling around Mrs. O'Shea's home, but they'd have no reason to go near Eltham Lodge. Having already gotten the money for their travel, Norah had only to arrange for Rose to be with her and her sisters for an outing. Then it was off to

Brighton Station and a train ride that would put prying eyes a good fifty miles away."

Holmes looked to Parnell and Watson as though bored by the simplicity of the problem he had deciphered, and poured himself a second small brandy. Parnell simply guffawed. "Mr. Holmes, your reputation is well and justly earned. As you promised, it is simple logic when explained, but I suspect it's a good deal like resolving the Irish Question. It can only seem simple after it is done. Until then it's God's own conundrum." Parnell frowned at hearing his own words, then brightened, becoming again the genial host in a house he might yet come to share. "Ah well, this puzzle, at least, is solved and most happily so. I suspect Katharine has had time to resolve the difficulties with the girls and we should invite them to join us." With that, he rang for a servant. When Mrs. Grafton appeared he asked her to summon the ladies, "if they're ready."

Moments later the men were joined by a far happier group of ladies than had left them. Clara and Katie still clung to their mother's hands, but were content to be kept at arm's length without any trace of the fright they'd shown earlier. Carmen and Norah trailed after their mother and sisters, gangly and a little self-conscious—two typical teen-aged girls. They took the same chairs they had occupied earlier, this time collapsing into them and falling back as far as the thinly tufted cushions allowed. On the settee, Katharine loosened the clinging hands of her little ones long enough for them to slide from where they'd been sitting and restock themselves with cakes from the tea cart.

The three men continued to drape themselves around the fireplace, smiling their satisfaction at the scene before them.

Katharine O'Shea confirmed what they saw. "We've had a good talk. And I think we all understand each other a little better now." She looked to Holmes with soft brown eyes that seemed to embrace his soul and, like Watson, he understood the woman's hold on a husband and a lover. "We have you to thank for all of this, Mr. Holmes, and I am deeply in your debt. I mean to be certain you are well rewarded for your assistance, but even more importantly, know that you have a friend for life and will be forever in my thoughts and prayers."

"And those are sentiments I share as well, Mr. Holmes," Parnell added.

The expressions of appreciation marked the time for Holmes and Watson to take their leave. There was nothing left to accomplish and no more glory in which to bask.

"Mrs. O'Shea, Mr. Parnell, I'm delighted that everything has worked out as it has. Dr. Watson and I thank you for your kind hospitality, and now I fear we will need to return to London to resume the work waiting for us there."

"Certainly, Mr. Holmes. I'll see you to the door." Katharine dislodged herself from the settee and the children, and together with Parnell walked Holmes and Watson to the small porch looking out to the road that would take her guests back to London. Carruthers had sent a footman to fetch the coach, and Katharine used the short wait to reaffirm her gratitude. Fearing Holmes had forgotten their charge from Mrs. Hudson, Watson inserted the housekeeper's request as tactfully as he could manage. "We are, of course, most pleased to have been of service. As it happens, Mrs. O'Shea, Mr. Holmes is engaged on another case in which you may, in fact, be able to provide invaluable assistance. I am afraid we're not at liberty to discuss its details with you at this time. And, of course, it goes without saying we won't ask you to do anything inappropriate or dangerous."

The coach pulled to a halt on the path below, its fresh team of horses ready to return Holmes and Watson to Baker Street. Watson's vague request added an unexpectedly sober note to Katharine's good-bye. "I should, of course, wish to do everything I can to return this very kind favor, Doctor. It remains only to be seen whether I can comfortably do so in the instance you are describing."

"We quite understand and will leave it at that until the time comes, if indeed it comes at all." Holmes and Watson descended the steps to the waiting carriage and waved good-bye to the couple whose own waves were less vigorous than they might have been only moments earlier.

As the coach started from the Lodge, Holmes clapped his hands together. "I'd say that went surprisingly well, Watson."

Watson's raised eyebrows and small smile made clear the need for Holmes's further explanation.

"I know what you're thinking, Watson. And Mrs. Hudson does unquestionably deserve some credit in all this. But as I now consider things, I believe my statement to Parnell was exactly right. The explanation was there to be seen the whole time. The woman just has a way of getting under my skin and I don't reason things out as I should. I sometimes believe it's purposeful on her part. Anyway, all's well if it ends well, if I might paraphrase Mr. Shakespeare. Speaking of which, Watson, I do appreciate your taking care of that little business at the end. I had quite forgotten about alerting Mrs. O'Shea that we might be needing her in the Coogan affair, although I must say I don't see how she can be of any use to us."

It would be a few days later that Holmes would learn what use Mrs. O'Shea could be.

Chapter 9.
The Puzzle Solved

Mrs. Hudson glowered at Holmes as he savored each spoonful of his lemon custard dessert. She and Watson had finished their dinners nearly a half hour earlier. Watson remained at the table, ostensibly to keep Holmes company; in fact, trying, without success, to hasten his digestion. Holmes had left the table after the fried sole muttering something about a new idea regarding the distinction between English and Indian hemp fibers that required his immediate attention. The meal had begun on a far more agreeable note. Servings of soup and fish were accompanied by discussion of the triumphs at Eltham Lodge. Mrs. Hudson said little while her two lodgers described the reunion of mother and daughters, giving unqualified, if unacknowledged, confirmation of her judgment. She was content with confirmation in whatever state. When Holmes found the siren call of science overwhelming, he interrupted the serving of Mrs. Hudson's special dessert and postponed her analysis of the events surrounding Coogan's death. Mrs. Hudson's impatience came from an awareness of all that needed to be done to prepare Holmes for the part he would play in unraveling the mystery Moira Keegan had presented to them. Having gotten him back to the table, she now took a position opposite Holmes and attempted to stare him to the bottom of his dessert plate.

Exchanging a smile for her glare, Holmes pronounced the custard excellent, running his spoon several times around the empty dish to emphasize the point, before dabbing his mouth with a napkin and declaring himself done. Mrs. Hudson motioned the men to stay seated while she snatched the dish and placed it in her tub.

Holmes pushed himself from the table and looked to the gathering dark beyond the kitchen window. "Now then, Mrs.

Hudson, Watson and I have had a terribly busy day. Might we not put this discussion off to morning?"

Mrs. Hudson had pulled her chair to a position where she faced both men. "I think not, Mr. 'Olmes. Tomorrow mornin' we will 'ave to be gettin' in touch with the people we'll want 'ere in the evenin' to work our way through Miss Moira's puzzle. If you'll take notes, Doctor, I'll share with you what I've discovered about Mr. Coogan's murder."

When she had finished, Mrs. Hudson took note of the hour, and excused herself to clean the supper dishes and clear away the rest of the kitchen before getting to bed. In the morning they would have Wiggins deliver invitations, and afterward they would rehearse their parts for the following evening. Holmes and Watson nodded, but said nothing. They appeared to be stumbling through a fog as they padded their way to the stairs. In the sitting room, Holmes selected a briar, scooped tobacco from the toe of its slipper container, sprawled across the settee newly freed of books, papers, and clothing, and lit a pipe that gave him none of its customary satisfaction. Watson sat at his desk, his own briar in hand together with the burley he stored more conventionally in a cubbyhole of his desk. He meant to transcribe the brief notes he had taken in Mrs. Hudson's parlor, but, like Holmes, he sat contemplating the tale they had just heard. Neither man was of a mind to question Mrs. Hudson's analysis—not after the day's experience at Eltham Lodge—but neither man could easily embrace the fantastic story he had just heard. Watson muttered the word "incredible" several times. Holmes grunted agreement and neither man spoke another word. Watson found a pen, dipped its nib into the inkpot and began to record the incredible. Holmes sat for a while, watching smoke from his pipe wend its way in slender curls to the ceiling, then went to get his violin from its place beside the bookcase. As night embraced 221B Baker Street, the only sounds from the apartments were the scratching of Watson's pen and a flawless rendering of Mendelssohn's Violin Concerto. An hour later, and for hours into the night, there was only the violin.

As Mrs. Hudson promised, there was a great deal of work to get done the following morning. The housekeeper's refusal to have a telephone installed complicated and slowed the process—unnecessarily as far as both Holmes and Watson were concerned. Mrs. Hudson had insisted their work depended on observation and she was not about to eliminate "the clues to be 'ad from just watchin'." It was an ongoing war, but the two men had long since fought and lost all the major battles. And so, while Watson and Holmes worked their way through mounds of eggs, rashers of bacon, piles of sausages, and small heaps of toast, supplemented by the ever-present pot of tea, Mrs. Hudson went to locate Wiggins, their substitute telephone service.

She found him directing the activities of two boys, both of them younger and taller than himself, armed with brooms and waiting curbside to sweep the paths of gentlemen and ladies preparing to hazard the crossing at Baker and George Streets. The boys were receiving instruction on the identification of gentry who would appreciate and properly reward their services, as well as the percentage of their earnings to be shared with their mentor. Having completed financial arrangements with his two protégés, Wiggins was ready to turn his attention to a position he deemed more appropriate to his talents. Before starting out however, Mrs. Hudson insisted Thomas have the breakfast she was certain he would otherwise go without, and he joined Holmes and Watson at the table, where they were as much amazed by his presence as they were by Mrs. Hudson's insistence on addressing him by his Christian name. After reducing the two lodgers' portions of eggs and bacon by greater than a third, Wiggins wiped his mouth with a sleeve well accustomed to the purpose, asked for and was provided a scone "to tide me over to supper," and was given his assignment.

Wiggins was dispatched first to Scotland Yard carrying a carefully worded and lengthy message to Inspector Lestrade, and instructed to wait for a written reply. He was to return to Baker Street with the Inspector's note, after which he would go again to Kilburn and the apartment of Mrs. Keegan with a brief message to which he was to get her verbal reply, and finally to Fleet Street to the offices of the *Times* to put a note into the hand of Mr. Parkhurst from whom he was also to receive a written reply. He engaged a four-wheeler whose driver had his eye on more affluent trade, but was persuaded by the shillings Wiggins waved at him as he climbed into the carriage. The four-wheeler passed the corner where his minions were providing safe conduct for a matron whose voluminous skirts, fur trimmed jacket, silk parasol, and wide feathered hat made clear her appropriateness for their attention. Wiggins nodded his approval to the sweepers and waved encouragement for their efforts. Open-mouthed, the two boys put up their brooms a reverent moment as the cab sped past. Then, they turned again to clearing manure and refuse from the lady's path.

At the appointed hour of 7 p.m., all parties had taken their places in the sitting room at 221B, happily unaware of the conflict between Holmes and Mrs. Hudson that had accompanied the room's modest straightening and cleaning from the day's wear. They were unaware, as well, of the several hours of patient explanation and painstaking rehearsal that preceded the performance they were about to witness. In accord with Mrs. Hudson's plan, the assembled guests were to be the first to learn the events surrounding the death of Liam

Coogan.

Watson sat in his accustomed place at the secretary's desk. Lestrade and Parkhurst had taken the two easy chairs after first nodding perfunctorily one to the other, uncertain whether they had met before, but observing the minimal social graces as a precaution. Mrs. Keegan and her brother sat on the settee, Seamus Keegan still dressed in his coachman's uniform. A third man, about Seamus's age with brown curly hair and a heart-shaped, smooth-shaven face, whose slight build was also clothed in a servant's livery, pulled the stool from Holmes's work table and sat apart from the others at the back of the room. Holmes alone remained standing, leaning against the wall beyond the fireplace as if his slender body was necessary to hold it in place.

Holmes scanned the room, appearing to notice for the first time he had visitors. "Introductions would seem to be in order, although I believe most of you know each other." As he spoke, Holmes cocked his head or swept a hand, or sometimes both, in the direction of the person he was acknowledging. "Inspector Lestrade of Scotland Yard has graciously assented to join us in an unofficial capacity. Mr. Parkhurst of the *London Times* is also forgoing his reporting duties while he's with us. Mrs. Keegan is, I am certain, known to all but Inspector Lestrade. The gentleman beside her is Mr. Seamus Keegan, her brother and coachman to the Shipworths in Bloomsbury. And the gentleman at the back is Mr. John Davies, a groom with the Shipworths, who has agreed to join us as well." Davies squinted hard at Holmes suggesting his agreement might not have come easily.

Seamus Keegan's eyes flashed when he learned the identity of the ferret-like man in the chair beside him. He jerked a thumb in his direction before speaking.

"Before we get on with this, Mr. Holmes, I'd be obliged to know what it means that this here bloke from Scotland Yard is 'unofficial,' and whether he ain't got a whole crowd of bobbies waiting outside, with every one of them being very official. His asking Lord Shipworth to have me and Mr. Davies excused from our duties so's we could come here for questioning didn't seem to me so unofficial."

Holmes responded to the accusation he knew to be as much about him as about Lestrade. "I have worked with the Inspector for a great many years and have never been given the least cause to doubt his word. I can assure you there is no crowd of bobbies, nor will there be. It's my understanding Inspector Lestrade made very clear to Lord Shipworth that you and Mr. Davies could provide a valuable service to the Yard, and were not in any way under suspicion yourselves. Moreover, Lord Shipworth was assured you both would be returning to Bloomsbury immediately after our meeting. The Inspector has been invited by me with the understanding his assistance will be significant to achieving our goals. That is as much as you need to know about his unofficial capacity. He is, as is each of you, my guest, and before the night is over we may all find cause to trust each other if there is to be a happy resolution to this difficulty." The last was accompanied by a fixed stare to Seamus Keegan, who stayed locked in visual combat with Holmes as the detective began his description of events surrounding the death of Liam Coogan exactly as they had been described to him the night before.

"Let us start with Mr. Coogan's arrival at the Lord Selkirk Inn in Wapping. He checked himself in for three days, requesting a room on the first floor, but agreeing to a room on the second that faced away from the traffic. He requested as well that the room be as near to the Inn's backstairs as possible. I'm told that is not an unusual request among the Inn's patrons and he was given room seventeen, facing the back and one door removed from the stairs. The first night of his stay he complained to Mr. Peacock, the clerk on duty, that he was having trouble sleeping when he joined him for a smoke. Mr. Peacock remembers Mr. Coogan talking at length about his family. The rest of his time at the Inn, he was, in Mr. Peacock's words, 'regular,' by which he meant Mr. Coogan had a pleasant word for everyone while keeping largely to himself. Mr. Peacock is himself regular, although in a different sense of that word. While he's expected to remain behind the registration counter at all times other than when making his rounds, Mr. Peacock feels a need to stretch and have a smoke periodically, and so, beginning at three, and on the chimes of every succeeding hour, he unlocks the front door and allows himself the luxury of a cigarette on the steps outside. I put it to you that our Mr. Coogan may simply have been a congenial man, sharing a smoke with Mr. Peacock when he had difficulty sleeping, and always having a pleasant word for his fellow guests, or he may have been establishing the night clerk's patterns and making certain the Inn's guests were aware of his stay."

Holmes paused in striding the small stage he had made for himself, and looked beyond the place footlights might have been to gauge the reaction of his audience. He found himself the object of a rapt, if wary, attention by all but Lestrade who puffed contentedly on his pipe while he waited the revelation he knew to be forthcoming.

"Let us then look more closely at the state of Mr. Coogan's room as I found it. More particularly, let's look at what was out of place about Coogan's room. For one, there was the room's fully opened window. The night of the attack was described by Mr. Peacock as chilly enough to convince him to plan on a shorter than usual cigarette break, and to be unsurprised at finding a tramp having lit a fire at the roadway for warmth. The open window is something I'll come back to.

"More puzzling was the arrangement of blood splatter in the room. If Mr. Coogan had been surprised in his bed and

197

murdered there, the bed should have been covered with blood, but there was none. If Mr. Coogan was awake and out of bed when his murderers entered, one would expect a violent struggle with blood splattered over a good portion of the room. Not only is there no such splatter, there's no report of the noise we'd expect from a man battling for his life. No screams or cries for help. In fact, no one at the Inn knew of Mr. Coogan's death until his body was discovered the next morning. And then it was found that virtually all the blood from this horrific crime is contained on a single carpet. It is as if Mr. Coogan conveniently laid himself down on the room's single throw rug to be brutally murdered. In short, we are asked to believe we have a murder that is noiseless and as tidy as could be wanted by the most fastidious housekeeper.

"Let us now consider two other events occurring on the night of Mr. Coogan's demise and having relevance for our story. First, we have the report of a body stolen from the undertaking firm of Septimus McCardle and Son on Holborn Street. Dr. Watson read aloud that item from the *Standard*'s listing of crime reports at our breakfast the day the murder of Mr. Coogan was reported. Second, we have the use of a cosh on Mr. Peacock while the clerk was taking his late night smoke one day after Mr. Coogan had opportunity to learn his routine." Holmes made a cathedral of his fingers and placed its spire to his lips. "I believe you all know what I'm suggesting, so allow me to detail the events of that evening as well as I can reconstruct them."

Each member of his audience had their own reaction to the scenario being developed by Holmes. Mrs. Keegan had again taken to throttling the handkerchief she held in her lap while eyeing Holmes with outward calm; her brother sat motionless and staring so hard at Holmes he seemed not even to blink. John Davies appeared intent on finding a comfortable way to arrange his feet while Parkhurst did his best to work his way deeper into the cushions of his easy chair. Lestrade alone was expressionless, but a close observer might have noticed the pipe he clenched had lost fire.

"Sometime well past midnight, when his employers, the Shipworths, and their staff were all in bed, Mr. Keegan hitched up a coach in the quiet of the stables above which he likely has his living quarters. The route from Bloomsbury to Wapping would require only a short detour to make a stop on Holborn Street. Somewhere along that route, Mr. Keegan stopped to pick up the confederate he would need for a visit to McCardle and Son, and to assist in the rest of the night's work. His confederate would be young, vital, reliable, and someone who had reason to know the names of the recently deceased and the funeral homes holding their remains. As, for example, a newspaperman with responsibility for reporting birth and death notices. With Mr. Parkhurst identifying a conveniently located funeral home, Mr. Keegan's skill in housebreaking, while long in disuse, could be called on to allow the two men to enter the establishment and remove the remains of the unfortunate Joshua Hobbes.

"From Mr. Coogan, Mr. Keegan and Mr. Parkhurst had been made aware of the night clerk's pattern and prepared themselves accordingly. Having obtained a cosh for their use, they now had to have a means of luring Mr. Peacock from the steps where he normally had his smoke to a place away from the Inn. That was the function of the tramp's fire out by the roadway. Mr. Peacock was duty bound to explore the fire on the Inn's property, and as soon as he did, he could be sapped by a person waiting in the shadows. I'm guessing Mr. Parkhurst played the role of tramp and Mr. Keegan assumed responsibility for the strong-arm tactics." Holmes looked from one man to the next, trading one blank stare for another.

"They then removed the keys from the unconscious man and opened the back door to bring the stolen corpse up the

199

back way to Mr. Coogan's room, locking it back up immediately after, and leaving the keys on Mr. Peacock's counter since Mr. Coogan would be able to open his door to them. They laid the body on the carpet where they savaged it beyond recognition, after first dressing it in Mr. Coogan's clothes and placing Moira's purse with his keys in a pants pocket. When the task was done, a note was pinned to the body with the single word, 'informer,' to make certain there would be no doubt as to the reason for the supposed murder. Mrs. Keegan would later identify the clothing and purse as belonging to her late husband. And Mr. Peacock and the Inn's residents would of course identify the guest in room seventeen as Mr. Coogan when shown his photograph by the police.

"Everything went exactly to plan until it came time to leave the Inn. The three men may have heard noises and been afraid someone was awake and might come to investigate. Whatever startled them, they decided they couldn't chance going back into the hall and down the stairs, and would have to make use of an alternative escape plan involving the drop from the second floor window to the ground, a relatively short drop given the rise at the back of the Inn. And that explains the open window on a chilly night.

"It worked well for Mr. Parkhurst and Mr. Coogan, but the larger Mr. Keegan did not have the same good fortune. His fall resulted in the small limp people noted at his brother-in-law's wake, and the creation of the rather improbable tale of an experienced coachman being kicked by one of his own horses. Mr. Keegan also reported a need to leave the wake a little before time to return the carriage the Shipworths had allowed him to borrow, and to resume supervision of his new groom. His new groom was, of course, the absent star of the wake he was leaving, and is with us today under the name John Davies. Would you be so good as to confirm your identity, Mr. Coogan?"

The object of Holmes's question drew inquisitive stares from Lestrade and Watson; everyone else in the room had eyes only for Holmes. The accused man pushed away from his stool, and began to pace at the back of the room, weaving dangerously close to Holmes's worktable, placing hemp, slides, beaker, assembled papers and microscope at risk. To Holmes's considerable relief, he came forward at last and screwed his body into the empty basket chair.

"I'll have nothing to say until I know the thinking and scheming of his nibs over there who's not said a word, and can take down any one of us what does. I know you say you've got his promise and he's never let you down. But I never met him before today and, with respect, I don't know why he's here or what his game is." Having given expression to the emotion he had been working to contain, Coogan again became quiet except for the small dance at his chair he now resumed.

Lestrade was not a man to be bullied into action, neither was he a man to be insensitive to concerns he deemed legitimate. He turned in his chair to look to each of Holmes's guests without seeming to take special interest in any one of them. "The investigation of the death of Liam Coogan is a concern for the Special Branch of the Yard. It falls outside my own area of responsibility, although I can't ignore a crime the Yard's got under investigation. Still, I have to wonder what's the crime here. There's certainly no murder, since our victim," Lestrade nodded to the sullen figure in the basket chair, "is very much alive. The counterfeiting of a murder seems to me in questionable taste, but doesn't rise to the level of being criminal. And the lying that's been done was intended to protect a life—and maybe a family—and not meant to hurt anyone, at least not anyone living."

Lestrade's words had an instant calming effect. The activity in Mrs. Keegan's lap and at her husband's chair slowed, and Seamus Keegan's hard squint softened to the extent of becoming a wary stare as Lestrade continued. "On the other hand, sapping citizens and stealing bodies are crimes with less shades of gray. At least for me. It's true the sapping isn't going to lead to any investigation or arrest because Mr. Peacock seems happy to let the whole thing die, what with him not wanting to publicize his taking liberties without his employer's knowing or approving.

"The body snatching and mutilation of that body are, however, things I can't ignore. I'm not a sentimentalist and I recognize there's no one to see the body, and it will be dust as we'll all be soon enough, but it's a crime and so is stealing a body no matter what the purpose. My first concern has to be protecting life, and I've no problem with seeing the Coogans safely away since they've committed no crime that amounts to anything, and Mr. Holmes has got me convinced Mr. Coogan will be in real danger if his enemies find out he's still alive. Putting that to one side, it's my duty to help apprehend the men responsible for the body snatching and mutilation. That's, of course, if those men are still in the country when I get around to looking for them." Lestrade spoke the last with soft deliberation, looking to the window as if he could spy the ocean somewhere beyond. "And I can tell you I'd feel a good deal more comfortable about things, and maybe move just a little slower if I could know for certain Mr. Hobbes was buried in the plot that's got his name on it." This time, Lestrade paused to look first to Seamus Keegan then to Winston Parkhurst, his eyebrows at full mast as he waited a response.

Parkhurst spoke for both men. "It's a matter that bears correction; we can agree it will be set right tomorrow night or the next at the latest." Seamus Keegan inclined his head the smallest amount; Lestrade had known such men and recognized his small nod to be sufficient.

"Fine. In that case, I am here only as a guest of my good

friend, Mr. Holmes."

Watson had never understood Lestrade and Holmes to be anything more than congenial, and hoped he was the only one who'd seen Holmes wince when Lestrade announced the introduction of warmth to their relationship.

Holmes felt it time to pull the group's attention back to himself. "Mr. Parkhurst, I believe we can safely say that you followed a more circuitous route than your colleagues in becoming Mr. Coogan's defender. Indeed, your original intention—your mission I might say—was to make certain it was Mr. Coogan who suffered the fate that befell the body of Mr. Hobbes. That takes us back to your days at the Royal Military Academy at Woolwich or "the Shop" as it was less formally called. You were one of three friends at the Shop. There was Peter Lassiter, Frederick Egerton and yourself. You became very close in the manner strong friendships can form among young men boarding together. School holidays you went to the home of Frederick, now Commander, Egerton, met the Admiral and Lady Egerton, and were treated very kindly by them. Doubtless, you met Lord Cavendish, Lady Egerton's brother and Frederick's uncle during some of those visits. And so, when Lord Cavendish was brutally murdered at Phoenix Park, the three of you took an oath to seek vengeance on the perpetrators of that outrage. It was the pledge of impressionable young men, but the three of you stayed in touch and no one ever renounced the commitment made eight years ago. Your own relationship with Peter Lassiter was apparent at Liam Coogan's wake when the two of you held a friendly chat within earshot of the very deaf James Burch." Holmes paused to acknowledge the nod from Parkhurst and the gasps from the Coogans.

"Over the years, Commander Egerton became a virtual invalid after saving the lives of others during a training exercise gone tragically wrong. He could no longer directly participate, but at the same time his desire for action could not be refused. Peter Lassiter had meanwhile become a member of the Irish Branch, now the Special Branch of the Yard and so was in a position to track the activities of any Invincibles who hoped to disappear into the warrens in and around London, while you joined the *Times* giving you opportunity to carry out your own investigations with people who might be willing to talk to a reporter, but be less inclined to talk to the police.

"All was quiet for a while, those conspirators in the Phoenix Park murders who lacked the resources to get beyond England had either been hung, or were serving long prison sentences. But then Liam Coogan fell into your lap. He had completed a relatively short prison term and lacked the money to get himself and his family beyond London. You finally had a target for the plot you'd concocted all those years before. You had probably drawn the short straw, and so had responsibility for carrying out the act. Being a *Times* reporter, you constructed the easy fiction that you were developing a story on the Brotherhood and, with information supplied by Lassiter, you found the Keegans and inserted yourself into their family to track Liam Coogan's movements. But then something happened. I admit I'm at a loss to know what it was. Somewhere along the way you became Liam Coogan's protector, and together with him and the Keegans you conceived a plan to rid Mr. Coogan of his pursuers. Of course, being an amateur in all this, you came close to committing one fateful error. You couldn't resist going back to Wapping to revisit the site of your action and learn what was being said about it. You went to the Fat Mermaid, knowing it was the pub used by those staying at the Lord Selkirk Inn. You did take the precaution of becoming again the reporter for the *Times* before asking whether anyone could provide information about the murder of Mr. Coogan. Still, if you had been recognized, you could only have done yourself and your cause great harm."

Having concluded Mrs. Hudson's analysis, Holmes strolled back to the mantel, ignoring an audience that, with the exception of Watson and Lestrade, sat dumbfounded. Parkhurst was the first to find his voice. "You make only one mistake, Mr. Holmes, in your extraordinary analysis. I did not draw the short straw. If that had been the case, committing the act would not have the significance it held for us. It would have been a matter of the least fortunate, and perhaps least willing, being assigned to seek the group's revenge. No, Mr. Holmes—and forgive me, Liam—it was seen as a privilege and one for which we all competed. We spent a long night in the Academy's gymnasium in a fencing competition to determine who would have the honor of acting on the group's behalf, and I won."

For the first time there came a female voice, weary, but firm, exactly as Holmes and Watson remembered it. "And it's God's own blessing that you did, Mr. Parkhurst."

The reporter nodded acknowledgement and looked back to Holmes. "You wonder why I turned away from vengeance and decided on a course to help the Coogans. The answer is simple: I came to know them. It's easy to hate in the abstract, it's much harder to hate when you come to know your supposed enemy. In truth, Mr. Holmes, I was having difficulty with the plans we made even before I met Liam and Patsy. I was a much younger man eight years ago, and life was more easily seen in black and white. I still believe the killings in Phoenix Park are indefensible, but Liam's sin was one of naivete and his role was minor. As I saw it, he'd been a driver at times for the Invincibles out of loyalty to the man who'd housed him, fed him, taught him the building trades, and hired and promoted him in that honest work. With all of that, it was wrong of Liam to participate in their vile acts, and he paid the price for doing so. Five years in Kilmainham Jail seemed to me adequate punishment; I had no justification for making him pay more dearly, and no wish to do so.

"After I met Liam and Patsy it became quite impossible to conceive of following through on those outdated plans. As you say, Mr. Holmes, I sought to be their protector and we planned the deception you have recognized. We had things organized such that Peter would be content I had carried out my obligation. As the Special Branch investigator, he was doing his best to focus blame for the crime on the Brotherhood while controlling the investigation to make certain no one could discover the part I was supposed to have played. That should have left me free to work on getting Liam and Patsy away from here. When Moira came to see you with her own ideas about what Liam was planning, and you chose to get involved, it changed everything. We had to track your progress and throw you off the scent as best we could. Obviously, we didn't do that very well." Parkhurst glanced to the Coogans and Seamus, and pursed his lips before speaking, "I will tell you this as well. I regret nothing that I've done in this whole affair and if called upon, I would do the same again."

"As would I, and I'm not caring who knows it," Seamus Keegan added.

Holmes waved off the two men's comments. "I'm not expecting you to have regrets and, in any event, I'm not much concerned whether you do or you don't. I can't entirely support the efforts that were made to assist Mr. Coogan, but I can understand them. However, none of that matters. I will remind you I have been hired to keep Mr. Coogan alive and I mean to give value for pay. Like you, I am convinced his staying alive requires his leaving England, and it is to achieve that end each of you has been invited here tonight. But to succeed we will need to rely on each other, and we will all need to agree on a single course of action. Can I depend on your cooperation?" The question was meant for just one person. No one but Lestrade had any option but to cooperate, and the Inspector was well aware of his singular position.

"I'll hear the plan and I give my word that what I hear will stay in this room. I'll not promise anything more until I learn what you have to say, Mr. Holmes."

"I can ask no more than that, Inspector." Knowing he would, in fact, be asking a good deal more than that before the evening ended, Holmes began to outline the plan to which all the earlier evening had been prelude. His face was drawn and every now and again he tapped the empty pipe he had taken from the mantel against his palm. "We are agreed the Coogans cannot stay safe in England and that an ocean voyage is in order." There were nods all around with a single exception. "In five days the Ludgate Hill sails from London to America. The ship is a cargo steamer, but carries a large number of passengers. I am convinced it offers our best opportunity to get the Coogans safely away before anyone realizes Mr. Coogan did not die at the Lord Selkirk Inn. Money for second class passage will be lent to you with an understanding it will be returned as soon as you are able." Holmes brushed past expressions of gratitude. "For the next few days, Mr. Coogan is to remain James Davies and a groom at the Shipworth Estate. I assume that poses no problem for you, Mr. Coogan?"

Liam Coogan stared hard at Holmes, but with none of the wariness of their earlier exchange. He avoided looking to Lestrade as they all did. "I'll do all what's needed to be back with Patsy and the cubs, and be safe away from these parts."

"Very good. Beyond that, I have a concern about Mrs. Keegan, as I'll continue to call her, getting safely aboard the Ludgate Hill. The house may be watched and her attempt to leave with the children and baggage could be questioned and perhaps blocked, or she might be followed and her plans to join Mr. Coogan discovered. The placement of a constable on Princess Street could help to discourage prying eyes." Holmes hazarded a glance at Lestrade, but got no response. There was nothing to do but proceed regardless. "Let me now detail the plan that I believe offers us the greatest opportunity for success."

In the end, Lestrade declared the plan agreeable to him and promised to do his part. What no one could foresee was how that plan, although carefully drawn by the director of London's premier consulting detective agency, was destined to come apart before its implementation could begin.

Chapter 10.
Best Laid Plans

Mrs. Hudson held herself to blame. She had made certain Holmes emphasized the need for secrecy with all those at the meeting. The problem lay with those who weren't at the meeting. She had failed to take into account the naivete of the youngest Coogan and the greed of his grandfather.

Cornelius Keegan had a coward's need for borrowed courage, and a drunkard's need to hide it from himself. He satisfied both needs with frequent trips to Caffey's pub. There, he could cultivate the company of men he saw as strong, the men of the Irish resistance. It hardly mattered that they reviled his son-in-law, regarding him as a Judas to the movement. Hadn't Liam gone into hiding, confirming the legitimacy of the strong men's charge, and bringing shame on the family from which Cornelius felt every right to separate himself—at least between meals and before bedtime.

There was still the matter of his thirst. Loyalty to the movement led to acceptance at Caffey's, but money was needed to buy drinks. His family's shame did not keep him from taking his daughter's money when he had to, which was most of the time. Occasionally, he could trade information for drink. The bits and pieces he brought to Caffey's pub could earn him a pint of bitter if Caffey found them worthy of being transmitted to Mr. Fogarty, and a whiskey if Caffey thought them of immediate interest to Mr. Fogarty. He'd gotten three whiskeys for reporting his daughter was keeping company with a newspaper man doing a story about the Brotherhood, and he'd been promised drinks for a full week in exchange for the information that led to the kidnapping of Holmes and Watson. The fact that drinks became available to the extent he endangered his family either never occurred to him or was of no great consequence.

He was on the steps outside the apartment having a pipe when Seamus brought Patsy home in the Shipworths' carriage. Little Liam had some kind of breathing problem and Patsy forbade any smoking in the house. She'd caught him once smoking around the boy and told him if she caught him again she'd throw him out, da or no. She'd even urged Big Liam to quit smoking for fear he'd forget and smoke around the boy, although he never had.

Seamus nodded to him from his seat on the box; it was as close to affection as the two of them ever got. Patsy sat for a while before climbing out of the coach. He thought there might be someone else inside, probably that reporter, but couldn't be certain it wasn't simply the shadows from the street lanterns playing tricks on him. She answered his question with a brusque, "Just out," and hurried past him to gather up Moira and Little Liam.

He was well accustomed to the two of them paying him little mind. He dismissed their treatment of him as the natural comeuppance of his having been too free and giving when they were young, and their resenting him for asking a little of his own back now when he was getting on—that, and their not appreciating a man's need to have a little bit of a nip with his friends every now and again. The two of them had no more understanding of the comforts of drink and time spent with good companions than their mother had, which was maybe why his daughter married a man who was practically a teetotaler. Still, she seemed sharper with him than usual, and was even short with the cubs. She put the two of them to bed with no more conversation than to hear their prayers. And she near took his head off when he asked a perfectly reasonable question, telling him he could get his own supper, she and the cubs had theirs while he was down at Caffey's.

There was something going on all right and whatever it was involved Seamus as well. The two of them hadn't been

210

together since Liam's wake and now here they were not just together, but with Seamus bringing her home on a day that wasn't even his regular day out, and in the Shipworths' own carriage to boot. The two of them were plainly cooking something up and, whatever it was, he'd be the last person in the world to find out about it—unless he did his own investigating.

Learning their secret, in fact, proved remarkably easy. The next day was Thursday, and Patsy had char duties every Thursday for two families the other side of St. Augustine's. She left for work right after Moira had started for school and she had taken Little Liam upstairs to Mrs. Hogan. This Thursday, Patsy came down from Mrs. Hogan's with Little Liam in tow well after Cornelius was out of bed. When he asked why she was still at home, he was told only that something came up. And when he asked why she stayed so long with Mrs. Hogan, she nearly bit his head off. He judged then that whatever "came up" was related to her being "just out" with Seamus, and that the neighbors knew more about it than he did.

On Friday morning the pieces started to come together. Patsy had to make a stop at the greengrocer and, with Moira in school, he was left to mind Little Liam while she was gone. He had it in mind to have a conversation with his grandson thinking the boy might have been told something of what was going on, but before he could begin there was a knock at the door. It would be Mrs. Hogan from upstairs wanting to gossip with Patsy, probably about him, and he had half a mind to ignore her, except she would tell Patsy he didn't have the courtesy to answer her knock. That would lead to a lecture from his daughter on how she had little enough chance to see anybody and would appreciate it if he didn't antagonize her friends. Then too, the knocking kept on with no sign of its ending, only of its getting louder and more frequent.

Cursing the demons that tormented his life, he went to admit his neighbor only to find the insistent caller wasn't Mrs. Hogan or anyone else he knew. The woman facing him was as tall as he was, but both more erect and built a good deal more substantially. She wore a nun's habit, and he judged her visit must have something to do with Moira and school. A nun had been to the house a few days before because of something about Moira at school. She announced herself as Sister Mary Margaret, expressed no interest in who he was, and asked if Patricia Keegan was at home.

Cornelius Keegan had never been comfortable around priests or nuns, always feeling himself being judged by them and always believing himself to be found wanting. He mumbled to Sister Mary Margaret that his daughter wasn't home at the moment, unnecessarily added that he was Mrs. Keegan's father, at the same time becoming aware of his unshaven face and rumpled clothes. Still, he was thankful he'd slept in them and therefore had answered the door fully dressed. She looked past him to the hall that ran the length of the small apartment, making him aware that he had not yet invited the Sister inside. He corrected his oversight, leading her to the parlor where he urged her to make use of the couch, the best and most substantial piece of furniture in the room. He sat in an easy chair across from her. He thought he should probably offer her something, but wasn't sure if Patsy had put up tea and so decided to ignore the amenities. "Is there something I can help you with, Sister?"

Sister Mary Margaret made it her business to know something of her students and their families. She knew about Mrs. Keegan's struggles and she knew about her father's contribution to those struggles. Still, she had come all this way, had several other stops to make, and she supposed Mrs. Keegan had shared some of her thinking with her father. "I'm wondering if you can tell me why Moira will be leaving school as of this Monday. The child was unable to give us a reason and we are very concerned about it. If it's a matter of finances, we would like to try to work something out although the family is already being charged our lowest fee."

Cornelius screwed his face into a pretense of concern and nodded several times. Sister Mary Margaret concluded he knew nothing of what she was telling him and regretted her own candor. "I appreciate your coming all this way Sister. I promise you I'll have a talk with my Patsy. I'm that sure it's some kind of mix-up as will happen with the cubs—even them as sharp as Moira. My daughter and me are both of us knowing what a wonderful job you sisters are doing and are wanting you to keep at it."

Sister Mary Margaret had already pushed herself from the couch and now Cornelius eased his way from his chair. "Yes, well, please tell your daughter—please tell Mrs. Keegan—that I called and I'd appreciate hearing from her. May the Lord be with you Mr. Keegan." She delivered the last with more form than conviction, but Cornelius did not take notice. Sister Mary Margaret put her card on the parlor table, then proceeded to the door without waiting for Cornelius to accompany her, and left the apartment without looking back.

Cornelius was now certain his daughter was planning a major change in her life, almost certainly a move of some sort, that it would be soon, and that it didn't include him. There was no good his asking her and there'd be no good trying to reach Seamus since he was part of whatever it was that was about to happen. It now made even more sense to find out what the children had been told. Moira must have been given some reason for leaving school, and Little Liam would have gotten some kind of preparation for whatever was coming. And for the moment, the boy and he were alone.

Little Liam had taken a puzzle from the stack in the

wardrobe he shared with Moira. When complete, the wooden pieces formed a sheep badly in need of shearing. It was a puzzle Liam had put together well over a hundred times before; nonetheless, his tongue hung out the side of his mouth and he squinted hard at the pieces before him. When he began, his hands moved quickly setting the familiar pieces in their proper places.

"I reckon as how you'll be taking the sheep puzzle with you when you go?" He let the question hang in the air as his grandson added the animal's back legs.

"I'm not supposed to talk about that."

"Well of course you ain't supposed to talk about that to them as are from outside the family. That's only right. But you and me can talk about it."

As the tail and hind-quarters were fitted into the one remaining slot, Liam was trying to figure out what he could and could not tell his grandda. He wasn't to talk about the trip they would be taking, but he was also supposed to respect his grandda and mind what he says, although nobody had told him that for a long time. Mostly, he was five years old and hadn't yet learned to distrust his grandfather as had the other members of his family.

He gathered up the finished puzzle and moved to put it back in the wardrobe. "Well, it's sort of like a secret from everybody."

"I'm your grandda, not everybody, and I already know you'll all be taking a trip real soon. I just want to be sure in my own mind about when so I can be there to say good-bye. It's not like you'd be telling me what I don't already know, you'd just be helping your grandda know when he can say a proper good-bye to you and Moira, and to your mam."

Little Liam's tongue again hung from the corner of his mouth as he screwed his face into concentration. It didn't seem so bad if grandda already knew the *big* secret, it wasn't

214

like he'd be giving away the really important stuff. But his mam had told him not to talk about it to his grandda, and he thought she might mean not to talk about any of it.

"Maybe we should wait until mam gets home."

Cornelius Keegan felt opportunity slipping away. "Now, you know your mam. She won't want any fuss made about your going, but I promise just to be there so's I don't miss seeing all of you off. You wouldn't keep your grandda from that just because your mam wants to keep things from being a big show, now would you, boy?"

His grandda looked awful upset and he was right about his mam not liking to make a big fuss about things. He couldn't see how his knowing a little of the secret could hurt. "I'll just say it's Monday and it's in the afternoon."

"Thank you, lad. And I promise I'll be good. I'll not make a fuss. I give my word. But it might be well not to tell your mam. I want to surprise her—but I'll do it quiet."

Whatever Cornelius Keegan's intentions, there would be nothing quiet about his family's efforts to leave London.

Knowing for certain his daughter's plans to leave, and leave soon, probably with the reporter she'd been seeing, he decided to make a search of Patsy's bedroom to learn what more he could. He reasoned he had a right to protect himself, and if nobody was going to tell him anything—as they surely weren't—he'd have to find things out for himself.

His daughter's room was neat as a pin just as he knew it would be, and there was nothing obvious to give a clue to her plans. The meager furniture—a rope bed, four-drawer chest and one basket chair much the worse for its frequent wear—looked as they always had. The chest of drawers held her clothes arranged in two small piles, they could have been ready for packing or just normal wear. There weren't more than three changes of clothes in any event. After searching the four drawers of the chest, he looked under the bed's blanket and pillow, its straw mattress, and finally under the bed itself. He ignored the coin jar, which he dared not touch in any event as Patsy knew exactly how much it contained and whom to accuse if the correct amount was not found. In its stead, he spied a treasure that would get him even more than a week's worth of whiskies at Caffey's, maybe a great deal more. Neatly stacked beneath the bed were two changes of his son-in-law's clothing, his pipe and a package of the burley tobacco he favored. The impossible had suddenly become possible. The clothes might be kept as a remembrance, but not the pipe and tobacco. There could be only one reason to save those, and it had to do with the shadowy figure in Seamus's coach whose identity was suddenly clear to him. Patsy wasn't leaving with the reporter, Patsy was leaving with her own husband.

Patricia Keegan returned home to find her father anxious to get to Caffey's. He was in such a hurry to leave he didn't even ask for money although she was almost certain he had none of his own. Cornelius Keegan told his daughter he'd be back for dinner; secretly, he expected the information he was carrying would get him drinks and dinner at Caffey's. He had hopes it would get him even more. The information he had secured would prove his resourcefulness and thus his value to the Brotherhood. It should lead to a spot on Mr. Fogarty's payroll. He was certain Mr. Fogarty had a payroll because neither he nor the people around him appeared to have any other jobs.

Late morning was always a quiet time at Caffey's. The landlord had spread his newspaper across a generous portion of the bar he would scour clean before the lunch time trade began to wander in. For now, the pub was empty except for two men, older than Cornelius, who were nursing half pints of bitter over a game of draughts. Neither man greeted Cornelius nor did he speak to them although he knew them both. Caffey's eyes drifted up from his newspaper, but no other part of his body stirred to welcome his new patron. "You're in a bit early, ain't you, Keegan?"

Cornelius looked back to the old men as he seated himself on a stool in front of Caffey. He made a best estimate about distance and their hearing, and leaned forward, careful not to touch the landlord's newspaper, before speaking to him in a hoarse whisper. "I've news. Important news. Important to you know who."

Caffey folded his newspaper, straightened himself, and clasped his arms across the full apron that covered his well-nourished form. He spoke without making effort to hide his skepticism. "Let's have it then and we'll see what it's worth, if it's worth anything at all."

The newspaper no longer providing a barrier between the men, Cornelius leaned his way further across the bar. "Not this time, Mr. Caffey. This time is big. This time is very big. It's worth a good deal more than a pint of bitter and has got to be shared with the man hisself. He'll thank me, and he'll be that grateful to you for arranging for him to hear what I got to say."

Cornelius sat back, meeting Caffey's stare with a look that he hoped was both grave and confident. He drew his lips into a firm line, but felt a twitch at the corner of his mouth he knew won't escape the landlord.

"Well now you know better than that, Keegan. It just ain't the way things are done. I have the boy take the messages to him. It's the way it's always been and you ain't exactly suffered by it. We can't have himself running up here every time somebody thinks they've got something important to share."

Cornelius recognized the legitimacy of the landlord's position and, more importantly, his ability to control the flow of communication to the man neither of them was willing to name. "I'll tell you this and only this, and then it'll be on your head whether to tell the man the things he needs to know. Everything he's believing about Liam Coogan and his dying is wrong, and I'm the only one as knows what's right. And if that's not worth the time of hisself, I'm sure I don't know what is."

If Michael Caffey was to enjoy the continuing patronage of those who guaranteed a full house every night, he had to fulfill certain obligations. One of those was to transmit information to Mr. Fogarty. It was Caffey's job to screen messages from the hangers-on like Keegan, and forward the useful communications to Mr. Fogarty, or more likely to one of his lieutenants. It was almost always trivial stuff, somebody was in town or had just left town, one constable had come and another gone, things Mr. Fogarty wanted to know, but things that weren't uncomfortable for Caffey to know as well.

Mr. Fogarty had made clear to Caffey his feeling that their arrangement had broken down after the fiasco with Sherlock Holmes and the char who wasn't a char, and Caffey had been instructed to put the potboy back to full time and pay to be certain he was always available to carry messages. Caffey understood the need to avoid any future breakdowns. With that in mind he took stock of the situation. He judged Keegan to be sober, and his daughter *was* married to Coogan—or had been—it was possible he actually knew something useful, and if it was something about Coogan's murder it was likely to be something that would interest the Brotherhood a great deal.

All in all, it was not such a bad idea to leave it up to Mr. Fogarty to decide whether or not he wanted to hear Keegan's story. He'd be doing his part by letting Mr. Fogarty know there was something about Coogan he might want to hear and Keegan refused to tell it to anybody but him. If it was something useful, Mr. Fogarty would be indebted to Caffey for making the arrangements, and if it turned out to be the nothing Caffey expected it to be, the fault would be Keegan's, not his.

Caffey smoothed his moustaches, and looked hard at Cornelius. "It's on your head then. I'll share your message and himself will decide what he wants to do. Write out exactly what you want him to know and I'll send the boy around."

Cornelius took a table in a far corner, well satisfied with what he had accomplished. Caffey again spread the paper across the bar and waited the arrival of himself.

Mr. Fogarty swept in 20 minutes later, a cigarette between his lips and blowing smoke like a train roaring into its station. He squinted through thick lenses at Caffey who pointed to Cornelius and, without losing stride, he continued to Caffey's private room, leaving it to the thick-set dark-bearded man walking behind him to gather up Keegan and follow him into the office. Fogarty took the seat behind Caffey's small desk while the bearded man framed himself before the closed door, and Cornelius took a seat across from Fogarty that left him blind to the big man's actions.

"Have Caffey bring us three whiskies if you would, Mr. Cavanaugh. I take it you won't object to having a whiskey with me, Mr. Keegan?"

Cornelius nodded his willingness to join Fogarty in a drink, but neither Fogarty or Cavanaugh paid him any attention, the burly assistant having already gone to place his leader's order. The two men waited for Cavanaugh's return, Fogarty tapped tobacco into a paper he then sealed while Keegan appeared to search for a soft place in the oaken chair on which he was seated. Cavanaugh returned carrying a tray containing a bottle and three glasses on the outstretched

219

fingers of one beefy hand as he had once seen done by a waiter in a cafe. He set the tray in front of Fogarty, then poured out three whiskies. Each man downed his drink after first raising his glass to a free Ireland. Cavanaugh returned to his place in the doorway and Fogarty fixed his squint on Cornelius. "Now, Mr. Keegan, what is the news you've got that's fit only for my ears?"

Cornelius drew himself up, trying hard to ignore the man at his back, but his mouth was still dry and vital parts of the speech he had carefully practiced now seemed lost to him. He raised his empty glass, tilting it to Fogarty. "My throat's that dry, Mr. Fogarty, I wonder if I might have another?"

Fogarty gave a wry smile and signaled his approval to the man at the door who came forward to refill Cornelius's glass. He downed it in a gulp after toasting his benefactor's good health. It only helped a little, but he dared not ask for another.

"Go on now, Mr. Keegan."

"Thank you, Mr. Fogarty. It's a rare story I want you to know, unbelievable except it's what I seen myself. And I share it with you only because of my feeling for the movement and my respect for the work you're doing."

"And what is your unbelievable story, Mr. Keegan?"

Cornelius told of his finding the evidence that his daughter was leaving, of its being confirmed by Sister Mary Margaret and his learning the day and time. "But that ain't the half of it, Mr. Fogarty." And he told of the indistinct figure in the coach he now described as definitely being his son-in-law, and of Patsy's saving his clothes, pipe and tobacco under the bed, explaining his daughter's aversion to tobacco, and citing its discovery as absolute proof of Liam Coogan's continuing existence. Hearing his own account of his daughter's plan, he became seized with a sudden paternal responsibility. "You do understand, Mr. Fogarty, the boy is the devil hisself and my poor Patsy is plain bewitched by him. I'm just saying she's an innocent in all this and, of course, so's the cubs. I just want to get her and the family free of the traitor. I wouldn't want them getting hurt by any of this."

Fogarty lit a second cigarette with the stub of the one he then ground out in the tobacco-stained saucer on Caffey's desk. He exhaled a trail of smoke down his narrow chest while waving away Cornelius's concern. "We don't make war on women and children, Mr. Keegan. It's for them the battle is being fought. They're the new generation that will make strong the nation ours brings to life. You've done us a good turn, Mr. Keegan. I'm obliged to you for bringing this to our attention. And rest assured we'll attend to Mr. Coogan."

Fogarty looked past Cornelius. "We'll need to know the sailings scheduled for Monday afternoon. I doubt there's more than one." The unseen presence grunted his understanding. Cornelius looked to Fogarty with surprise. It hadn't occurred to him they would be making their escape by ship. He had assumed they would be taking the train to another part of England or perhaps Scotland.

"You've earned yourself free drinks for a week, Mr. Keegan, although I won't allow more than five whiskies a night. I'll not have public drunkenness, no matter the circumstances." Fogarty came from behind Caffey's desk, still squinting behind his thick glasses as though he might have difficulty navigating his way around Caffey's meager furnishings, belying the speed and agility of his movements.

"Might I ask a moment more, Mr. Fogarty, sir?"

The local head of the Irish resistance paused in his progress to the door his bearded colleague had opened. He signaled approval for the door to be closed once again, and looked with eyebrows raised and a faint smile to his still seated informant. "And what more have you to say, Mr. Keegan?"

221

"Mr. Fogarty, sir, I was wondering ... I mean now that you see what a help I can be to the movement, I was wondering if you could see your way clear to having me in a position to do yourself and the movement a bigger service. What I mean to say, sir, is I'd be that honored to join the Brotherhood and be a part of your work." Cornelius sensed his hands becoming clammy and felt a need for one of the five drinks he'd been promised. He wondered if the two he'd had counted against the day's five.

"Well now, that's a fine sentiment, Mr. Keegan, and one I greatly appreciate. But let me point out you are already an important part of the movement as seen by what you've done for us today. I want you to continue that work. We're in need of men like you who can keep an ear to the ground. And now I really have to be going, Mr. Keegan. There's business waiting for me back at headquarters. I'll tell Caffey about the arrangements we've made and I thank you again for your help." With that, Fogarty smiled down to the seated man, turned sharply toward the reopened door and this time hurried through it, stopping to whisper instructions to the waiting Caffey, then scurrying to the street with a wave to the several patrons who had come to catch a glimpse of the man whose exploits were the stuff of hushed conversations over their kitchen tables.

Keegan shuffled his way from Caffey's office, drawing curious stares from the few in the pub who took notice of him. He accepted a whiskey from Caffey, then amazed the landlord by rejecting another. Cornelius Keegan needed a clear head. If Mr. Fogarty and the Irish Brotherhood could not assure his future, the inspector from the Special Branch, who'd been twice to question Patsy, might just provide a packet for his here and now.

Getting an audience with Inspector Lassiter proved a far

easier task than had getting an audience with Mr. Fogarty. Cornelius told the officer at the desk he wanted to speak to Inspector Lassiter about Liam Coogan and the Irish Brotherhood, and minutes later he was being ushered to the threshold of an office that could have held three of the one he had just left at the Winking Duck. He was equally ill at ease in Inspector Lassiter's office, but for different reason. Everything in the Inspector's office appeared at risk of being sullied by his touch, if not by his mere presence. In front of him, and on either side of windows facing out to the Victoria Embankment and the Thames, there were oversized pictures of the Queen and the Prime Minister, and a smaller picture of a man he didn't recognize, each of them staring with grim resolve into the distance beyond him. A sideboard stood beneath the Queen, its surface bare except for a tea service of bone china painted with a delicate floral design. A two-shelf bookcase was on the wall to his right, the books on each shelf arranged by height, the books on the top shelf held in place by a pair of gilded falcon heads. A fireplace occupied the center of the wall to his left, a small grandfather's clock on its mantel tolled the quarter hour, sounding to Cornelius like Big Ben in the silent room. A long table extended from near the fireplace to the room's center with three straight back chairs set in a perfect line on each of its sides.

An elegant figure with dark wavy hair was hunched over a roll-top desk set in the corner between the window and bookcase. The figure took no notice of either Cornelius or the officer with him, but continued reading the single sheet he was holding. The officer stood with Cornelius after advancing one step into the room, watching the figure at the desk and waiting for a signal. At length the figure turned, gave the officer a perfunctory nod and, with a hand firmly grasping Cornelius's upper arm, the two men came forward. In his office the Inspector seemed to Cornelius even more the dandy than he had in the Kilburn apartment. In spite of the warmth of the room, he wore a frock coat over a red checked waistcoat, and high-collared white shirt setting off a pale blue tie. Cornelius felt certain a silk top hat and walking stick were not far off.

Without a second look, Inspector Lassiter waved his visitors to the long table. The officer took a seat near the fireplace, while Lassiter and Keegan took seats opposite each other at the other end of the table. The officer produced a pencil and small notebook and waited for direction.

Lassiter spoke in the flat, gray tone that suited the routine nature of his inquiry and his distaste for the man across the table. "Officer Carpenter will be recording our conversation. I'll need you to answer a few questions before we start. First, your full name." Although he described them as questions, they sounded to Cornelius as a series of demands. After learning his name, birthplace, current address, length of time living at that address, persons with whom he was living, length of time living in London and England, foreign travel if any, occupation, relatives in Ireland, and activities in Ireland, Lassiter folded his hands on the table and continued in his same detached manner. "Now what is it you have to tell me."

Cornelius was determined not to play the fool a second time. "What I've got to tell you is worth good money."

Lassiter closed his eyes for a moment and when he reopened them his face held a rueful smile. "And what exactly is 'good money'?"

"What I've got is worth 10 quid."

Lassiter's smile widened. "You must know of a plot against the Queen."

Cornelius had come too far to be put off by ridicule, which was not, in any event, unique in his experience. "What I've got is a plot all right but it's not against the Queen, it's a game what's been played against the whole of Scotland

Yard."

The policeman's smile was gone, replaced by a cold stare. Cornelius tried to return the stare, failed, tried again, and turned finally to a study of the Prime Minister's photograph.

Lassiter hated the bargaining for information, as he hated the people with whom he had to bargain. They were men without a trace of honor, and they usually brought him information he already had or that was of no use to anyone. Even so, he had to give them a shilling or two because there was the slender chance that next time they'd have something that wasn't totally worthless. "I'll need to know something of what you have to tell us to understand the value it has, if it has any value at all." He nodded to Officer Carpenter who raised his pencil in readiness.

Cornelius again felt the moisture in his palms, and the need for a drink he suspected was available somewhere in the inspector's office. He worried that sweat might be showing at the armpits of his shirt, but dared not look. It was hot and stuffy in the closed up office. The policeman named Carpenter was in shirtsleeves. Lassiter, in jacket and vest, seemed not to notice. "I'll tell you this much and this much only. It's to do with Liam Coogan and how I know he's still alive."

Lassiter tried to read his man, but he couldn't get past the mix of fear and avarice that would have been evident to anyone. He made the same calculation as had Caffey almost three hours earlier, and came to the same conclusion. The man was Coogan's son-in-law and he seemed in his right mind and sober. However outlandish his claim, he guessed it was worth hearing the old scoundrel out. "I'll promise you two quid if your information is important, more if it's really important. And I'll kick you out the door myself if you're in here with a cock and bull story hoping to get money you don't deserve."

Cornelius dismissed the risk of forcible ejection, and decided Lassiter could be persuaded to go a little higher than his two quid offer. "I'd be obliged for another half quid. I guarantee it's worth at least that."

Lassiter sneered a response. "Two sovereigns and more if it's worth more. Now tell me what you've got."

When Cornelius had finished, a furious Peter Lassiter pounded a fist on the table and glared at him so fiercely he thought the inspector had found his report unbelievable and was now prepared to make good his threat to throw him out bodily, or maybe even call for his arrest on some trumped up charge. He'd heard of that happening. He began to wish he had never started the whole business.

But Cornelius Keegan was not the focus of Lassiter's contempt. Cornelius Keegan was beneath his contempt. Without looking at the informer, the Inspector pushed away from the table and growled his command to Officer Carpenter, "Pay this man his two and a half sovereigns and get him out of here. Then get me the shipping schedules for Monday afternoon. I want Liverpool, Southampton and London covered, and make sure you get all the lines, not just White Star and Cunard. I want the information on my desk in an hour." As Keegan was prodded from the room by Officer Carpenter, Peter Lassiter turned his back on both of them and stared blindly from his window, waiting for the rage to subside sufficiently to plan his revenge on Liam Coogan and Winston Parkhurst, one of them a traitor to his country, the other a traitor to his friends, and each of them deserving the retribution he meant to deliver.

Patsy Keegan found the reason for her father's hasty departure immediately on entering the parlor. Sister Mary Margaret's card was still on the table where she had left it. She went to question Little Liam and her worst fears were realized. He had heard a lady talking to his grandda although he hadn't come out to see who it was. Grandda did ask him some questions after, but it turned out he already knew they were going away and Liam only told him when so he could come to tell them good-bye. She wondered how to get in touch with Mr. Holmes or Mr. Parkhurst, but her concerns on that score proved unnecessary. Within an hour of Cornelius's visit Lestrade knew of Lassiter's intention to have a flying squad Monday afternoon at the pier where the Ludgate Hill was docked. Lestrade explained to Holmes the Special Branch was treating it as a clandestine operation, thereby ensuring its being known to everyone at the Yard.

As Holmes later described to Watson, when he told Mrs. Hudson the news he thought it certain she muttered, "bloody hell," although on reflection both agreed it was quite out of the question. Whatever her initial response to Holmes, her later words triggered a flurry of activity extending from Baker Street to Fleet Street, and to the Fox Hotel where Charles Parnell and Katharine O'Shea were staying.

Chapter 11.
The Ludgate Hill

At two o'clock on Monday, Pier Eight of the Royal Albert Docks was crowded with voyagers and their well-wishers. The Ludgate Hill, a steamer bound for New York, was preparing to take on passengers for its three o'clock departure. Men with silk top hats, frock coats, and striped trousers stood together with women wearing voluminous skirts, starched white shirtfronts, and velvet jackets; and apart from men with workman's caps, linsey-woolsey shirts, and rumpled trousers who were themselves accompanied by women in long cotton dresses. The separation at the pier would become still more pronounced when all were on board, and one group proceeded to their first and second class cabins while the other went below decks to third. For the moment all were joined in equal anticipation of a great adventure and the sorrow of leaving friends and family.

At 2:10 a whistle sounded, and a ship's officer appeared at the foot of the gangplank signaling the ship's readiness to take on passengers. Bales of wool were still being lowered into the ship's hold as voyagers untangled themselves by slow degrees from family and friends and, with a succession of smiles and waves, climbed the gangplank to stand at the deck rail and search out the people they had just left so they could resume the exchange of smiles and waves.

Two groups of men patrolled the dock without smiling or waving, melting into the crowd periodically to study the faces of those newly arrived and review the faces of those they'd studied earlier. Both groups searched for the same man, and each sought to bring him to their own conception of justice. Members of the crowd they surveyed regarded them with curiosity, but only for a moment before turning back to the people they were leaving or who were leaving them. The men of the Irish Brotherhood could have passed for steerage passengers; the Special Branch Inspector was fit only for first cabin. His half dozen charges wore the helmets and uniforms of the Yard's constabulary.

At 2:15, members of a third group arrived at the docks in a collection of four-wheelers and hansoms. Reverend Farnsworth and the members of the National Society for Christian Union wore sullen expressions identical to those of the Irish Brotherhood and the Special Branch, and drew scowls from both of them. The Union was gathered to oppose, and as necessary to suppress, a show of support for papal authority that was to be unveiled at Pier Eight of the Royal Albert Docks. Word had been received late that morning in an anonymous message sent by "a friend in Christian Union" who dared not share his identity for fear of his life. They stood in a body aloof from the crowd, providing yet another distraction for those taking leave of friends and relatives.

Across the roadway from the pier a single hansom sat, to all appearances waiting to take home any who had tired of waving and smiling their good-byes, and now wished to make their leaving more final. Hidden from view were the cab's two occupants, Sherlock Holmes and Dr. John Watson, who waited to play their roles in the drama contrived by Mrs. Hudson.

A little after half two, a four-wheeler arrived at the pier from which there exited three adults and a girl of twelve and boy of five. Two of the adults were recognized by several in the crowd who whispered their intelligence to those around them, and soon virtually everyone was aware that the woman and her two children were being accompanied by Ireland's leading advocate in the British Parliament and his lady, although the precise description of each varied with the individual's political affiliation and social views. As the five of them approached, the crowd parted as the sea before Moses and the noise on the dock subsided to a murmur, or more accurately to dozens of murmurs, and even the passengers aboard ship ceased for the moment their waves and shouts to watch the scene below unfold.

For their part, Parnell and Katharine O'Shea directed their attention solely to the gangplank of the Ludgate Hill, and the pink funnel identifying the ship as belonging to the Hill Lines. With one hand Parnell kept a tight grip on the arm of Patsy Keegan, with the other he struggled against the weight of a battered portmanteau, while Patsy carried a well-stuffed, but less ponderous carpetbag in her free hand.

Parnell pressed forward carrying Patsy Keegan with him, never speaking to her or to any in the crowd, ignoring even those who recognized and cheered his presence. Katharine O'Shea held the hands of Moira and Little Liam, smiling confidence and encouragement to the children who looked at everyone they passed with a mixture of fear and wonder. The children wore clothes that were slightly large on them, but in which they nonetheless took great pride. Knickerbockers, long stockings, waistcoat, and jacket were wonderfully new to Little Liam even if they had been the everyday clothing of Gerard O'Shea many years earlier, while the pale blue dress with a huge dark blue bow at its back and real silk stockings made Moira feel quite the lady, despite the clothes having been pushed well to the back of Carmen O'Shea's wardrobe a long time before. Patsy Keegan's clothes were new to her as well although the pleasure she took in her brown silk dress was mixed with worry about its getting ruined by being dragged along the ground. The dress would need to be taken in later when she got to her new home, but the gift had quite overwhelmed her as she had made clear to Mrs. O'Shea through a succession of thank you's and not a few tears.

Their way to the Ludgate Hill became blocked by a

clean-shaven young man in top hat and impeccable dress, holding his cane across his body as if it were a gate he was refusing to open. He identified himself as Inspector Lassiter of the Special Branch of the Metropolitan Police, then proceeded to his task. "I regret I must detain you as we have an interest in this woman." He nodded toward Patsy Keegan. An expression of police interest was sufficient to cow the people with whom Peter Lassiter normally came into contact. He had not, however, previously come into contact with the likes of the Honorable Charles Stewart Parnell.

The face of the uncrowned king of Ireland reddened as he glowered at the man who would halt his progress. "You choose to detain me. On what grounds, Mr. Lassiter, would you detain a Member of Parliament and his company?"

Parnell spoke as though he was dismissing the ludicrous claim of one of his several adversaries in Parliament, employing a volume capable of reaching the distant galleries of that body. Lassiter was aware that a portion of the crowd was beginning to mass behind Parnell. They appeared to be almost exclusively men wearing workmen's caps. Among them, he made out the undersized figure of Fogarty, nearly obscured by the oversized figure of the bearded man standing with him. Behind himself, Lassiter believed he could only be certain of his own small force, and the questionable support of Reverend Farnsworth and the men of the National Society for Christian Union.

As Peter Lassiter weighed limited and unattractive options two things happened that eliminated any need to choose between them. A small group of constables under the command of Inspector Lestrade swept around the crowd and mounted the ship's gangplank. He would learn later that Lestrade had received a report of smuggling aboard the Ludgate Hill and the Inspector was taking the lead in its investigation.

At the same time Lestrade and his constables were hurrying past, a huge banner was unfurled from the roof of the low building at the edge of the pier used to take and store baggage. The banner appeared to consist of four bed sheets stitched together and nailed to the wooden eave at the top of the building. A small tow-headed man, or more likely a boy, stood on the roof, hammer in his raised hand, proclaiming a call to arms. To what objective arms were to be taken up was lost in the breeze from the Thames. Whether for the words they thought they heard, or for those on the banner, part of the crowd cheered lustily while others stared stone-faced at the sentiment expressed. Across the bed sheets there was printed in words as red as blood:

One true Nation: Ireland
One true Religion: Roman Catholic

The confrontation between Parnell and Lassiter was forgotten. The banner had captured the crowd's attention, and galvanized activity by Reverend Farnsworth and the men of the Christian Union. Had he a sword, the Reverend Farnsworth would have held it high in leading the charge against the heresy printed across the bed sheets. The clergyman let out a whoop of indignation, and with umbrella pointed to the Heavens he supposed surely to be in his support, he marched toward the offending banner as quickly as his massive frame permitted. He was joined and quickly overtaken by the men of the Union and several others who formed temporary alliance with their cause, all of whom let out an equally unintelligible roar and surged forward in a great mix of umbrellas, walking sticks and clenched fists to put an end to plans for papal domination.

While the Union roared and charged, Fogarty, looking to the same banner, was bemused. The boy with the hammer looked familiar to him, although he couldn't place him, and he had no more understanding of what the boy said than anyone else in the crowd. The slogans across the banner made no sense to him, and there had been no call for an action at the pier. Nationhood was, of course, the objective but no one proclaimed Ireland to be the "one true nation" whatever in the world that meant. And as for "one true religion," Fogarty could not remember the last time he'd been to church nor was it counted as essential or even important to the movement. What Fogarty couldn't know was that the boy charged with putting words to the banner had a somewhat imperfect notion of the issues involved in the struggle for Home Rule, and simply did his best to make them sound as incendiary as possible. In that at least, he was an unqualified success.

The men of the National Society for Christian Union, together with their top hatted allies, were racing to tear down his banner supporting, however vaguely and inaccurately, the Cause. Fogarty found himself the center of attention from their opposite number for whom the enemy was clear, if the stimulus to battle was opaque. The men of the Brotherhood, and those who might follow them into battle, waited only his command. Fogarty knew he had a single course of action open to him and he took it. With an unintelligible roar differing only in dialect from the Union's unintelligible roar, he urged his men forward in a great wave to defend the integrity of the inarticulate banner.

The imminent conflict between the two small armies forced Lassiter's hand as well. While in principle he was not averse to the two groups destroying each other and reducing the burden each created for the Special Branch, he recognized that strategy had not yet risen to the level of policy, and he would be expected to restore order. Ignoring his earlier confrontation with Parnell, who seemed in any event to have disappeared, he turned in the direction of the two groups, rallying the constables he had brought with him and, sounding his whistle, called on Lestrade to leave the ship and help an officer in need. Parnell, Mrs. O'Shea and the Keegan family meanwhile made their unhurried way through the crowd to the gangplank where Parnell showed their tickets to the ship's officer who waived them through while continuing to track the activity occurring behind them. They began a search for the second cabin accommodations that had been purchased for the Keegans. The various members of the ship's company they passed along the way offered them no assistance being as wholly engrossed in the activities on the pier as their colleague dockside.

As Lassiter hoped, Lestrade and the constables with him joined his force on hearing the whistle. Lassiter thought he counted one less constable than earlier, but he had been too focused on his confrontation with Parnell to be certain of his count. Together, the two forces of police separated the near combatants with threats of jail, fines and a use of truncheons against the unarmed Christians and the Brotherhood who, while better armed, were intent on keeping that detail from the police.

The battle found a permanent truce when someone sighted the boy who had unfurled the banner, attempting to take advantage of the negotiations between militants and peacemakers to steal away from the pier. The Union members, exhausted by their preparations for conflict, hung back, as did the Brotherhood, uncertain of their allegiance to the stranger and therefore unwilling to do battle with the police on his behalf.

The members of the Special Branch had no conflict over mission, and were newly energized by the appearance of the individual who had not only disrupted their efforts to capture Coogan, but had created a near riot on the London docks. Lassiter and his men began to race down the pier after the boy, nearly tripping over Lestrade and his men in their haste.

Hearing the commotion, the boy turned to see a half dozen men or more charging after him, one of them carrying a top hat in one hand and walking stick in the other, the rest, uniformed constables carrying truncheons. It was a race on terms with which he was familiar. As always in such situations, they called on him to stop, as always, that led him to increase his speed. He had a head start of at least 30 meters, but considerably shorter legs and the police were gaining on him until he was able to get just beyond a hansom that had started from the end of the pier, blocking for a critical moment the path of his pursuers. When they emerged on the other side of the cab, they were in time to see the boy enter a second hansom improbably occupied by an older woman all in black, with coils of gray hair topping a doughy face. Lassiter recognized them both just as he recognized the passengers of the hansom that had blocked his way. He recognized as well that his discovery came too late to be of any use to him.

The sound of the Ludgate Hill's foghorn caused Lassiter to turn back to the ship just as the gangplank was being taken up. The crowd on the pier returned to its first duty of spirited waving of hands and handkerchiefs, and calling their good-byes to friends and relations at the deck's rail. Reverend Farnsworth and his allies went in search of someone who could remove the offending sign that still fluttered in the wind from the Thames. Members of the Special Branch of Scotland Yard and of the Irish Brotherhood stood together and apart, searching the ship's deck for the enemy they were powerless to capture, their good-byes unspoken, but no less heartfelt and permanent.

Chapter 12.
The Slate Wiped Clean

It was more than a week after the sailing of the Ludgate Hill before Lestrade was able to join Holmes and Watson at Baker Street for all to share their thoughts regarding the death and resurrection of Liam Coogan. The Inspector was greeted by a short young man with brown curly hair that looked to have been brought into a semblance of order through frequent brushing, and wearing a navy blue jacket that buttoned to his neck, close-fitting trousers of an identical color, and spit-polished shoes. The jacket, pants and shoes were all new, spotless and to Lestrade's thinking wholly unprecedented in the young man's experience.

"Mr. ... Wiggins, is it?"

"It is, Inspector Lestrade, sir. Thomas Wiggins, sir." The words were enunciated in a cadence appropriate to the rigid attention at which the Baker Street page stood. "Mr. Holmes and the Doctor is expecting you, and Mrs. Hudson is just now gone up to bring tea and some of them raisin scones she says you fancy. You can go straight up or I can 'nounce you. It's up to you, sir."

"That's alright, thank you, Thomas. I'll go straight up."

Lestrade rapped softly on the door and was rewarded with a hearty, "Please come in Inspector. The door is open as it always is to you."

Holmes gestured to the settee, customarily his own choice and waited while Mrs. Hudson poured the Inspector's tea, set out the lemon he favored and placed a scone on a plate for him. Holmes then chose an easy chair while Watson drew over the chair from his desk. As the housekeeper poured tea for her lodgers, Lestrade smiled his incredulity to Holmes. "I see you've taken on a page."

"Yes, it's really Mrs. Hudson's idea. She's convinced he

can make a go of it. I tend to agree although Watson feels it unlikely."

Lestrade delayed responding until he had savored the corner of his scone. "I do hope you're right about that, Mr. Holmes. If you are, I'm certain it will save the Yard a great deal of difficulty in the years to come." Before taking a second bite from the scone he turned to find the housekeeper, then held his pastry aloft. "Plain and simple, Mrs. Hudson, this is another triumph. I tell Mr. Holmes I come for his company, but it's really your scones that are the draw, ma'am."

Mrs. Hudson blushed just enough to astound her lodgers before speaking. "You are too kind, Inspector, I'm sure there's many as 'ave tastier bakin' than mine."

Lestrade dismissed her humility with a wave and turned again to Holmes.

"And may I take it, Mr. Holmes, that your reward for the Coogan investigation was everything you expected?"

Holmes searched the Inspector's face for evidence of the sarcasm he was certain lay behind his words, but found him absorbed in admiration for the scone he held. "Exactly what we negotiated with our client."

Lestrade grinned broadly with his suspicion confirmed.

"Now tell us, Lestrade, did Mr. Keegan and Mr. Parkhurst fulfill their promise to bury the unfortunate Joshua Hobbes?"

"Indeed they did, Mr. Holmes, and it caused quite a stir I can tell you. The man in charge of the graveyard called the Yard to let us know a fresh grave had been dug during the night in the place reserved for Mr. Hobbes. He said he didn't know how to report it. He'd called us often enough about folks being taken out of graves in the middle of the night, but having somebody put into a grave was new to him. We agreed it wasn't a crime, just highly unusual, which saved everybody a lot of paperwork and explaining." The three men shared a laugh and Mrs. Hudson grinned.

Lestrade asked, "What have you heard about the two of them? I know from the Shipworths that Seamus Keegan is no longer on their staff, and from Moberly Bell that Winston Parkhurst left the *Times* without even waiting to collect his wages. Of course, the Shipworths lost a groom as well, but they informed me he wasn't working out and they were going to let him go anyway."

"We did learn something of that," Holmes replied. "A young lady in the Shipworths' household, who described herself as a particular friend of Seamus, was good enough to visit us on her day out to deliver a message from Mr. Keegan which I was to be sure to transmit to you as well. It seems both he and Mr. Parkhurst are no longer living in London and are waiting passage across the ocean, at least they were a week ago. She wouldn't give us their ultimate location, if she even knew it, but I suspect they are already on their way to wherever it is."

"I take it you're thinking it's either America or Australia?"

"Or perhaps Canada. All those places seem to capture the best and the worst of us."

The Inspector had drawn a pipe from a jacket pocket and was preparing to fish out his tobacco when Holmes, after locating the Persian slipper where he stored his own tobacco, offered some to Lestrade. With an appreciative smile, he filled his pipe and lit it, taking a long, satisfied draw before speaking.

"Well, I would say it's a happy ending to our little problem. Speaking of people leaving us, my informants tell me that Mr. Fogarty has been recalled to Dublin for 'further instruction' and will likely be there a while. As it turns out, he'll have company familiar to him. Inspector Lassiter has requested and been granted a transfer to work with the force in Dublin. He hasn't spoken to me since the excitement at Prince Albert's Docks, but I understand from others he feels there is nothing to keep him in London any longer, and he can do better chasing down the Brotherhood from 'inside their stronghold' as I'm told he put it." Lestrade took another long draw on his pipe and watched a plume of smoke snake its way toward the ceiling then fall apart in a thin cloud.

In the quiet that enveloped the sitting room, each of them considered the turn of events they had witnessed and helped to create. Mrs. Hudson finally broke the silence to ask if the Inspector would like more tea or perhaps another scone. Employing a hand to each purpose, Lestrade gratefully accepted her offer, then turned his attention to the housekeeper.

"And Mrs. Hudson, I trust you will be receiving the Constable's uniform back very soon. I'll tell you, Mr. Holmes, it was nothing less than sheer brilliance to dress up Mr. Coogan as one of my constables. And of course, with the confusion created by young Wiggins and his sign, it was child's play to get him on board and then leave him there. I'm just glad the captain had to cast off when he did or there might have been quite a stir at the Yard. He was not happy about being accused of smuggling and informed me he would be lodging a 'vigorous protest.' Fortunately, he'll have a few weeks at sea to cool down."

Watson directed a question to Lestrade that had plagued him since the day at the pier. "Inspector, how in the world did you pull that off? The constables with you had to know that one of their number was in disguise and being helped to escape the country."

Lestrade covered his mouth as laughter and digestion entered into a possibly embarrassing competition. When he had completed both, he grinned his response to Watson. "Well, first of all, Doctor, we have to remember that Liam

Coogan wasn't involved in any crime. He'd served his time for a relatively minor part in Brotherhood activities, had no part in their goings-on here in London, and wasn't wanted for anything. The most you could say was that he had knowledge of the activities of his brother-in-law and Mr. Parkhurst. And like I said earlier, there was no great crime there either, at least none that was going to surface, so to speak.

On top of that, Doctor, you have to understand there's constables at the Yard who have a pretty good notion of what it means to be an Irishman in London. For that matter, being named Lestrade, every stranger I run into thinks I must be a Frenchy and gets either standoffish or extra polite, so even I get some sense of what our Irish boys have to put up with. Knowing that, I put together a squad of men named O'Mahoney, Quinlan, Grimes and Foley. All of them good lads and good constables, besides sharing a certain understanding of the situation with our Mr. Coogan. They knew what we were about and the risks we ran, and every one of them did himself and the Yard proud."

"And speaking of doing themselves proud, Mr. Holmes, have you heard anything from Mr. Parnell or Mrs. O'Shea?"

Holmes accepted a second cup of tea from Mrs. Hudson who ambled in the direction of his worktable and outside Lestrade's sight. "Not a word, Inspector, although I never expected to. They're rather busy between affairs of state and ... other affairs."

Lestrade smiled and nodded, "I dare say."

Silence again descended on the sitting room as each man attacked what remained of his scone, and took pleasure in sharing with colleagues and friends a rare lull in the work they shared. At length, Watson sought to tie up still another loose end. "And what of that scoundrel, Cornelius Keegan? I can't imagine a man—if he can be called a man—who would sell his daughter for thirty pieces, but I can't help but be curious as to what's become of him."

Lestrade grimaced at the name and shook his head in answer. "I've heard nothing, Doctor, although I can't say I'm either surprised or much concerned. Men like that near always come to a bad end. Somewhere along the way they end up informing on the wrong man, and we go to fishing another body out of the Thames."

Lestrade was determined to find a more cheerful subject. "But we're forgetting our hero of the moment. You did a grand job, Mrs. Hudson, rescuing young Wiggins and carrying the poor lad to safety. I dare say between Inspector Lassiter and the Christian Union he would have been either arrested or converted if you didn't scoop him out of the crowd and carry him off. I only hope this doesn't lead to any plans on your part to get into a life of fighting crime. Down at the Yard we have all we can do to keep up with the likes of Mr. Holmes. I'd hate to see him get an assistant and me lose out on getting the best scones in London." With that, the last of Lestrade's second scone disappeared into his mouth.

"You're much too kind, Inspector. Let me set your mind to rest. There'll always be scones for you in Baker Street, and there'll never come a day you'll find me becomin' Mr. 'Olmes' assistant." Mrs. Hudson raised her teapot high. "Another cup, gentlemen?" This time there were no takers.

Also from Barry S Brown

The Unpleasantness at Parkerton Manor
(Mrs Hudson of Baker Street Book 1)

Mrs. Hudson In The Ring
(Mrs Hudson of Baker Street Book 3 – available through reissue by MX Publishing November, 2018)

Mrs. Hudson In New York
(Mrs Hudson of Baker Street Book 4)

Mrs. Hudson's Olympic Triumph
(Mrs Hudson of Baker Street Book 5)

Also from MX Publishing

MX Publishing is the world's largest specialist Sherlock Holmes publisher, with over a hundred titles and fifty authors creating the latest in Sherlock Holmes fiction and non-fiction.

From traditional short stories and novels to travel guides and quiz books, MX Publishing cater for all Holmes fans.

The collection includes leading titles such as *Benedict Cumberbatch In Transition* and *The Norwood Author* which won the 2011 Howlett Award (Sherlock Holmes Book of the Year).

MX Publishing also has one of the largest communities of Holmes fans on Facebook with regular contributions from dozens of authors.

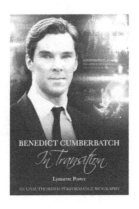

www.mxpublishing.com

Also from MX Publishing

  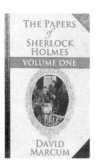

Our bestselling books are our short story collections;

'Lost Stories of Sherlock Holmes's , 'The Outstanding Mysteries of
Sherlock Holmes's, The Papers of Sherlock Holmes Volume 1 and 2,
'Untold Adventures of Sherlock Holmes's (and the sequel 'Studies in
Legacy) and 'Sherlock Holmes in Pursuit', 'The Cotswold Werewolf and
Other Stories of Sherlock Holmes's – and many more......

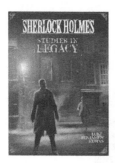  

www.mxpublishing.com

Also from MX Publishing

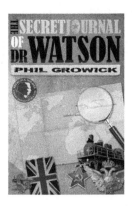

"Phil Growick's, 'The Secret Journal of Dr Watson', is an adventure which takes place in the latter part of Holmes and Watson's lives. They are entrusted by HM Government (although not officially) and the King no less to undertake a rescue mission to save the Romanovs, Russia's Royal family from a grisly end at the hand of the Bolsheviks. There is a wealth of detail in the story but not so much as would detract us from the enjoyment of the story. Espionage, counter-espionage, the ace of spies himself, double-agents, double-crossers...all these flit across the pages in a realistic and exciting way. All the characters are extremely well-drawn and Mr Growick, most importantly, does not falter with a very good ear for Holmesian dialogue indeed. Highly recommended. A five-star effort."
The Baker Street Society

Also from MX Publishing

The Missing Authors Series

Sherlock Holmes and The Adventure of The Grinning Cat
Sherlock Holmes and The Nautilus Adventure
Sherlock Holmes and The Round Table Adventure

"Joseph Svec, III is brilliant in entwining two endearing and enduring classics of literature, blending the factual with the fantastical; the playful with the pensive; and the mischievous with the mysterious. We shall, all of us young and old, benefit with a cup of tea, a tranquil afternoon, and a copy of Sherlock Holmes, The Adventure of the Grinning Cat."
Amador County Holmes Hounds Sherlockian Society

Also from MX Publishing

The American Literati Series

 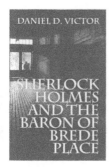 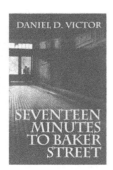

The Final Page of Baker Street
The Baron of Brede Place
Seventeen Minutes To Baker Street

"The really amazing thing about this book is the author's ability to call up the 'essence' of both the Baker Street 'digs' of Holmes and Watson as well as that of the 'mean streets' of Marlowe's Los Angeles. Although none of the action takes place in either place, Holmes and Watson share a sense of camaraderie and self-confidence in facing threats and problems that also pervades many of the later tales in the Canon. Following their conversations and banter is a return to Edwardian England and its certainties and hope for the future. This is definitely the world before The Great War."
Philip K Jones

Also from MX Publishing

The Detective and The Woman Series

 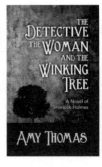 

The Detective and The Woman
The Detective, The Woman and The Winking Tree
The Detective, The Woman and The Silent Hive

"The book is entertaining, puzzling and a lot of fun. I believe the author has hit on the only type of long-term relationship possible for Sherlock Holmes and Irene Adler. The details of the narrative only add force to the romantic defects we expect in both of them and their growth and development are truly marvelous to watch. This is not a love story. Instead, it is a coming-of-age tale starring two of our favorite characters."
Philip K Jones

Also from MX Publishing

The Sherlock Holmes and Enoch Hale Series

 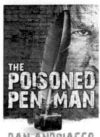 

The Amateur Executioner
The Poisoned Penman
The Egyptian Curse

"The Amateur Executioner: Enoch Hale Meets Sherlock Holmes", the first collaboration between Dan Andriacco and Kieran McMullen, concerns the possibility of a Fenian attack in London. Hale, a native Bostonian, is a reporter for London's Central News Syndicate - where, in 1920, Horace Harker is still a familiar figure, though far from revered. "The Amateur Executioner" takes us into an ambiguous and murky world where right and wrong aren't always distinguishable. I look forward to reading more about Enoch Hale."

Sherlock Holmes Society of London

Also from MX Publishing

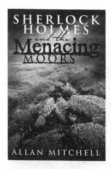  

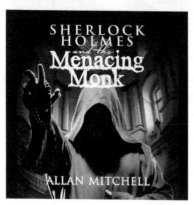

All four novellas have been released also in audio format with narration by Steve White

Sherlock Holmes and The Menacing Moors
Sherlock Holmes and The Menacing Metropolis
Sherlock Holmes and The Menacing Melbournian
Sherlock Holmes and The Menacing Monk

"The story is really good and the Herculean effort it must have been to write it all in verse—well, my hat is off to you, Mr. Allan Mitchell! I wouldn't dream of seeing such work get less than five plus stars from me..." **The Raven**

Also from MX Publishing

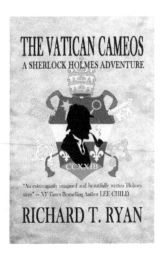

When the papal apartments are burgled in 1901, Sherlock Holmes is summoned to Rome by Pope Leo XII. After learning from the pontiff that several priceless cameos that could prove compromising to the church, and perhaps determine the future of the newly unified Italy, have been stolen, Holmes is asked to recover them. In a parallel story, Michelangelo, the toast of Rome in 1501 after the unveiling of his Pieta, is commissioned by Pope Alexander VI, the last of the Borgia pontiffs, with creating the cameos that will bedevil Holmes and the papacy four centuries later. For fans of Conan Doyle's immortal detective, the game is always afoot. However, the great detective has never encountered an adversary quite like the one with whom he crosses swords in "The Vatican Cameos.."

"An extravagantly imagined and beautifully written Holmes story"
(**Lee Child**, NY Times Bestselling author, Jack Reacher series)

Also from MX Publishing

The Conan Doyle Notes (The Hunt For Jack The Ripper)
"Holmesians have long speculated on the fact that the Ripper murders aren't mentioned in the canon, though the obvious reason is undoubtedly the correct one: even if Conan Doyle had suspected the killer's identity he'd never have considered mentioning it in the context of a fictional entertainment. Ms Madsen's novel equates his silence with that of the dog in the night-time, assuming that Conan Doyle did know who the Ripper was but chose not to say – which, of course, implies that good old stand-by, the government cover-up. It seems unlikely to me that the Ripper was anyone famous or distinguished, but fiction is not fact, and "The Conan Doyle Notes" is a gripping tale, with an intelligent, courageous and very likable protagonist in DD McGil."
The Sherlock Holmes Society of London

Also from MX Publishing

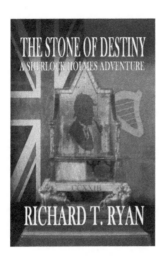

During the elaborate funeral for Queen Victoria, a group of Irish separatists breaks into Westminster Abbey and steals the Coronation Stone, on which every monarch of England has been crowned since the 14th century. After learning of the theft from Mycroft, Sherlock Holmes is tasked with recovering the stone and returning it to England. In pursuit of the many-named stone, which has a rich and colorful history, Holmes and Watson travel to Ireland in disguise as they try to infiltrate the Irish Republican Brotherhood, the group they believe responsible for the theft. The story features a number of historical characters, including a very young Michael Collins, who would go on to play a prominent role in Irish history; John Theodore Tussaud, the grandson of Madame Tussaud; and George Bradley, the dean of Westminster at the time of the theft. There are also references to a number of other Victorian luminaries, including Joseph Lister and Frederick Treves.